ABHIMANYU

ABHIMANYU

The Warrior Prince

Deepak M.R.

BLOOMSBURY
NEW DELHI • LONDON • OXFORD • NEW YORK • SYDNEY

BLOOMSBURY INDIA
Bloomsbury Publishing India Pvt. Ltd
Second Floor, LSC Building No. 4, DDA Complex, Pocket C – 6 & 7,
Vasant Kunj, New Delhi 110070

BLOOMSBURY, BLOOMSBURY INDIA and the Diana logo
are trademarks of Bloomsbury Publishing Plc

First published in India 2021
This edition published in 2021

ISBN: PB: 978-93-54351-11-2; eBook: 978-93-54350-05-4

2 4 6 8 10 9 7 5 3 1

Typeset in Fournier MT Std by Manipal Technologies Limited
Printed and bound in India

MIX
Paper from
responsible sources
FSC® C016779

To find out more about our authors and books visit www.bloomsbury.com and sign up for our newsletters

A hero is someone who has given his or her life to something bigger than oneself.

—Joseph Campbell

The mighty-armed Abhimanyu is a leader of leaders of [chariots]. Indeed, that slayer of foes is equal in battle to [Arjuna] himself or [Krishna]. Endued with great lightness of hand in shooting weapons, and acquainted with all the modes of warfare, he is possessed of great energy and is steady in the observance of vows. Remembering the sufferings of his own father, he will put forth his prowess.

—Bheeshma describing Abhimanyu
'Udyoga Parva, Section CLXXI',
The Mahabharata of Vyasa, English Prose
Translation by K.M. Ganguli

A sculpture of Abhimanyu and the Chakravyuha
from the Hoysaleshwara Temple in Halebeedu, Karnataka

CONTENTS

PREFACE

The story of Abhimanyu is not new. Neither is the story of the Mahabharata. Everyone knows that Abhimanyu was a brave warrior who entered the Chakravyuha but did not know how to get out, and as a result, died. What is not known is the valour he exhibited when he broke through the Chakravyuha. The details of his heroics on the thirteenth day of the Great War explain why he is not just a warrior but one of the heroes of the Mahabharata.

Here is a tragic hero, who lived for just sixteen years. This sixteen-year-old boy was considered a maharathi or great warrior, a title ordinarily given to the best among the best, like Arjuna, Bheeshma, Bheema, Drona and other greats. He is truly a hero who has not been given the credit he truly deserves. The story of Abhimanyu is the story of a prince who could have been an emperor. It is the story of a warrior who did not hesitate to take a decision that he knew could be fatal.

Abhimanyu's story needs to be told because here is a hero who has always been underrated. While listing the great heroes of the Mahabharata or Indian epics, he is unlikely to make it to the top of the list. The reality is different! Abhimanyu's heroics, in fact, make him one of the greatest warriors of the Kurukshetra war. His tragic death played a role in changing the course of the war.

The story of Abhimanyu is being retold in the form of this novel. The story and heroics of Abhimanyu are based on the Mahabharata. The battles he fought, the warriors he defeated and his exploits are entirely based on the original text. And you will find new tales in this novel, which you may not have heard of. These are not entirely fictional but are based on the rich folktales of our country.

The legend of Abhimanyu is one we must cherish. He is truly a hero we need to celebrate. The saga of bravery of this warrior prince is presented in the pages to come. Through this novel, I hope to change the common perception of this brave hero. I hope you will enjoy reading this book as much as I enjoyed writing it.

I would like to express my sincere thanks to my parents, Shylaja and Rajashekar, who inculcated the habit of reading in me. This helped me fall in love with books and also created a desire to write. My thanks to my beloved wife Rashmi and wonderful daughter Aishwarya for their support for my career choice.

I would like to express my gratitude to author Saiswaroopa Iyer who forwarded my manuscript to Bloomsbury India and helped me in my quest to become a published author.

My gratitude to the amazing team at Bloomsbury India who work at blazing speed. Thanks to Praveen Tiwari and Nitin Valecha. Sincere thanks to Shreya Chakraborti and her editorial team, including Megha Arora and Dr Pallavi Narayan, who did a great job with the editing. My thanks to Syed Dilshad Ali for the cover design.

This is a book about heroes and I would like to dedicate this book to all the real-life heroes in our country—especially those in our armed forces and police—who heroically battle adversity every single day so that we may remain safe.

MAIN CHARACTERS WHO APPEAR IN THIS STORY

Abhimanyu: The brave and heroic son of Arjuna and Subhadra.

Arjuna: The third of the five Pandava brothers. His mother was Kunti and his father Pandu. He was born with the blessings of Indra, the king of the gods.

Ashwatthama: Son of Drona.

Balarama: Krishna's elder brother. He had a soft corner for Duryodhana.

Bheema: The second Pandava was known for his strength and mastery over the use of the mace as a weapon.

Bheeshma: Grandsire of the Pandavas and Kauravas. He had taken a vow of celibacy and loyalty to the Hastinapura kingdom.

Dhrishtadyumna: Brother of Draupadi, who commanded the Pandava army in the Great War.

Dhritharashtra: Emperor of Hastinapura and father of the Kauravas. He was born blind and had a "blind" affection for his eldest son.

Draupadi: Daughter of King Drupada of Panchala. As a result of a boon from Lord Shiva in her previous life, she was destined to have five husbands hence was married to all five Pandavas.

Drona: The teacher of the Pandavas and Kaurava, who taught them warfare. Arjuna was his favourite student.

Drupada: King of Panchala.

Durmasana: Son of Dushasana.

Duryodhana: Eldest son of Dhritharashtra and the crown prince of Hastinapura. He had a hatred for the Pandavas from childhood as he felt that the Kuru elders were biased towards them.

Dushasana: Duryodhana's younger brother.

Karna: The son of a charioteer, who, in reality, was the son of Kunti with Surya, the sun god. He was made king of Anga by Duryodhana and was loyal to his friend.

Kripa: Brother-in-law of Drona, who also taught the Pandavas and Kauravas.

Krishna: The eighth incarnation of Lord Vishnu. Krishna's aunt was Kunti and he was, thus, a cousin of the Pandavas.

Lakshmana: Son of Duryodhana.

Nakula and Sahadeva: Twins who were the children of Pandu's second wife Madri.

Pradyumna: Son of Krishna. He taught Abhimanyu archery and warfare skills.

Shakuni: Brother-in-law of Dhritharashtra. He nursed a grievance that his sister Gandhari had been forced to marry a blind man. He is believed to be the mastermind behind the evil deeds of the Kauravas.

Shalya: King of Madra and uncle to Nakula and Sahadeva.

Susharma: King of Trigarta Kingdom. He formed the first suicide squad in history with the objective of killing Arjuna.

Subhadra: Sister of Krishna and Balarama. She fell in love with Arjuna and eloped with him (with the support of Krishna).

Virat: King of Matsya Kingdom.

Uttarakumar: Son of Virat, who loved to brag about his non-existent courage.

Uttara: The beautiful and intelligent daughter of King Virat.

Yudhishtira: Eldest of the Pandavas and the emperor of Indraprastha. Born of Kunti and Yama, the god of death and justice, he was addicted to dice and gambling.

KURU FAMILY TREE

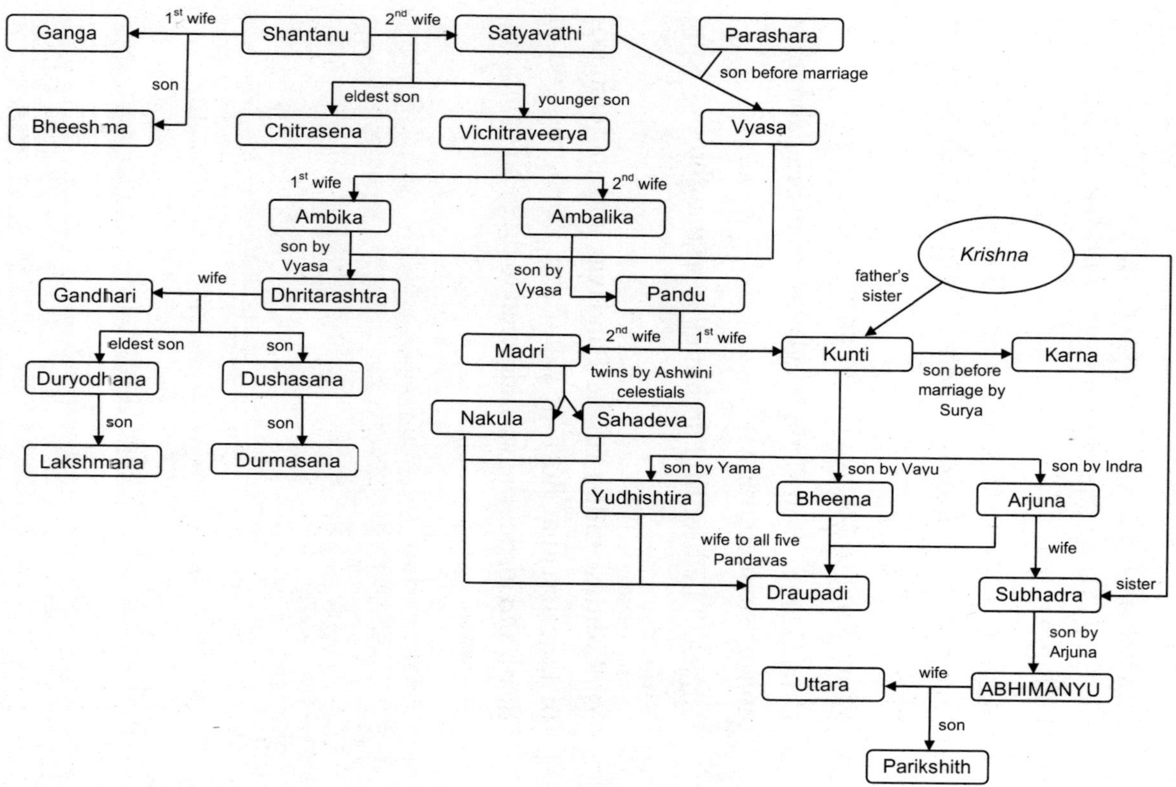

PROLOGUE

Krishna looked at the dark sky that was slowly turning red. All eyes were raised towards the east, awaiting the first rays of the sun. It was the fourteenth day of the Great War. The Pandavas, assembled on the Kurukshetra battlefield, were restless and nervously awaited the sunrise.

Everyone's eyes were on Krishna or rather on the warrior who sat behind him. Krishna looked back at Arjuna and smiled. Arjuna looked tense but Krishna could see the determination in his eyes. Arjuna's hands tightly gripped his great bow, the Gandiva. His eyes awaited the morning sun.

The previous night had been a terrible one. Neither Arjuna nor Krishna had slept. Arjuna should have been exhausted after the long day of battle, coupled with the sleepless night. He, however, seemed charged with energy, eagerly awaiting the start of the day's battle.

Krishna could not only see the determination in Arjuna's eyes, but also his heartache. His tears had not dried up completely. His eyes were bloodshot. The combination of unendurable pain and resoluteness did not augur well for the enemy.

Krishna looked at the opposite side and saw the Kauravas awaiting the start of the battle as well. It was clear that there was tension in their camp. The tensity in both camps were palpable. Everyone knew that this day would be decisive. Something big was going to happen. Soldiers on both sides were nervous. None of them knew if they would return to their respective camps by the end of the day.

Krishna looked back and saw Daruka, his charioteer, seated atop a great chariot whose flag had the symbol of the Garuda. It was Krishna's own chariot and was empty. Krishna had instructed Daruka to keep his chariot, a backup, ready with all his weapons.

Arjuna had to fulfil the fearful vow he had taken. If he could not, Krishna would have to break his vow not to fight in the war so as to save his beloved friend and cousin Arjuna. He hoped such a situation would not arise. In fact, he knew it would not arise. The chariot was there as a reminder to both him and Arjuna of what they needed to do.

The early rays of the sun were now visible. They were a few minutes away from the start of what would be a terrible day's battle. Thousands and thousands of soldiers would die today. The day would end with the triumph of the Pandavas or in a disaster. Krishna was determined to ensure that the latter did not happen.

He turned to Arjuna and said, "Partha[1], it is time to forget the terrible incidents of yesterday. Don't think of what has gone by or what may happen. Think of the present. You have a clear goal. Focus on it. Today is the day you show the world why Arjuna is the greatest warrior in the world. Yesterday's events have changed the course of the war. Today, you will move the war

[1] Arjuna is called Partha as he was the son of Pritha (Kunti). Since Krishna was Partha's charioteer (sarathy), he is also known as Parthasarathy.

towards its end. Leave the results to me, just focus on your goal."

Arjuna bowed his head reverently. "Vaasudeva[2], what happened yesterday is not easy to forget for either of us. The desolation will remain in my heart as long as I live, but I will heed your advice. I will not rest a second until I achieve my goal. With your blessings, I know it will happen. But…."

"But what, Partha?"

"But it always rankles in my mind. If only Subhadra had not fallen asleep that morning, maybe things would have been different."

Krishna smiled sadly. "Partha, all that happened is ordained. You know that. Nothing could have changed the events of yesterday. Once again, I remind you, forget the past and focus on the present. It is nearly time now."

Arjuna nodded his head and once again, his expression turned grim. His one hand gripped the Gandiva while the other reached for his conch, to blow it and signal the start of the battle.

Krishna held the reins of the chariot in one hand while holding his conch in the other. It was time! They were moments away from the most terrible battle of the war. Even as everyone geared up for the battle, Krishna pondered over Arjuna's words.

Krishna's mind went back some sixteen years as he remembered that hot and humid day in Indraprastha.

[2] Krishna is called Vaasudeva as he was the son of Vasudeva.

I

Lessons in the Womb

Krishna's sweet voice sounded like music to Subhadra. Pregnant with Arjuna's son, she lay on her bed and rested, listening to Krishna. Her beloved brother's voice was like music to her. She felt refreshed hearing him speak. He would spend time with her daily and talk about every topic in the world. He spoke of polity, governance, philosophy, God and art. There was no topic that Krishna did not know. After all, he was the Lord incarnate.

Today he was talking about warcraft. Subhadra understood the reason for Krishna's selection of topics. He was not talking to her. He was addressing her child, the son of the greatest warrior on Earth. She knew her son would one day become the emperor and rule wisely, bringing glory to his parents and to the people.

Krishna loved Subhadra, and he had a deep affection for Arjuna. This was the reason he had played a key role in allowing her to elope with the Pandava prince, despite their brother Balarama's opposition to the alliance. It was Krishna who had convinced their furious elder brother. He loved her unborn child and wanted him to be an emperor ruling over the greatest kingdom on Earth.

Thus, he was preparing him for his future role by instructing him in Subhadra's womb. Krishna had told her how the foetus could hear, and even though it could not understand what was being said, everything would be registering in its subconscious mind. A day would come when her son would have the power to unlock his subconscious. On that day, his knowledge would increase tenfold.

She smiled, thinking about her son and how he would be as great a warrior as his father. She was feeling sleepy. It had been a hot and humid day. She struggled to keep awake while she listened to Krishna. He was now talking about vyuhas or battle formations. He explained how armies made formations to fight battles and how a warrior could intelligently breach the formations to defeat the enemy. He elaborated on their construction.

He spoke about great battle formations like the Kurma (turtle) vyuha, Sarvatobhadra (protection from all sides) vyuha, Trishula (trident) vyuha, Makara (crocodile) vyuha, Garuda (eagle) vyuha, Krauncha (crane) vyuha, Suchimukha (eye of the needle) vyuha and many other such formations.

He further explained how a commander could set a formation that matched the one the enemy had set. He narrated how the Garuda vyuha could be arranged to counter the Krauncha vyuha. He talked about how a warrior could break the formation open, attack it and exit from it easily.

He was now talking about the Chakravyuha, the wheel formation. She had heard about it earlier from Arjuna who had described what a powerful battle tactic it was. The Chakravyuha was an incredible formation that comprised seven concentric circles. Within each circle were powerful warriors standing close together.

The infantry formed the outer circle, with the next circles formed by chariots, cavalry and elephants.

The innermost circle had the key warriors of the army waiting collectively like a spider at the core of the web. The commander was at the centre and his assistants used the sounds of the conch and the beat of the drums to synchronise the movement of the soldiers. Every soldier moved continuously within the formation while moving forward. The wheel thus moved relentlessly and ruthlessly and anyone trying to enter had to breach it. The moment he attacked a solder and created a gap, the others immediately moved in to fill the gap.

If he somehow entered the formation, it would be closed behind him, making an exit almost impossible. The movement of the formation would overwhelm even the best of warriors when they encountered layer after layer of soldiers tightly packed together. By the time a warrior had entered the inner circle, he would be completely exhausted. That is when he would face the best warriors of the enemy.

The Chakravyuha was a deadly formation and if breaking into it was difficult, breaking out from it was almost impossible. In the entire world, only five warriors were capable of doing this as they had intricate knowledge of the Chakravyuha—Krishna, his son Pradyumna, Arjuna, Drona (the guru of the Pandavas and Kauravas) and Pitamaha (grandsire) Bheeshma.

Forming the Chakravyuha itself was a challenge as setting up the seven layers and ensuring that soldiers move in the right way could be managed only by a veteran commander. The Chakravyuha needed thousands of soldiers. If formed by fewer soldiers, it could be broken into easily. This is why it was a battle tactic spoken about frequently, but not used very often.

Krishna was now explaining how to break into the Chakravyuha.

"The Chakravyuha has an entry point that is meant to deceive the opposition. Anyone who tries to enter through it will be quickly engulfed by the moving formation. At the entry point is the most fearsome soldier of the enemy or the commander himself. Thus, anyone trying to enter from here is defeated quickly. It is foolhardy to try to enter from the opening. The first thing you need to know about entering the wheel is to find the weak link."

Subhadra was listening with interest. "How can a warrior do that, Krishna?" she asked.

"It takes time and planning to breach the Chakravyuha. The warrior needs to quickly move around the ring and inspect the formation. No formation is perfect; there will be a weak link or two. That's the starting point. One more thing—only an archer can break through the Chakravyuha."

"Why? Can't a gadadhari (warrior with a mace) break through?"

"No! The soldiers in the outer layers are tightly packed together. The moment you kill one, the others quickly move to the right, filling in the gap. To break into the Chakravyuha, you need to simultaneously create two or three gaps. That can only be done by an expert archer who has to shoot a volley of arrows. He should do this not only at the soldiers in front of him, but also to the ones on his left and right. The moment these soldiers fall, the others move to fill the gap and the circle rotates."

"Yes," said Subhadra, nodding her head.

"When the circle rotates, the gap that is created comes right in front of the warrior. He can then enter the formation and shoot a volley of arrows at the second circle, creating a gap there. In this way, he can break through the circles. The moment the lead warrior breaks through the circle, his army must quickly follow him. This is crucial. If this doesn't happen, the gap gets filled in and the warrior is trapped."

Subhadra continued nodding, her eyes half-closed. Sleep was gently pulling her away from Krishna's narration.

Krishna continued, "The second and third layers have archers who attack the incoming warrior. This is the reason I said only an archer can lead an attack against the Chakravyuha. The archer must be a master who should breach each layer of soldiers, be it on foot, horse and elephant. His army has to support him and there must be archers behind him to support him as well."

Subhadra nodded her head gently. She was half-asleep now; the intricacies of the battle tactics did not interest her.

"Soldiers with spears should lead the charge against elephants so that the warrior can breach into the inner circle. Meanwhile, the warrior's elephant division must attack the infantry at the outer layer and kill them thus stopping the wheel from moving. This ensures the warrior can go right up to the centre of the formation to face the commander in battle. Getting in is easy but getting out is difficult, do you know why?"

"Mmmmm...." mumbled Subhadra, barely replying to Krishna's question.

"The moment anyone gets in, he not only has to face the soldiers in the inner layer, but he also has to face the soldiers behind him who would now turn in his direction. It is easy to find weak points in the outer layers. The inner layers have champion soldiers. Breaking through them and exiting is extremely difficult. However, it is not impossible to exit the Chakravyuha. Do you want to know how it can be done?" asked Krishna.

He waited for a response but all he got was a gentle snore. Subhadra was fast asleep. Krishna got up and covered her with a blanket. He gently caressed her forehead for a few moments until he heard her breathing deeply. She was now fast asleep. Krishna quietly tiptoed out of her chamber, not wishing to wake her up.

2

The Birth of Abhimanyu

After leaving Subhadra, Krishna walked down to the palace when he met Arjuna, who was returning after an expedition to the nearby villages. Arjuna got down from his chariot and bowed to Krishna.

"Vaasudeva, I hope Subhadra is keeping good health," said Arjuna.

"Yes, Partha, I am spending every day with her and talking to her. I am also talking to your son who is listening to me from inside his mother's womb."

"I am amazed to hear this, Krishna! How can an unborn baby understand what is being said?"

"There is nothing impossible, Arjuna. The mind has three parts—the conscious, the subconscious and the superconscious. The conscious mind is what you perceive, like when you are listening to me. The subconscious mind registers things that the conscious mind is not aware of. Your son's subconscious is registering what I have said. He does not understand what I speak but everything is being registered in his mind. His subconscious will be activated one day and all that he has heard will be transformed into knowledge."

"What is the superconscious, Krishna?"

"The superconscious is your innermost mind. It is the mind that links you to the cosmos and to the mind of God."

"Are all human minds linked to that of God?"

"Yes, all minds are one, Partha. They are all connected to the energy of the ultimate power, that of the Supreme Being. Most people don't know this. Hardly a handful can access the superconscious. It is the gateway to the world of God. Only true yogis[3] can access the superconscious. You are a yogi, Arjuna, you can access the superconscious. You can channelise its powers and achieve anything you want."

"With your blessings, Krishna, nothing is impossible. Having learnt from you in the womb, I am sure my son will be the greatest warrior prince on Earth."

Just then, there was a commotion as some people tried to enter the palace to meet Arjuna. The guards tried to prevent them. Arjuna was furious. He charged towards the guards, rebuked them and asked them to allow the people to come inside.

The people rushed in and fell at Arjuna's feet. He asked them to get up and state their problem. One of them stood with folded hands and said, "My Lord Arjuna, we are traders who sell our produce to the cities in the north. For the past one month, bandits have been attacking us and looting our produce. Those of us who tried to defend ourselves were brutally killed."

"Why didn't you complain to our soldiers?"

"We did, my lord. A group of soldiers came to the valley through the mountains where we were attacked. The bandits attacked them so furiously that they fled.

[3] A yogi is one who has mastered the art of yoga and has attained complete control over his mind and body.

We have lost everything. If our trade stops, our families will die of hunger. Save us, Lord Arjuna."

Arjuna summoned the general who was in charge of ensuring law and order, and questioned the cowardice of his soldiers. The general shamefacedly admitted that he had sent new soldiers who got scared of the bandits and ran away.

Arjuna said, "We are here to serve the people, not to wear fancy headgear, hold great titles and live in opulent luxury. If we cannot serve the people, we have no right to be called princes or kings. This is the last time I want to hear such complaints. If you cannot help our citizens in distress, you have no right to continue."

Turning to Krishna, he said, "I will go with these people and solve their problems and be back."

Krishna smiled at him and said, "I will come with you, Arjuna. Let us go. All royals need to learn from you. The problems and needs of the people take precedence over everything else. Bravo Arjuna, let us go and defeat those bandits."

Arjuna escorted Krishna into his chariot and he led from the front along with his trusted soldiers. The traders followed behind. They travelled to the north for many hours before they reached a huge mountain. They had to cross the valley to reach the other side and it was in this valley that the bandits had attacked the traders.

Arjuna entered the valley holding his great bow, the Gandiva, in his hand. As he looked around, he saw that there were caves on the sides of the mountains. He noticed there were ropes hanging down from the mountains. He knew that this was the place from where the bandits attacked. He fixed an arrow on his bow and aimed it at the path ahead to clear the way.

Hearing the sound, the bandits thought their victims had arrived. They came out of the caves and slid down from the ropes. They had positioned the ropes in such a way that they would land on carefully constructed canopies on the tree. From there, they would mount their attack on wayfarers. Once they were killed or had fled, they would loot all their belongings.

Little did they know that Arjuna was observing them. As the bandits slid down the ropes, Arjuna fixed five arrows and released them, aiming at the ropes. He quickly fixed five more arrows and released them. He repeated this until he had cut down all the ropes. The bandits came crashing down to the ground.

He then aimed crescent-shaped arrows at the canopies on the tree. He drew the bowstring of his mighty six-and-a-half-foot bow until his ear, and released the arrow. The missiles went at top speed and smashed the canopies. With no cover, the bandits stood exposed. His soldiers then attacked them, killing those who resisted and capturing those who surrendered.

The bandit chief, who was watching from the top, was furious. He picked up a huge boulder and flung it at Arjuna, whose senses were so acute he could even hear the flutter of a bird faraway. Arjuna sensed the movement and looked up. He saw the boulder hurtling towards him. It was too late to fix an arrow to his bow.

He quickly picked up his shield in his left hand and covered his head with it. The huge rock struck his shield with a powerful impact which any other soldier would have been crushed by. Arjuna's shield was strong and he pushed at the rock with his shield using his powerful muscles. His strength was so great that the stone broke into three pieces and fell harmlessly to the side.

He quickly fixed a special arrow that had been made for this purpose. He shot it, with great force, at the bandit chief. The arrow hit the chief on his leg, going in deep. The arrow was attached to a long rope. Arjuna hurled its other end around the branch of a tree and pulled hard. The chief came racing upside down and just as it seemed he would break his head, the rope pulled him up the tree.

He was hanging upside down from the tree and screaming in pain. Arjuna turned back and said, "Let him hang here. It will be a lesson for anyone who dares to attack the good people who live under the protection of King Yudhishtira of Indraprastha."

The traders fell at Arjuna's feet and thanked him profusely. He asked them to continue their journey. Krishna was fulsome in praise of Arjuna, "Bravo Partha, you have demonstrated how a ruler should be— caring for his citizens and leaving no stone unturned for their welfare. Your prowess in archery and your effortless defeat of the bandits will have people singing your praise for years."

Arjuna smiled at Krishna, "It is all your blessings, Krishna. As long your blessings are with us, the Pandavas will always be victorious."

They returned to Indraprastha and the citizens lined the streets, welcoming them by showering them with flower petals. As they reached the palace, Sahadeva, who had been waiting for them, came running to Arjuna.

"Subhadra devi has developed labour pains, Arjuna. We are waiting for the midwife to arrive. Mother Kunti is tending to her right now."

Arjuna ran towards his palace and anxiously waited near the door. Krishna walked up to him smilingly and said, "Relax, Partha, your wife is not the first woman to have given birth to a child. Stop walking around nervously and sit down and let us wait for the good news."

Yudhishtira, who had heard the news, joined them. The night set in as they waited anxiously. Soon the door to the palace opened and Kunti came out, holding her grandson proudly. Arjuna ran to Kunti to see his son. The child shone in the light of the moon. The lustre of the moon's light made Arjuna's son look like a divine being with a halo surrounding him.

Kunti handed over the child to Arjuna who cradled the baby in his arms. He proudly showed his son to Krishna, "Look at your nephew, Krishna, the son of your beloved sister. Brother Yudhishtira, look at the pride of the Pandavas. He will make our family name shine."

Yudhishtira blessed the child and hugged Arjuna, "I am very happy for you. Your son will grow up to be a great warrior just like his father. You must name your heir. His name must be one that makes the world wake up and take notice of him."

Arjuna turned to Krishna, "Vaasudeva, you have been the first teacher to my son. You must name him."

Krishna picked up the child and blessed him. He smiled at Arjuna and said, "This son of yours has a broad chest and large arms just like you. He will grow up to be a great warrior and exhibit heroism and courage of the highest order. He will be filled with passion and self-respect. He will have no fear and exhibit fury against enemies. So, let his name be Abhimanyu."

"It is a great name, Krishna," said Yudhishtira. "It is a name that will be remembered for many years thanks to the heroism he will exhibit before the world."

Arjuna took his son Abhimanyu in his arms and went inside to meet his beloved wife Subhadra. Yudhishtira discussed his plans for Abhimanyu's naming ceremony. He insisted that Krishna should be present and conduct all the rites himself.

There was a celebration throughout the kingdom to welcome the heir of Arjuna. The people of Indraprastha rejoiced and celebrated the birth of their future king. The proud parents were happy seeing their son who shone like the moon. Krishna's brother Balarama visited Indraprastha to bless his nephew.

Balarama was upset about the way Arjuna had married his sister without his permission. He was also upset about Krishna's role in it. However, the birth of his nephew had mollified him and all was forgiven.

Yudhishtira organised a grand naming ceremony on the twelfth day after Abhimanyu's birth. All the residents of the kingdom were invited, as were the rulers of friendly kingdoms. They all came and blessed Abhimanyu, returning to their homes with their stomachs full of food and arms full of gifts.

Yudhishtira gifted 10,000 cows to the Brahmins. He presented gold coins to all those who came to bless the child. The pomp and splendour of the ceremony impressed all the royal guests who attended the ceremony. Many great kings and princes came to wish Arjuna and bless the child. All of them returned singing praises of Yudhishtira and Arjuna.

The guests were happy seeing Arjuna's heir. Impressed with the lustre on his face, they sang praises of the young prince. They all blessed him to be a great warrior and achieve immense success in life. Arjuna's happiness knew no bounds when his grandfather, the great Bheeshma, arrived to bless his great-grandson.

The birth of Abhimanyu brought great happiness to the kingdom of Indraprastha. Arjuna and Subhadra spent most of their time with their son. Krishna too visited Indraprastha frequently to spend time with his dear nephew. A happy childhood awaited Abhimanyu.

3

A Happy Childhood

Abhimanyu's childhood was pleasant. He was the apple of his father's eye. His mother doted on him and spent all her time bringing him up with loving care. His parents, uncles, aunt Draupadi and grandmother Kunti showered him with unlimited love and affection. Even though Draupadi had a son of her own, she treated Abhimanyu as her own.

Abhimanyu was lucky to receive the love of his illustrious uncle, the great Krishna. Even though he stayed at Dwaraka hundreds of miles away, he regularly visited Indraprastha for the sole purpose of spending time with his favourite nephew.

Subhadra knew that her son would be a great warrior. She fervently hoped that one day he would be the king of Indraprastha and maybe even Hastinapura. She looked after him with the belief that she was bringing up a future king and great warrior. She fed her son with the richest and most nutritious food made with pure ghee.

The milk and ghee used for Abhimanyu's food came from the cows that were from Dwaraka. Krishna had gifted those cows to his sister. Arjuna was proud of his son and loved him a lot. He spent every free moment playing with him and watching him grow.

Abhimanyu was clearly destined to achieve big things in life. He grew fast, just like the moon grows from the time of amavasya (dark night of no moon) to poornima (full moon). One day Arjuna spotted his son taking infant steps towards his great bow Gandiva and trying to play with it.

Arjuna was pleased. His son was truly going to be a great warrior, there was no doubt about it. He would become an archer and Arjuna would train him personally. Arjuna was determined to teach him all that he knew about archery and make him an archer whose skills would match his own. He had made a lot of plans for Abhimanyu's education and training in warfare. The only thing left was for Abhimanyu to grow up.

Subhadra would tease Arjuna, "Your son cannot grow at the speed you want. He needs to be five years old before he starts learning and you cannot teach him archery so early. Have patience, dear husband. Let our son enjoy his play time before you make him a great archer."

Abhimanyu loved playing with weapons, and Subhadra had to take care to keep the child away from the sharp ones. Arjuna carved a toy bow of wood for his son with arrows made from plant stems, which became the child's favourite toy. He would start crying if separated from his bow and arrow. Arjuna couldn't wait for his son to grow up so he could teach him archery.

Abhimanyu had a happy childhood, with all the palace maids lining up to play with him. There was never a dull moment in the little one's life. Abhimanyu's childhood seemed to have only joy in it. The kingdom was abuzz with activity as King Yudhishtira decided to perform the Rajasuya yagna.[4]

On Krishna's advice, it was decided that the evil Emperor Jarasandha had to be defeated if Yudhishtira's Rajasuya had to succeed. Krishna, Bheema and Arjuna went disguised as Brahmins to Jarasandha's palace in Magadha. They challenged Jarasandha to a duel, and with Krishna's help, Bheema killed him.

The victorious Pandavas then set out to conquer other kingdoms. They did not want to topple the kings but only wanted to make them accept Yudhishtira's supremacy. All those who accepted this were allowed to continue to rule after giving a tribute. Those who resisted were defeated in battle. Arjuna, being a great warrior, was sent on a conquering expedition to the north.

He defeated King Bhagadatta of Pragjyotisha and King Vrihanta. One by one, he conquered all the lands he visited. He conquered Kashmira, Uluka, Modapura, Puru, Trigarta, Avisari, Uraga, Kambhoja and the mystical land of the Kurus of the north. He returned bearing tributes from all the kingdoms with caravans full of gold, precious gems, coins and other gifts that he offered to Yudhishtira.

Bheema travelled to the east and conquered the Gandhakas, Videhas, Dasaranas, Kosalas, Vatsabhumi, Videha and Karusha. Sahadeva travelled south and conquered the Matsyas, Surasenas, Adhirajas, Avanti, Vinda, Anuvinda, Mahishmati and Lanka. Nakula

[4] The Rajasuya yagna was a sacrificial ritual that was performed by a king who wished to become an emperor.

travelled to the west and conquered the Karnatas, Malavas and Mlecchas. The kingdoms of Dwaraka and Madra gladly accepted Yudhishtira's rule.

Having conquered almost the entire country with the exception of Hastinapura, Yudhishtira was now the emperor of the land. He organised the Rajasuya yagna and all the great sages and saints visited his palace to conduct the yagna. All the kings under his suzerainty attended the yagna. He invited his uncles and cousins as well. Bheeshma, Drona and Duryodhana attended the yagna along with other Kaurava princes.

All the guests who arrived for the yagna were given the best accommodation with all facilities to ensure they had a good stay. As they moved around the city, they marvelled at the beautiful palaces and the well-administered city. Their interactions with the satisfied citizens made them appreciate Yudhishtira's leadership.

The guests were taken to the Palace of Illusions. The Pandavas had built the city of Indraprastha by burning down the Khandava forest as per the wishes of Agni, the god of fire. Arjuna had slain the Nagas who lived there. Only one among them, Maya, had been spared. He was an architect, skilled in the art of creating illusions.

Maya created an amazing Palace of Illusions that mesmerised the visitors. The illusion generated in his architecture was brilliant. Some rooms had mirrors that looked like doors. Other doors turned out to be mirrors. There were water bodies in the palace, which actually was the floor. There were forests within the palace, which were again Maya's illusions.

All the guests were astounded after visiting the Palace of Illusions. Usually, someone would accompany guests to the palace so that they would not face any problems. The palaces in the city, the opulence and the excellent hospitality had guests singing praises of the Pandavas.

The yagna commenced and it was time to worship the elders and important guests. Yudhishtira's quandary over who should be worshipped first was resolved by Bheeshma who endorsed the name of Krishna. When Krishna was being worshipped, King Shishupala of Chedi objected and hurled abuses at Krishna, who silently listened to him without exhibiting even a little anger.

Arjuna was outraged and told Krishna, "How can you keep quiet when this vile man abuses you? I will slay him in an instant, permit me."

Krishna smilingly asked Arjuna to remain seated. He allowed Shishupala to continue to say what he wanted and then stood up to address the audience of kings, celestial beings and sages, "Shishupala is ordained to be killed by me. However, for his mother's sake, I had allowed him a hundred mistakes. I had given a boon to Shishupala's mother saying that I will pardon him a hundred times for whatever mistakes he will make. Now, he has completed a hundred offences and his time is up."

Krishna then raised his finger and the Sudarshana Chakra appeared spinning like a blazing disc. Krishna released the golden disc towards Shishupala and it blazed in the air towards the horrified Chedi king and beheaded him.

Once this ugly incident was over, the yagna was completed peacefully. All the visiting dignitaries blessed Yudhishtira, his brothers and their children. Subhadra proudly stood next to her husband, carrying Abhimanyu in her arms. The sages and kings blessed Abhimanyu to be a great prince and warrior.

The ceremonies and celebrations lasted weeks. The Pandava family was busy attending to the guests and ensuring that everything went well. Draupadi had not been able to spend time with Abhimanyu for many weeks. After all the guests had departed, she visited Subhadra to spend time with Abhimanyu.

Arjuna's two queens were discussing the yagna and all that had happened. The beheading of Shishupala had stunned everyone. It was an incident that marred the otherwise successful event.

"Did you know something very funny happened when our guests were here?" said Draupadi.

"What was it, sister?"

"The great crown prince of Hastinapura visited the Palace of Illusions."

"Hope he was impressed with what he saw."

"The Pandavas were impressed and delighted with Duryodhana's adventures in the palace. Krishna revealed his naughty side."

"What did my brother do?"

"He asked the Pandavas to send Duryodhana inside the palace with an escort and then asked the escort to leave midway. Poor Duryodhana had no idea where to go and what to do. He tried to open a door but it was already open. He then tried to walk through the door, but it turned out to be a door made of crystal and he bumped against it. Everyone laughed merrily."

"I don't think he would have liked it."

"All my husbands were there as well as Krishna and his queens. I was there too. I tried to control my laughter but couldn't. Everyone burst out laughing."

"Poor man. I know it is funny, but he is a very proud and arrogant man. I think it was wrong to make fun of him."

"Come on, Subhadra, sometimes a bit of humour is needed after a tiring day. I haven't finished narrating the antics of Duryodhana. He came across a stream in the middle of the palace and lifted his clothes to avoid them getting wet. It was not a stream but a glass floor. He then saw another stream and thinking it was glass, stepped on it. The floor actually was a stream and he fell into it and was fully wet. How everyone laughed!" said Draupadi, chuckling at the memory of the incident and tickling Abhimanyu, making him laugh uncontrollably.

"Hmm, I still think it was not good to humiliate that man. He seems to be vengeful."

"You don't have to feel pity for him. He is not fit to be the prince of the Kuru clan. He lacks even one good quality that my husbands have. Even though he is my brother-in-law, he looks at me with lust in his eyes. He is a depraved man. He had come to my swayamvara[5] to marry me but couldn't succeed. Since then, he looks at

[5] The swayamvara was an occasion where a princess would choose her own husband from various invitees, usually after a contest or competition.

me with evil intent in his eyes. He deserved this insult and it was good of Krishna to entertain us in this way."

Subhadra dropped the unpleasant topic and both the queens played with Abhimanyu, who was delighted by the attention he was getting.

Little did they know that Subhadra's fears were about to come true. Duryodhana was vengeful and jealous in nature. He had always hated the Pandavas and could not tolerate their successes. He had tried to kill them in the Lac Palace and failed. Now they had a huge empire of their own. It was bigger and better than the kingdom his father ruled. He was jealous of the grand city that the Pandavas had built.

He burned in the flame of envy, seeing how everyone praised the Pandavas for the way the yagna was conducted. Above all, he seethed in rage at the way he was humiliated in the Palace of Illusions. He blamed the Pandavas for this and unjustly held Draupadi at fault.

His wily uncle Shakuni, his mother Gandhari's brother, spared no effort to add fuel to the fire that burnt in Duryodhana's heart. Uncle and nephew, along with their trusted aides, spent hours together plotting ways to avenge Duryodhana's insult.

The Pandavas spent their days happily exultant at the success of the Rajasuya yagna. Yudhishtira was now the emperor of the greatest empire in the land. The Pandava brothers and their family rejoiced at their victory. Their citizens lived in peace and prosperity. Little did they know what fate had in store for all of them.

4

Bad Times for the Pandavas

One day, Arjuna came to Subhadra and informed her that they were leaving for Hastinapura. She was surprised and asked Arjuna for the reason of their visit.

Arjuna, who was playing with Abhimanyu and helping him shoot arrows from his toy bow, said, "King Dhritharashtra has invited us. All five of us and Draupadi are going. He has organised a gambling match and you know how my brother Yudhishtira loves the game of dice. Let us enjoy their hospitality, and hopefully, the relations between our families will improve."

"After you humiliated Duryodhana in Maya's palace, I don't understand how things will improve. Let us hope he does not intend to avenge the humiliation. He is not a man to be trusted."

"Quiet, Subhadra," said Arjuna sharply. "It is not Duryodhana who has organised this. Our invitation came from our uncle King Dhritharashtra. He has the wise Vidura as his prime minister. They will not allow Duryodhana to do any mischief. We will go for a few days and enjoy their hospitality and the gambling matches. We anyway have so much wealth, even if brother Yudhishtira loses some money gambling it does not matter."

Arjuna got ready to leave. He hugged and kissed Abhimanyu and asked Subhadra to take care of him. A large retinue left with the five Pandavas and Draupadi in it.

Subhadra was bored being alone at the palace. She was also worried about what would happen at Hastinapura, at the gambling match. She knew in her heart that her brother Krishna had made a big mistake by allowing Duryodhana to be humiliated. Abhimanyu could sense the fear in her eyes and kept asking her why she looked unhappy.

She waited eagerly for any news from Hastinapura, but none came. Finally, after a few days, the Pandavas returned. A maid came shouting that the emperor had returned. Subhadra ran to the window and was shocked to see Draupadi. Her hair was unkempt and left loose. She looked terribly distraught. The five Pandava brothers had their heads bent and did not lift them even once. Very clearly, something terrible had happened.

Arjuna entered the palace and, ignoring Subhadra, went into the sleeping chamber and lay down. He gruffly asked her to allow him some rest. She was surprised that he did not even greet his dear son Abhimanyu. He slept through the evening and night, refusing to even take food. The next day morning, she found that he had left on his horse without telling anyone where he had gone.

Seriously worried and unable to control her anxiety, Subhadra carried a sleeping Abhimanyu with her and went to meet Draupadi. She was shocked by what she saw. Even Draupadi ignored Abhimanyu. Her eyes were red from weeping and her hair was still unkempt.

"Sister, I know something terrible has happened. You seem to be extremely upset. Probably you do not want to be disturbed, but I am very tense and worried. None of you seem normal after your return from Hastinapura. Please tell me what happened there."

Draupadi gestured to Subhadra to sit down. She placed Abhimanyu on the bed and patted him while he was asleep, as she waited for Draupadi to speak. After a long period of silence, Draupadi started speaking.

"You said that Duryodhana was a vile and vengeful man. You had feared he may retaliate for the way he was humiliated in the palace of Maya."

"Yes," said Subhadra apprehensively.

"Your fears came true. His vengeance has shattered me. I am mentally devastated by what happened in the palace in Hastinapura."

Now Subhadra was scared. She knew that something terrible had happened and waited anxiously to hear about it. Both the queens did not know that Abhimanyu had woken up and was listening to them. He did not understand everything that was said, but it was all registering in his mind.

Draupadi narrated what had transpired in Hastinapura.

"We reached Hastinapura and were given a royal welcome. We were given excellent quarters to stay in and experienced hospitality at its best. Duryodhana, Dushasana and his other brothers greeted us effusively.

All the arrangements were excellent. After a few days of relaxation, the gambling match commenced in the court of King Dhritharashtra in the presence of the Kuru elders."

Draupadi paused and then continued, "I was in my living quarters but found out later what had happened. Shakuni of Gandhara played on behalf of Duryodhana. Jewellery, rare gemstones, silver coins, gold coins, elephants, horses were all used as wagers for the gambling competition. The king kept losing all the wagers but did not stop. He kept gambling and began to lose everything."

"What happened then?" asked Subhadra.

"Duryodhana then offered the greatest wager, the kingdom of Hastinapura against Indraprastha."

Subhadra was horrified, "How could Duryodhana wager Hastinapura when he is not the king?"

"The Kuru elders sat silently. King Dhritharashtra is not just physically blind, his affection for his son has made him mentally blind and he tolerates all that his son does. The dice were rolled and yet again my husband was defeated. In one instant, everything was lost. Duryodhana had won Indraprastha."

"So Indraprastha no longer belongs to us?"

"Wait, there is a lot more that happened. Duryodhana commiserated with our loss. He offered another chance to win back everything."

"But ... but ... we did not have anything left to wager?"

"He asked the king to wager himself and his brothers."

Subhadra couldn't believe what she was hearing.

"My husband accepted the wager. The dice were rolled and Shakuni won again. My five husbands were no longer free men. They were now slaves of Duryodhana. He and his brothers laughed, made merry and humiliated my husbands. However, he was not done yet. The vile man offered one more chance for Yudhishtira to win back everything. He asked him to wager me. The bet was that if Shakuni lost, everything would be returned to us. If Shakuni won, then I would belong to Duryodhana."

Subhadra closed her ears, unable to hear the wicked thing that had been said, "How dare Duryodhana ask for someone else's wife to be put on wager? How did the Kuru elders allow this? Didn't the grandsire Bheeshma stop it?"

"I told you, Subhadra, the Kuru elders were blind, deaf and dumb. My great husband, Dharmaraja[6] Yudhishtira, agreed to place his wife on wager. The dice were rolled and the wily Shakuni won. The wicked Duryodhana then asked a servant to bring me to the great hall."

Draupadi was now in tears, remembering the terrible events, "I naturally refused to come. I demanded an answer. I wanted to know if Dharmaraja had wagered himself first or me. If he had wagered himself and lost, then he had no right to put me on wager. My answer made Duryodhana furious and he sent his brother to me."

Tears rolled down Draupadi's eyes and Subhadra embraced her and wiped the tears from her face as little Abhimanyu looked on, not understanding why his mothers were crying.

[6] Dharmaraja is the name given to Yudhishtira as he was the son of the god Yamadharma, the god of dharma who dispensed justice in the world.

"The wicked Dushasana demanded I come to the hall. When I refused and repeated my question, he caught me by my hair. He pulled off the ornaments that I had braided into my hair. He grabbed my flowing hair and dragged me all the way to the great hall as the soldiers and servants looked on in shock."

Draupadi tried hard but could not control her tears. "He dragged me through the hall even as I resisted in vain. He threw me on the ground in front of the vile Duryodhana. The Kaurava brothers laughed wickedly and Duryodhana ogled me in the vilest possible way. I looked at my five great husbands. They all sat on the floor bareheaded, their crowns on the floor, their heads bent in shame. I looked at the Kuru elders, none of whom could look me in the eye."

Draupadi took a deep breath and continued her narration, "Duryodhana looked me with the most despicable expression in his eyes. He patted his thigh, said I was his slave and asked me to sit on his thigh. Bheema and Arjuna got up and charged at him, but Yudhishtira stopped them. Bheema could not be stopped. He said that one day he would break Duryodhana's thighs."

"I cannot even imagine the horror of the situation. I can only imagine how much pain you would have felt."

Draupadi laughed aloud, "Subhadra, what I have narrated is nothing. This was just the beginning. More horrors were to follow."

Subhadra felt a sinking sensation in her stomach, wondering what more depravities could have occurred.

Draupadi looked up and closed her eyes, desperately trying to get rid of the picture that was appearing before her. She continued, "Karna, the son of a charioteer, was furious hearing the words of brave Bheema. He told Duryodhana that not only was I his slave but that I was also a harlot. He humiliated me, saying that I belonged to five men and hence I have no rights to stand wearing such grand clothes before the great kings."

Draupadi could not control herself and cried piteously as Subhadra embraced her once more and tried to console her. She could not believe that all this had happened in the court of Hastinapura.

"The wicked Duryodhana had always lusted for me. He now leered wickedly and agreed with Karna's ugly words. He asked Dushasana to disrobe me in front of everyone."

Subhadra could not control herself. She wept listening to the terrible incident. Seeing her cry, little Abhimanyu started crying as well. Both the queens of Arjuna then consoled Abhimanyu and put him to sleep before continuing their conversation.

"I ran towards my husbands and appealed to them to save me. They could only look down at the ground. I ran to the Kuru elders and demanded them to stop this. No one could even look me in the eye. I appealed to everyone to stop it and wept. Vidura meekly asked Duryodhana to stop everything, but he rudely ordered him to sit quietly."

"Only one person came to my support," said Draupadi. "It was Vikarna, Duryodhana's brother. He protested but Duryodhana shouted at him and asked him to get out. The wicked Dushasana then caught hold of my saree and started disrobing me. Arjuna and

Bheema tried to get up, but the righteous Dharmaraja held them by their hands and stopped them. For him, his dharma mattered more than my dignity."

Draupadi sighed deeply, "My dignity had been stripped completely, Subhadra. It was now the turn of my clothes to be stripped. I realised that no one there would save me. I then remembered the only person in the world who would save me."

"Who?" asked Subhadra.

"Your brother Vaasudeva," said Draupadi and folded her hands with her eyes closed. "I stood like this, with my eyes closed and a prayer to Krishna on my lips, desperately hoping for a miracle, as Dushasana kept stripping away my clothes."

Draupadi opened her eyes and smiled, "Then a miracle did happen. Krishna heard my prayers. Dushasana kept pulling at my saree, encouraged by the vile Duryodhana, but even as he stripped off large lengths of cloth, more appeared miraculously. My dear friend Krishna protected me that day. Exhausted, Dushasana finally fell on the floor."

"I lost control and decided to speak everything in my mind," said Draupadi. "I shouted at my husbands that their respect for their brother's addiction to gambling was more than my dignity. I shouted at Dushasana for daring to touch me. I took a vow that I would never tie my hair until he was dead."

"Then Bheema got up," said Draupadi, clearly relishing the one memorable moment from that terrible day. "He said he would kill Dushasana, rip his intestines out, comb my hair with Dushasana's blood and finally tie my hair with his intestines."

Draupadi laughed, "The blind king suddenly woke up, now that serious death threats had been hurled at his sons. He apologised to me and said that with his authority as the king, he cancels the results of the game. He released my husbands from their slavery and returned our kingdom."

Draupadi sighed again, "So we have returned, our kingdom intact but our dignity lost. Our bad times have started and I don't know when they will stop."

5

Bidding Goodbye to Indraprastha

Subhadra was shattered hearing about the shameful incident in Hastinapura. Arjuna returned after a few days from wherever he had gone. He was clearly disturbed by what had happened and was humiliated. He spoke very little and spent his time in silence. He did not even play with Abhimanyu as much as he used to before. Realising his state of mind, Subhadra did not refer to the terrible incident.

The days of joy, happiness and peace were clearly over for the royals of Indraprastha; now only a tragic silence remained. None of the Pandava princes ventured out and preferred to spend their time in quietude and meditation. Subhadra did her best to console Draupadi. She tried to help her come out of the terrible mental anguish she had suffered.

It was nearly a month since the terrible incident when Subhadra saw Arjuna pack his belongings. He looked at her and said, "We are off to Hastinapura."

Subhadra was shocked, "After all that happened you are going again?"

"Yes, King Dhritharashtra has invited us again for a gambling match. King Yudhishtira has accepted."

"How can Yudhishtira do this? He will gamble away the kingdom and Draupadi again. You must stop him."

"Quiet, Subhadra, you are speaking of the emperor. Right or wrong, he is our brother and our ruler. We have no option but to obey his orders."

"They will once again humiliate you. I have heard from a maid that the wicked Shakuni uses black magic. I heard that his dice are made of the bones of his dead father and he invokes spirits to make the dice do what he wants. You cannot hope to defeat him in gambling."

"I know that Subhadra, and probably so does Yudhishtira. We have no option. We are Kshatriyas. To refuse the invitation would be cowardice, that's what my brother says. We will do what he says. As far as what will happen there, we are prepared for the worst. You too need to be prepared for unpleasant times."

Arjuna and his brothers left for Hastinapura. This time they did not take Draupadi with them. Subhadra waited anxiously, feeling sick about what evil plans the Kauravas would have hatched against her family. All this affected little Abhimanyu. Other than Subhadra, no one played with him. Everyone was in a state of shock and worry.

It did not take long for the Pandavas to come back from Hastinapura. Arjuna returned with his head bent low yet again. Seeing her husband, Subhadra knew something terrible had happened to him. She ran to him and held his hand, "Please tell me what happened. I know that something bad has happened again."

Arjuna picked up Abhimanyu, cradled him, kissed him fondly and hugged him tightly. Little Abhimanyu squealed in delight at the affection shown by his father after such a long time. Arjuna smiled wanly at Subhadra and said, "Look around you and see the beautiful city of Indraprastha. How does it look to you?"

"It is truly heaven on Earth for me and my son."

"It is time to bid goodbye to this heavenly kingdom, my dear wife. As you rightly expected, Shakuni defeated us at the game of dice. At stake was our empire. We lost and we now have to bid goodbye to this great city."

Subhadra couldn't control her tears at the thought of leaving the city. Where would they go? What would they do?

Arjuna continued, "There was one more condition. We are to go into exile for twelve years in the forest and after that, spend the thirteenth year incognito, without being discovered. If we are discovered, then we have to spend twelve more years in exile."

Subhadra's heart sank. The unspoken question in her mind was what she and her son would do.

Arjuna hugged Subhadra and Abhimanyu. He said, "We five brothers are going with Draupadi tomorrow. We leave for the forests to spend twelve years in exile. You will not be coming with us."

"Why not? Am I not your wife? Should I not be with you?"

"You are first a mother and then a wife. I do not want to expose my Abhimanyu to the rigours of life in the forest. Draupadi has chosen to come with us as she is wife to all of us and believes it is her dharma to be with us. Her children will be in her father Drupada's kingdom."

"What about me?" asked Subhadra.

"I have sent a messenger to Krishna. I have requested him to send someone to take you and Abhimanyu to Dwaraka. It is your home. Stay there in peace and bring up my son to be a great warrior prince. That's all I ask of you."

"How will my son and I live without you?"

"There is no option. It is the will of the gods that things should happen like this. Thirteen years will pass in no time and then we will be reunited. We cannot break our exile else I would have visited Dwaraka to meet my son."

Tears were shed as the Pandavas prepared to leave for exile. The citizens of Indraprastha were grief-stricken and they mourned the exit of their beloved rulers. The next day, Krishna's son Pradyumna came to Indraprastha to escort his aunt Subhadra and cousin Abhimanyu to Dwaraka.

There was a tearful parting as Arjuna hugged Subhadra and Abhimanyu and bid them farewell. Abhimanyu's lovely childhood had been brutally disrupted. He was now going to be cruelly separated from the land of his birth and his father.

The Pandavas, along with Draupadi, left for the forest. They moved from one place to another during their exile. Arjuna pined for his son but knew that he had to wait a long time to meet him again.

In Dwaraka, Subhadra pined for Arjuna. The presence of her beloved brothers Krishna and Balarama and their wives helped reduce her grief. Abhimanyu demanded to see his father, cried and sulked for many days but soon adjusted to life in blissful Dwaraka.

There was no shortage of affection for Abhimanyu as everyone in Dwaraka showered love on him. He became the favourite of Krishna, who would spend time with him regularly. Balarama, Pradyumna, Rukmini and Satyabhama all regularly visited Subhadra to spend time with Abhimanyu.

As Abhimanyu grew, plans were made for his education. It was decided that he would be taught by a guru at the palace. He soon learned to read and write. Like his father, he was a quick learner and grasped all that was taught to him. The Yadavas regarded Abhimanyu as heir to the Pandavas and brought him up like a future emperor.

He was taught the scriptures, the art of governance and statecraft. He enjoyed spending time with the sons of the Yadava princes. Like his uncle Krishna, Abhimanyu loved to spend time amidst nature, wandering to the nearby forests and playing with the cows and calves. He enjoyed his games with the Yadava cowherds during his free time.

As he grew older, along with his studies, he was taught the art of warfare. While Subhadra protested that it was too early to teach him to fight, Krishna assured her that Abhimanyu was a quick learner and powerful warrior. He again pointed out that she was bringing up the heir to the Pandava kingdom and that Abhimanyu should be trained accordingly.

Krishna personally trained Abhimanyu on the basic aspects of warfare. It was his son Pradyumna who was

Abhimanyu's guru. Just as Dronacharya had taught archery and other skills to Arjuna, Pradyumna taught warfare to Abhimanyu.

Abhimanyu's lessons on warfare started with the basics of sword-fighting. Keeping his age in mind, he was given a small sword made of wood so that he would not get hurt. He was taught how to hold the sword, how to swing it, how to block an attack and how to get through an opponent's defences.

Apart from sword-fighting, there were also lessons on wrestling and hand-to-hand combat. Abhimanyu was sufficiently strong for his age thanks to his broad chest and huge arms. He quickly learnt the art of hand-to-hand combat. He could easily defeat boys of his age and even sustain an attack from a stronger wrestler.

Sword training continued every day. Hundreds of wooden swords and shields lay broken during the training. The warrior Satyaki was his teacher and was a hard taskmaster. He would defeat Abhimanyu in a minute, breaking his sword and shield. Abhimanyu would be reduced to tears but would not be allowed to stop. He had to pick up another sword and shield and continue training.

This went on for weeks until he could defend himself from Satyaki's attacks with his sword intact. He was then given a metal sword whose edges were blunt. Satyaki's forceful attacks broke through his defence many times, and he was hit all over his body by the metal sword. Even though it did not have a sharp blade, the metal left behind marks and hurt him severely.

Abhimanyu did not flinch or cry but took the blows on his young body and fought on bravely. At night, Subhadra would look at the marks on his body and cry. She would apply medicine to reduce the pain. She complained to Krishna and asked him to go back to the wooden swords for Abhimanyu's training.

Krishna smiled and said, "My dear sister, when Abhimanyu goes to war, he cannot ask the opponent to use a wooden sword since he cannot tolerate the pain. A warrior's learning will be accompanied by pain and injuries. Your son is very tough and will soon become an expert. Don't worry. Have faith in me and allow your son to train to become a great warrior."

Soon Abhimanyu could not only fend off Satyaki's attacks but also could hit him back. Then Pradyumna and Satyaki would attack him simultaneously. The blows they delivered with the blunt swords were enough to make any boy run away from the training. Abhimanyu was mature beyond his years and knew that every blow he took now would help him become stronger.

Soon, he was able to fend off the joint attack of the two powerful Yadavas. One day during training, he fought back so ferociously that he broke Satyaki's sword and hit him hard on the chest, causing him to fall. He charged at Pradyumna and hit him repeatedly on his shield, causing it to break.

Satyaki ran to Abhimanyu and hugged him in joy. "Brave son of Arjuna, I am proud to have been a teacher to you. Keep training and be focused, you will become the greatest warrior in this world, I have no doubts about this."

Pradyumna congratulated Abhimanyu on his quick mastery of sword fighting. Now they started using real swords and Abhimanyu was covered in heavy armour to prevent serious injuries. By then, he had become an expert and could fight without being hit even once on his body.

Once the training in fighting with a sword was completed, the next lessons were on the use of the spear. For this, he was given a real spear and targets in the form of a number of logs were lined up, each with a sketch of a human being on them. All the sketches were made using a dye made from fruit. He had to throw the spear and hit the heart of the man sketched on the log.

At first, he could not even throw the spear halfway. But Pradyumna was a good teacher. He encouraged his student and showed him how it should be done. He taught him how to aim and to use his muscles to impart power to the javelin. It took days before Abhimanyu could hit the target. He was then asked to move back and throw the spear, thus increasing the distance. It did not take long for Abhimanyu to master the use of the spear.

In this way, under Pradyumna's tutelage, Abhimanyu learnt sword fighting and the use of a spear. Then the main training commenced. Like his father, Abhimanyu wanted to become a great archer. Pradyumna would not allow him to pick up the bow until he had first mastered hand fighting, sword usage and use of the spear.

It was now time for Abhimanyu to be trained to become a great archer.

6

Training to Be a Great Warrior

Pradyumna was a great archer himself and he ensured that Abhimanyu learnt all that was needed to become a great archer. He first taught Abhimanyu how to string the bow, starting with a small bow and then moving on to bigger bows that were almost as big as the little prince himself.

He was taught how to hold the bow, how to pick the arrow from the quiver, how to fix the arrow and how to shoot it at the target. Pradyumna made him understand the importance of doing all this at top speed.

"Remember, Abhimanyu, when you go to war, you will find opponents older and more experienced than you. If you have to defeat them, it is not enough knowing how to shoot an arrow or even delivering it on target. What is important is speed and power. If you want to beat your opponent, you need to release your arrows quickly so that they reach your opponent faster than he draws his arrows."

Abhimanyu was diligent and determined. He put in hours of training and learnt how to fix and release an arrow quickly. Once this was done, Pradyumna started with target practice. The logs were brought back and Abhimanyu was asked to hit the heart of the drawing from different distances.

After finishing a hard day of training, Abhimanyu would rest, have his food, go out at night and continue training in the moonlight. When there was no moon in the sky, he would light a torch fire and train in semi-darkness. He would do this until his mother forced him to go to bed.

Both Krishna and Pradyumna were happy to see Abhimanyu's dedication and hard work. This made their job of training him easy. In the next round of training, a variety of fruit—melons, apples, smaller oranges and even grapes—was tied to and dangled down from trees. Abhimanyu had to hit them all.

Hitting the small grapes took a lot of practice. Under Pradyumna's training, Abhimanyu learnt quickly. He was able to hit targets perfectly and could do it from quite a distance.

Sometimes Krishna would himself attend the training. He trained Abhimanyu on hitting moving targets. He would throw a fruit in the air and ask Abhimanyu to shoot it down. Once this was learnt, he would hurl wooden arrows at Abhimanyu and ask him to shoot each down before it reached him. In time, real arrows replaced wooden arrows.

Abhimanyu was hit many times on his armour and it hurt him badly. But he did not change his expression and went ahead with the training as though nothing had happened. He knew that if he showed pain, his mother would cry and he did not want to cause her any grief.

One day Krishna took Abhimanyu for a walk. They saw a dog nearby. Seeing them walk towards it, the dog turned to run away. Krishna asked Abhimanyu to shoot his arrow at the fleeing dog and kill it.

Abhimanyu lifted his bow, fixed an arrow but did not release it. He put down his bow and said, "Uncle, is it right that for me to learn target practice, a dog should die?"

"It is a dog, after all, kill it! What does it matter?"

"Uncle, it is a living being and is not harming me in any way. It is not attacking me nor is it dangerous. In fact, it is running away in fear. Isn't killing in this way cruelty?"

Krishna embraced Abhimanyu and said, "Bravo, my child, I am proud that you have proven yourself to be a true warrior. A warrior is not one who uses his power to kill wantonly. You have shown that you have understood what it means to be a warrior."

Abhimanyu was happy that he did not have to kill the poor little dog.

Krishna continued, "That's the differences between manavas (humans) and danavas (demons). Danavas kill for pleasure and to satisfy their blood lust. Humans kill only when it is necessary."

"What about hunting? Is it right to kill animals?"

"Why do people hunt? They do it for food. It is justified to hunt and kill animals for food. It is also justified to kill wild animals like tigers, boars, wolves, hyenas and other such animals that are a danger to mankind. Hunting for sport or pleasure is not right. It should only be for a justified reason."

Krishna continued to explain the law of nature. "Animals multiply rapidly. Too many animals in the forest would create a situation where the food supply of animals would be less. They would finish off all the plants and move on to the villages to feed on crops grown there. This would cause a serious imbalance. Nature intends a balance to be maintained between humans, animals that eat plants and wild animals. Hunting helps maintain that balance."

"So, it will not be considered adharma[7] if a warrior kills his opponent?"

"When a war is fought, the goal is to defeat the enemy. If you do not kill an opponent, he will kill you—it is as simple as that. If the opponent is defenceless, weak and has no weapons, then it is not justified to kill him. He can be taken prisoner. Of course, a good warrior would not want to be defeated or taken prisoner. He would prefer to die on the battlefield."

"If war leads to so many deaths, why fight?"

"My child, war is fought for a cause. Your uncle Yudhishtira wanted to expand his kingdom. He did not intend to conquer his opponents and humiliate them. He asked other kings to accept his suzerainty and give tributes. Those who refused had to face war. Similarly, when you face the forces of adharma you have to fight a war. In the earlier yugas, wars were fought with the asuras or demons as they were evil and had to be killed to protect the good. In the same way, evil kings are abundant today. They need to be killed to reduce the burden on Earth."

[7] Adharma is that which is unjust, unfair or evil. Dharma is the opposite of adharma. Dharma is not just good and just, it also refers to doing one's duty.

"Now I have a question for you," asked Krishna. "Supposing I had overruled your views and ordered you to kill the dog, what would you have done?"

"You are my guru now and I have to listen to you. I would have done it."

"Good! A warrior must obey the king or his teacher or his parents. Parashurama killed his mother without thinking when his father ordered him to do so. A warrior has to do his duty as ordained by his king or his general."

"We are now reaching the end of this yuga," continued Krishna. "As we step into the Kali Yuga, we will come across kings and generals who do not think about dharma but only about their own selfish needs. Their orders may be against dharma. When such selfish, cruel and evil leaders give orders, in the interest of dharma, one can defy their orders. The future will see more and more such instances."

"What will happen during Kali Yuga, uncle? How will it be different from the previous yugas?"

"In the Satya, Treta and Dwapara yugas, the gods would visit Earth to bless their devotees. As we move into the Kali Yuga, sinners would be found in abundance. Selfishness, lust, gluttony and greed will become the predominant traits of humans. Soon gods and celestial beings will not enter Earth."

"In the Kali Yuga," continued Krishna, "women will be disrespected; people will behave like animals and kill each other for no reason. People, however good they may be, will no longer able to see God with their naked eyes. The gods will not come to the rescue of people when they pray like it happens in this yuga. The law of karma will prevail."

"What is karma?"

"It is action. When you act in a particular way, you get the result you deserve. As you sow, so you will reap. If you do good, good karma will accumulate and help you in your next birth. The more good you do, the higher is your chance of reaching heaven and becoming one with the Supreme Being. The bad deeds done will ensure you will continue to remain on Earth so that you face the consequences of those deeds."

"Will all bad deeds be punished?"

"Yes, my child, punishment for bad deeds will have to be faced. It can be either in this life or in the next. Those who are evil and have anger and hate in their hearts will never be free from the cycle of birth and rebirth. They will continue to be born to experience the results of the actions of their previous life."

"I learn so much from you, Uncle," said Abhimanyu. "I have a question on war. What are the divyastras or celestial weapons and when can they be used?"

"You have asked a good question. Celestial weapons are given by the gods to their devotees if they are convinced that they deserve them. The divyastras are meant to be used properly. They must be used on an opponent who is strong and must never be used on ordinary soldiers or on someone weaker than you."

"Which are the different celestial weapons, Uncle?"

"There are many celestial weapons that the gods bestow. There is the Agneyastra that emits fire against the opponent. The Varunastra releases water and can be used to nullify the effects of the Agneyastra.

The Sammohanastra renders the enemy unconscious. The Vayavyastra causes a gale storm that will blow away the enemy. The Shilastra can be used to dispel the effects of the Vayavyastra. The Suryastra dispels darkness and creates light. The Sarpastra releases snakes that will tie up the enemy. The Mahendrastra causes a rain of flaming arrows to destroy the enemy."

"Which is the most powerful astra, Uncle?"

"The trinity of Brahma, Vishnu and Shiva are the most powerful gods. The weapons they have are the most powerful. The Brahmastra and the Brahmashirastra are similar and can destroy an entire army. The Narayanastra releases thousands and thousands of missiles and other weapons on the enemies and can wipe out an entire army. The Pashupatastra is a potent weapon that can destroy everything it encounters."

"These astras are extremely powerful and dangerous," said Krishna. "Only a very few warriors possess them. They are weapons of mass destruction. The Brahmastra and Pashupatastra create an explosion through the atoms that surround us. They release deadly radiation that can destroy an entire civilisation. These weapons have to be used cautiously else nothing will be left on Earth."

"How are these special weapons used, Uncle?"

"Abhimanyu, there are two kinds of weapons—shastras and astras. A shastra or regular weapon like an arrow can be converted into an astra by invoking the deity. There is a mantra or a chant to invoke a celestial weapon. When that is chanted, any object can be converted into an astra. It need not even be hurled at the enemy. A great warrior can control the astra with his mind and command it to do what he wants."

"How can I get celestial weapons?"

"You are too young to possess celestial weapons, my child. You need to master the art of warfare. You have not yet learnt the art of archery warfare. Master that and then learn how to use it. You need to prove that you are a great warrior capable of handling these weapons. You can then get the weapons either from your guru or from the god whom you need to please through meditation."

Abhimanyu bowed to Krishna and said, "Every moment I spend with you is instructive. I learn a lot from you."

Krishna smiled and said, "You will get a chance to use all that you have learnt. It is now time to go ahead with your training and complete it."

7

Abhimanyu's Training Is Complete

Now that Abhimanyu was adept at using the bow and arrow and could hit any target, it was time to teach him to use archery in warfare. Pradyumna got arrows with blunt edges wrapped in cloth and dipped in a dye. The number of coloured marks on the armour or body would indicate how many times the weapon had hit its target.

This time the targets were real soldiers. Archers from the Yadava army were involved in the training. Abhimanyu had to target them, get through their defences and hit them in the chest. Once this part of the training was complete, it was time for him to learn how to defend himself.

The archers who helped in his training shot their dye-dipped arrows at Abhimanyu who only had a shield for defence. He had to avoid being hit by the arrows using the shield. Any dye mark on his armour indicated that an arrow had penetrated his defence.

During the next stage of the training, he had to counter the arrows shot by the opponent through his own arrows, avoid them and breach his opponent's defence to hit him. The training was arduous and it took many months for Abhimanyu to be able to break through his opponent's defence and hit him.

The training had two objectives. One was to prevent Abhimanyu from being hit. The other was to ensure he successfully hit the opponent by breaching his defence. During the training, Pradyumna taught Abhimanyu how to cut down the arrows of his opponents and break their bows.

"When you hold the bow, fix an arrow and pull the bowstring back until your ear, the maximum extent possible. Release the arrow with as much force as possible. Use the muscles of your arm and chest to impart power to the arrow. This will send the arrow at top speed with great force."

"It is not as easy as you say, Cousin Pradyumna."

"Who said warfare is easy? It is not easy becoming a great archer. Do you know how your father learnt archery? Focus, dedication, determination and hard work with constant practice has made him the greatest archer in the world, whose skills equal that of Lord Rama himself."

The training continued with multiple levels in this way until Abhimanyu was able to defeat the opponent. In the initial levels, soldiers would come one by one to take him on. In the next level, he had to face two soldiers at a time, then three at a time and even ten at a time.

Pradyumna taught him how to hold the bow in the best position to shoot arrows in all directions. He demonstrated how Abhimanyu should twirl around, releasing arrows and reloading them quickly. He stressed that fighting more than one soldier needed great speed and accuracy. This was the toughest part of the training.

By the time Abhimanyu hit two soldiers, others would hit him. Pradyumna pointed out that in a real war, this could mean death. He had to be faster to succeed. He also had to use more than one arrow at a time. It took many months for Abhimanyu to master the art of taking on multiple opponents at a time. Pradyumna spent hours every day watching as Abhimanyu tackled soldiers who came relentlessly at him.

Once this level was complete, the next level was even difficult. Instead of ordinary soldiers, trained archers would attack Abhimanyu and he had to first defend himself and then counter-attack. Here, again, they would attack together, testing his abilities to the maximum.

Abhimanyu would have a hard day. He would get up in the morning, finish his morning routines, offer pooja to the gods, eat his food and attend classes. His learning of the scriptures would get over in the morning and then his archery training would go on through the day. At night, after completing his dinner and spending time with his mother, he would continue training by the light of the moon.

Residents of the palace were used to the thudding sound of his arrows as he practised his skills on various targets throughout the evening until late in the night. His commitment made him a favourite of Pradyumna's, who worked hard to ensure that Abhimanyu would become an archer with unparalleled skills.

Abhimanyu also learnt to ride a horse and practise archery skills from a chariot just as he would need to do in a real war. Every month, he would be tested on all his skills. He would be given targets to hit, and opponents would launch a surprise attack on him and he had to defeat them. He would perform well in each of the tests and make his teacher proud.

As his archery training continued, more advanced levels had to be completed. Instead of archers, he would face the leading warriors of the Yadava army like Kritavarma and Satyaki. Defeating them was an extremely difficult task as they were the best in the land. Every session with these great warriors would result in hits from the blunt arrows all over his body.

His mother would call the physician, who would apply herbs and soothing balms to help Abhimanyu get relief from pain. The physician was also impressed by Abhimanyu's strength. For a young boy, his body was strong and he could withstand the pain that Satyaki's blazing arrows inflicted on him.

After he finally managed to defeat Kritavarma and Satyaki, he had to fight his master Pradyumna. The arrows released by Pradyumna scythed through the air, often breaking Abhimanyu's bow. Pradyumna would defeat him several times through the day, reducing Abhimanyu to tears.

But he never complained and continued his efforts. This phase of his training would take not months but years and would only be complete when Abhimanyu was able to defeat Pradyumna, break his weapons and hit him with the arrows. Pradyumna pointed out that if Abhimanyu was able to defeat him, he could defeat anyone in the world.

By the age of fourteen, he had grown tall and strong and could defeat anyone in battle, though he had yet to defeat Pradyumna. One day Pradyumna took Abhimanyu hunting. There were reports of a group of fearsome wild boars which were creating havoc in nearby villages.

Abhimanyu was excited. This was his first experience using his arrows on live targets. Pradyumna allowed him to go ahead. He rode his favourite horse and charged into the jungle. He spotted the boars and quickly released an arrow at them. The arrow was not the usual blunt one but razor-sharp; one boar fell dead.

The other boars ran in different directions and Abhimanyu was confused as to which one to pursue. Even before he could decide what to do, he heard a whizzing sound behind him. Arrows flew in all directions and all the fleeing boars fell dead. It was Pradyumna and he had shot arrows at the boars to kill them.

"You should have fixed more than one arrow and killed more boars initially. You should have used the skills I taught you to kill the boars all at one time. Indecision is costly, Abhimanyu. In a war, you can die if you waste a second thinking instead of acting."

"I promise to learn from this mistake, Cousin," said Abhimanyu.

Pradyumna smiled and said, "You did not observe properly, the alpha boar is not dead. We need to kill it before we leave this forest."

"Where is it?" asked Abhimanyu.

"Right behind you," said Pradyumna.

Even before Abhimanyu could turn, a huge boar with large tusks charged at Abhimanyu and struck his horse from behind. Abhimanyu fell to the ground with his horse, his bow flying away from him. The boar turned and looked at him. Abhimanyu was weaponless and looked on as the boar charged at him. He looked at Pradyumna who watched silently.

This was a real test for him and he had to pass it successfully. In an instant, Abhimanyu leapt in the air and kicked at the boar, taking it by surprise. The boar fell but got up quickly. Grunting in anger, it charged at him again, but Abhimanyu was ready this time. He grabbed the boar by its tusks and wrestled with it. He remembered his wrestling lessons and fought the boar that was trying to gore him with its tusks.

The tusk pierced his arm, causing it to bleed. He was enraged. He pushed his legs back into the ground for support and used all his might to lift the huge boar, flinging it into the air. The boar somersaulted and fell. It got up unsteadily and charged once more. Pradyumna threw a spear at Abhimanyu. He held it and waited for the boar.

He threw the spear with great force as it came near him. His training proved to be of use. The spear struck the boar in its throat and came out through the back. It fell dead.

His opponent was a boar, nevertheless, he had won his first battle. He came out of it scarred with an injury but wise in experience. As he picked up his bow and arrows, he heard a growl. It was a tiger!

It had smelt the dead boars and come prowling there. Pradyumna shouted at Abhimanyu to quickly retreat but he stood still.

The tiger crouched, ready to leap. Abhimanyu quickly fixed three arrows and released them, drawing his bowstring to his ears, pushing his chest forward and using all the force at his disposal. The arrows went at blazing speed and as the tiger leapt, they found their mark. One arrow hit the neck of the tiger and the other two hit its chest.

The tiger was in the air when it died. A worried Pradyumna shot another five arrows at the tiger but it was already dead. Before Abhimanyu could move, the dead tiger fell on him. He did not flinch although his body ached with the tiger's weight. He used all his might to lift the tiger and throw it aside. Getting up and brushing the dust off his clothes, he put his foot on the dead tiger's head and looked at Pradyumna proudly.

"Bravo Abhimanyu, I now have no doubt you can take on any opponent. Well done, you have learnt your lessons well and you have the bravery that no one of your age can have."

"Whose student am I after all?" asked Abhimanyu gaily.

Both of them returned to the palace, dragging the dead tiger with them. The Yadavas were astounded to learn that the young Abhimanyu had slain a tiger. He later learnt that particular tiger was the most ferocious and one of the largest that had been killed. There was a celebration that night in honour of Abhimanyu's kill.

This would be the first of many kills for Abhimanyu. He regularly went hunting to kill wild animals. He would also go hunting to kill deer when meat was required. As he turned fifteen, he was allowed to hunt on his own without being accompanied by any of the Yadavas. Even though Subhadra was worried, he came back without a single injury during his hunts.

Then one day, there was news of a gang of bandits who had attacked a nearby village. Pradyumna took Abhimanyu along with him. It was Abhimanyu's first battle with real opponents. There were ten hefty bandits in the group but all of them together were no match for Abhimanyu. He took hardly a few minutes before he had broken their weapons.

He had decided not to kill the bandits but to capture them alive. As Pradyumna watched, he expertly shot arrows that had ropes tied to them. Soon all the bandits were on the ground, a sharp arrow through their feet with a rope jutting out of it. Abhimanyu tied the other end of each rope to a carriage on his horse and dragged the bandits all the way back to Dwaraka.

The citizens of Dwaraka looked on in awe as the son of their beloved princess Subhadra rode into the city, dragging the bandits behind him. A proud Pradyumna allowed him the privilege of moving ahead. Abhimanyu's training was now complete.

8

Pining for Father

A grand event was arranged for the people of Dwaraka where Abhimanyu demonstrated his skills in warfare. He expertly hit targets, shot down flying objects with his arrows and defeated soldiers who attacked him. The Yadavas watched his performance with pride.

Balarama, who attended the event, was pleased with Abhimanyu's showing. He promised to teach him to fight using the mace. The next day, he gifted one of his own maces to Abhimanyu and trained him to fight with it.

At first, Abhimanyu found it difficult to even lift the mace; he needed a few days to practise lifting and swinging it on his own, using wooden logs as his targets. Balarama trained him to use the mace to defend himself and defeat his opponent.

His nephew's ability to learn quickly impressed Balarama. It did not take much time for Abhimanyu to learn to fight using the mace. A pleased Balarama presented him with a special mace that he had used in battle.

Balarama blessed his nephew, saying, "You can be a great fighter with the mace just like your uncle Bheema. Keep this mace with you when you fight. As long as it is in your hands, you will never lose. You are destined to be a great warrior."

Abhimanyu was now fully skilled in warfare. He could fight anyone in hand-to-hand combat. He knew how to use the spear. He could fight using the sword and the mace. He could fight on foot and on horseback. Most importantly, he could now match Pradyumna in an archery bout. He was a complete warrior who at his young age could take on any experienced warrior.

Years of training and hard work had helped him gain expertise in archery. He had the strength and focus that many of his age did not have. He was grateful to Pradyumna and Krishna for their efforts. Guided by Subhadra, he offered gurudakshina or a gift to his teachers and sought their blessings.

He washed Krishna's feet, anointed them with turmeric, vermilion and flowers, and sought his blessings. Krishna hugged his favourite nephew, praised his dedication and blessed him to be a great warrior. He also gave him a special blessing that allowed him to access all that his subconscious mind held.

On receiving Krishna's blessing, he felt energised. He perceived hundreds of thoughts, images and words before his eyes. He now remembered all the lessons he had learnt in his mother's womb, particularly Krishna's lessons on statecraft and warfare. He recalled the lessons on different war formations and how to break through each.

He felt fortunate to have been endowed with so much knowledge. He then realised that one lesson was not complete, which was on the way to break through the Chakravyuha formation. He reminded Krishna of it.

"Uncle, you taught me how to enter the Chakravyuha but did not teach me how to exit it. This knowledge will complete my lessons."

"Don't worry about it," said Krishna. "You will learn it from your father very soon when you meet him."

Abhimanyu knew that one day he would make his father proud. The thought of his father made him sad. It had been nearly twelve years since he had seen him. The last image he remembered of his father was when he had hugged and kissed him before leaving for exile. He kept hearing of his father's valour and skills from everyone he met, which made him pine for his father even more.

He fought with Subhadra, demanding to meet his father. She told him that his father was in the forest in exile, moving from one place to another, and no one knew where the company was. She reminded him that exile meant that he could not leave the forest and come to Dwaraka else he would have surely come to meet his beloved son.

Then, Abhimanyu went to Krishna, expressing his wish to meet his father. Krishna had been to the forest many times and met Arjuna.

Krishna said, "You must have patience, Abhimanyu. The time to reunite with your father is very near. Yudhishtira has forbidden any of the children to enter the forest. Your father has been very busy all these days and if you go there, it may disturb and distract him from what he has set out to do."

"What has my father been doing, Uncle?" asked Abhimanyu.

"Your father has been obtaining celestial weapons from the gods. He has travelled far and wide. He has visited the abode of the gods and met his divine father Indra. He has travelled to the world of the Gandharvas[8] and spent time there."

"Which celestial weapon did my father obtain?"

"Let me tell you what happened. Your father set out to worship Lord Shiva to take his blessings. He engaged in penance and prayers to please the destroyer. One day, as he was meditating, there was a commotion. A wild boar rushed towards him and he could hear kiratas (tribal hunters) behind it. Your father was angry with the boar for disturbing his penance."

"Did he kill the boar?"

"He shot the boar with an arrow, but before his arrow could hit the boar, another arrow came at an unbelievable speed and killed the boar. The kiratas arrived there with their leader and his wife, and she claimed that it was her husband who killed the boar. This irritated your father who claimed that he was the greatest archer on Earth. The kirata's wife scoffed and asserted that her husband was the greatest."

"What happened then, Uncle?" asked Abhimanyu. "Did my father teach that arrogant kirata a lesson?"

"The kirata challenged your father to a duel and they both fought for a long time. He destroyed every single arrow that your father hurled at him. Arjuna used all the weapons at his command but nothing affected the kirata. He even used celestial weapons but the kirata destroyed them effortlessly."

[8] The Gandharvas are celestial beings who live in the abode of the gods.

"How did this happen? Isn't my father a great warrior? How was an ordinary kirata able to resist his attack?"

Krishna smiled and continued, "As the fight continued, the kirata's arrows hit the mighty Gandiva bow, causing it to fly away. Then Arjuna attacked the kirata by hand. A fierce hand-to-hand combat followed. The kirata effortlessly defeated your father as his wife and followers cheered him on. Your father was humiliated and suddenly recalled what he had set out to do. He had come here to take the blessings of Shiva, and he would invoke Shiva to defeat the kirata."

"What happened then?"

"Arjuna sat down and prayed to the mud Shiva linga he had constructed. He took a garland of flowers that he had made and placed it on the linga. Feeling charged with energy, he decided to attack the kirata afresh and did so, roaring like a lion."

"Was my father able to defeat the kirata?"

"Your father was surprised when he saw the kirata. The garland he had placed on the linga was on the kirata's neck. At this point, he realised that the kirata was none other than Lord Shiva himself, his followers were his ganas[9] and the lady who taunted him was none other than the Mother Goddess herself."

Krishna continued as Abhimanyu listened in awe. "Arjuna was ashamed at his bravado, and falling at the feet of Parvati and Parameshwara, he sought their blessings. Shiva, who was pleased with Arjuna's valour and devotion, blessed him and gave him the all

[9] Ganas are the followers of Lord Shiva.

powerful Pashupatastra and Raudrastra. Your father now has all the celestial weapons and he even proved it to Yudhishtira."

"How did that happen?"

"Once Duryodhana had gone to Dwaitavana Lake along with his brothers and Karna. There he met some Gandharvas and asked them arrogantly to leave. When they refused, he attacked them. The furious Gandharva king Chitrasena attacked and defeated the Kauravas. Even though Karna fought bravely, they forced him to flee. They captured Duryodhana and took him prisoner."

"Ha, he deserved that for all the evil he has done."

"That's what Bheema also said. Your uncle Yudhishtira rebuked Bheema, stating that Duryodhana is their cousin and was in trouble, and they should save him. He sent Arjuna to fight the Gandharvas. There was a fierce battle between Arjuna and Chitrasena. Ultimately, your father defeated Chitrasena and freed Duryodhana. Chitrasena used his powers of illusion, but Arjuna used his celestial weapons to counter them."

"I hope Uncle Duryodhana realised that he stands no chance against my father."

Krishna smiled and shook his head, "After everything was over, Lord Indra came and restored all the dead Gandharvas and Kauravas. Duryodhana refused to believe all this had happened and returned, convinced it was a dream. But your father proved his mastery over the celestial weapons again."

"How did he do that, Uncle?"

"There was an aerial city called Hiranyapura that floated in the sky. It was ruled by the clan of a rakshasi

Puloma who headed the Kalakeyas and they used to trouble the gods. Indra asked your father to defeat them. Arjuna used the Raudrastra and destroyed Hiranyapura. He also defeated the Nivatakavacha demons who lived beneath the ocean."

Abhimanyu sighed, "Everything you say about my father makes me long to meet him. I cannot wait for the day."

Krishna said, "It won't be long, Abhimanyu. Meanwhile, your cousins the Upapandavas are coming here. I have briefed Arjuna about your training. He now wants the sons of Draupadi to be trained by Pradyumna."

The Upapandavas were Draupadi's sons by the Pandavas. Abhimanyu warmly welcomed them to Dwaraka. They received training from Pradyumna. The eldest of the Upapandavas was Yudhishtira's son Prativindhya. Even though Abhimanyu was younger than Prativindhya, he was taller and stronger.

Pradyumna asked Abhimanyu to join him to train the Upapandavas. It was a proud moment for Abhimanyu to help his cousin train Draupadi's sons. He spent many happy months with his cousins and had a special affection for Shrutakarma, Arjuna's son. After completing their training, the Upapandavas returned to Panchala, where they lived with their grandfather Drupada.

As the days passed, Abhimanyu's longing to meet his father increased. He was now nearly sixteen, and it had been more than twelve years since he had last met his father. Krishna told Abhimanyu that now the time was very crucial for the Pandavas as they had finished their twelve years of exile.

They had to spend their last year of exile incognito without being detected by anyone. They had disguised themselves and left for a place that no one knew. No one could meet them for the next one year. Duryodhana had sent spies all over the continent to search for them. He desperately wanted to discover them so they could be sent to exile again.

Abhimanyu spent many months continuing his archery practice. He went on hunting expeditions on his own and travelled to different places in and around Dwaraka. As much as he tried to distract himself, he could not. His mind kept going back to Arjuna. He longed to meet him.

He would spend hours together looking at paintings of his father and uncles. He was very young when his father had been exiled, but he could never forget the moment of parting. His father's face came before him often. He shed tears in his room at night wondering why fate had played such a cruel game and separated him from his father.

After some months, he went to Subhadra and Krishna and said that he would go to search for his father. Subhadra remonstrated with him and refused to allow him to go. Abhimanyu was adamant. He was determined to meet his father. Knowing that Arjuna was in exile and probably would not have his weapons, he was worried that something could happen to him.

He insisted that he should be allowed to go and search for his father, promising not to do anything to reveal their location. Krishna remarked to Subhadra, "He has now reached the age where he is independent. His mind is restless and he cannot be stopped. Let him go."

With a heavy heart, Subhadra allowed him to leave. Abhimanyu disguised himself as a soldier and climbed on his horse. As Subhadra looked on tearfully, he took Krishna's blessings and left, determined to find his father.

9

Searching for Arjuna

Abhimanyu left Dwaraka to search for Arjuna. He had no idea where Arjuna was and he knew he couldn't get a clue from anyone since no one knew anything. He also knew that they would be in disguise so he could not ask for the Pandavas. He had to think of other ways to find them.

He had forced everyone to agree to his going in search of Arjuna. But as he left the ramparts of Dwaraka city, he did not know where to go. He closed his eyes and prayed to Krishna. Suddenly, he heard a screech. It was a peacock! It flew above him and moved in the northeastern direction.

He took it as an omen and decided to go towards the northeast. He moved on, travelling through dense forests and mountains. Whenever he came across villages or towns, he narrated the story of him being a soldier of the Vrishni army who was searching for his lost father. He tried to enquire if anyone had heard of any new people who had arrived nearby and of any unexpected events.

Not receiving a positive response anywhere, he continued onwards. His mother had packed many delicacies for him to snack on. He bathed in the streams and waterfalls, ate his fill and rested in temples at night.

He travelled for days together which turned into weeks and he had no idea what to do next. There was no information about Arjuna or the Pandavas. Soon his food supplies ran out. He had to forage and hunt for food. He found it challenging but thanks to his training, it was not much of a problem.

Sometimes he encountered wild animals and thieves but faced no problem with them. The sight of him mounted on a horse with a huge bow and quiver of sharp arrows was enough to keep both animals and men at bay. Whenever an animal or thief did dare attack him, it took him seconds to be rid of them.

It was now nearly two months since he had left home. He wandered from one place to another and met many different kinds of people but could not find any information about the Pandavas. He met many sages and travellers but none of them could help him.

One day, as he was passing through a town, he overheard two men enquiring about the Pandavas. He stopped and listened. They were describing the Pandavas to the town dwellers and were asking if they had seen them. The response was negative. He followed the men and eavesdropped on their conversation.

They were spies sent by Duryodhana to search for the Pandavas and were talking about how desperate Duryodhana was that no one could locate the Pandavas. Abhimanyu was tempted to kill them as they were from the enemy army but realising that they were simply soldiers doing their duty, he proceeded on his way.

He continued on his travels but could not find any information about his family. They must have been well disguised or in some hidden place. It was now three months since his journey had begun. He knew his mother would be worried. Many times he felt like returning but then he was not one to quit a mission. He was determined to find his father at any cost.

One day, as he was moving through a forest, he heard wolves howling and panting as they did when they saw their prey. Registering the feeble sounds of a man shouting and trying to ward off the wolves, he quickly moved towards the cries and saw an old man surrounded by wolves and desperately trying to keep them off with a stick.

Abhimanyu fixed five arrows and released them, and all the sharp arrows found their mark on the five wolves, which fell dead. The old man saw Abhimanyu and thanked him profusely, telling Abhimanyu that he had gone to his daughter's house and was returning home in a hurry, as he had to harvest his crops. He had taken a shortcut through the forest and had been trapped by the wolves.

Abhimanyu asked him to climb onto his horse and took him to his village, dropping him home without any further incident. Since it was getting dark, the farmer invited Abhimanyu to eat with them and stay the night. Abhimanyu, who was exhausted by his travels, readily agreed.

The farmer's wife was a good cook; the hot meal she served was filling and refreshed Abhimanyu. Soon, the farmer entered into a conversation with Abhimanyu.

"Who are you, young man? Where are you from and where were you going?"

"My name is Abh … Abhi … Abhijit. I am from the Vrishni clan. I am a soldier searching for my father who is missing. He is tall, strong and well-built. Have you seen or heard of anyone like him?"

"No," said the farmer, shaking his head.

Abhimanyu was disappointed. He asked, "Have you heard of any strangers who have come or any unexpected or strange incidents that would have occurred recently?"

The farmer shook his head but his wife fidgeted, she seemed to know something.

"Good lady, have you heard anything?" asked Abhimanyu.

"Yes," said the lady. "My brother had come yesterday. He was telling me of strange incidents that happened in his city."

Abhimanyu was excited. "What were the incidents and where does your brother live?"

"My brother is from the Matsya Kingdom ruled by King Virata. Its capital is Viratanagar."

"What was the strange incident, please tell me. I am very curious to know."

"The kingdom had a great commander called Keechaka, who was the king's brother-in-law. He was a mighty man, built like a mountain. He had defeated many kings in battle and was known for his strength. Recently he was killed at night and no one knew how it happened. He must have been killed by a very strong man. The next day, all his brothers were killed. The killer was so strong that he had uprooted a huge tree, walloped it on the heads of Keechaka's brothers and killed them. The entire city was abuzz with this news."

Abhimanyu's heart filled with joy. It could only be his uncle Bheema who could exhibit such strength.

He was now sure that Bheema and maybe the rest of the Pandavas were in Viratanagar.

The next day he inquired about the route to Viratanagar and the farmer gave him the directions. Abhimanyu thanked him for his hospitality and left, but not before the good lady gave him food to eat on the way.

Abhimanyu rode his horse fast and was in a hurry to reach Viratanagar. Every passing moment, he felt confident that he would meet his father very soon. He did not know what he would do once he reached there. It also dawned on him that the city was the capital of a major kingdom; it would be heavily guarded, and they might not permit a soldier to walk in.

He travelled for a day, hardly stopping for a few minutes; he was determined to reach Viratanagar as soon as possible. As he descended a hill, he saw the great city towering in front of him. It had huge walls that were difficult to breach; he would have to go in through the main gates.

He had to cross a forest before entering the city; as he was hurrying through it, he heard noises. There seemed to be people fighting with swords. He rode quickly towards the source of the sounds.

When he reached a clearing, he saw a fight ongoing between a group of hefty bandits and a couple of soldiers who were bravely trying to defend someone in a chariot. Bodies of many soldiers were lying on the ground. The person in the chariot seemed to be a royal and was cowering in the chariot. His charioteer was dead.

Abhimanyu did not wait. He pulled out his sword and charged towards the bandits who were surprised to see him. He flashed his sword and two of the bandits lay dead, their heads severed from their bodies. The rest of the bandits were outraged and three of them charged at him with swords in their hands. He cut off the hand of one of the bandits while the other bandit tried to kill his horse.

He threw his sword at the bandit; it stuck into his heart and he collapsed on the ground. Abhimanyu quickly pulled out an arrow from his quiver as the third bandit attacked him. He grabbed the bandit's sword hand with his left hand to block his blow and pushed the arrow into his neck, killing him instantly.

Three more bandits charged at him. He quickly took three arrows from his bow and even before they came halfway near him, released them. The arrows zipped through the air and hit the three bandits in their necks, beheading them. Three more bandits were left—two were fighting with the soldiers while one who seemed to be the leader had climbed into the chariot and was threatening the royal in it.

The person in the chariot took out his sword and tried to fight with the bandit chief but he struck the sword out of the royal's hand. The bandit chief looked at Abhimanyu charging towards him and put his sword's tip at the royal's neck.

"Stop," shouted the bandit chief. "If you take one step further, I will cut your prince's throat."

Abhimanyu stopped and suddenly looked towards his left. The bandit chief was distracted for a moment and turned. That was all the time needed for Abhimanyu to fix an arrow and shoot it. Even before the bandit chief realised what was happening, the barbed arrow hit his wrist, severing it, and his sword fell harmlessly.

Abhimanyu's next two arrows hit the two bandits fighting with the soldiers, killing them. He ordered the soldiers to seize the bandit chief who was writhing on the floor and tie him to the chariot.

He walked over to the chariot and the prince in it gave him a wan smile.

"Thanks for your help, soldier. I could have defeated the bandits easily if I wanted to. Since you came, I thought I would allow you to fight."

Abhimanyu smiled and bowed to the prince.

"Who are you?" asked the prince.

"I am Abhijit, a soldier in search of my father. I have been travelling to many places but have not found him anywhere."

"Come with me," said the prince. "You fight well. I will make you my bodyguard. My charioteer is dead, take me home."

"No, my prince, accept my apologies. I have a mission to complete. I...."

Before Abhimanyu could complete his sentence, the prince cut him off, "You dare defy the order of the crown prince of Matsya Kingdom?"

Abhimanyu was pleasantly surprised to hear this information. "Oh, are you the prince of Matsya Kingdom? I am sorry, my lord. I did not know this."

"Yes," said the prince, puffing up his chest. "I am Uttarakumar, crown prince of Matsya Kingdom and son of King Virata."

Abhimanyu was happy. This was a golden chance for him to enter the kingdom and search for his father.

He bowed low before the prince and said, "Accept my salutations, great prince. It will be an honour to serve you."

Uttarakumar said haughtily, "Come, take the reins of the chariot and drive me home. My soldiers will bring your horse. We are in need of good soldiers. My uncle Keechaka who was the commander of the army was killed with all his brothers. I can use your services in my army."

Abhimanyu jumped into the chariot and sat in the charioteer's place. He patted the horses, pulled at the reins and moved ahead towards the city of Viratanagar. He surely had the blessings of the gods. He was now easily going to enter Matsya Kingdom where he would find his father.

He drove the chariot speedily towards the gates of Viratanagar, his heart racing in anticipation of meeting his family.

10

Unexpected Meetings

Abhimanyu reached the gates of the city and the guards bowed and opened the gates. Everyone gaped at the sight of the unconscious bandit chief who was being dragged in the chariot. Soon Abhimanyu reached the palace. The soldiers came running to the chariot.

Uttarakumar addressed them and said, "Look, I have defeated the bandits who were harassing our citizens. Here is their chief, his hand cut off as punishment. Throw him into the dungeons."

The soldiers took the bandit away and Uttarakumar got down from the chariot and walked with his head held high; Abhimanyu looked at him, his mouth open in astonishment at his false bravado. The prince turned to Abhimanyu and beckoned him to follow.

Abhimanyu quickly kept his weapons inside the chariot and ran behind the prince with his hands folded.

"I like you, young man," said Uttarakumar. "You can be with me as my personal guard. I will teach you how to be a great soldier. Then one day maybe you can head this great army."

Abhimanyu chuckled to himself and said, "It will be my honour to serve this kingdom."

He followed the prince inside the palace. Everywhere guards and maids bowed to the prince and looked curiously at the handsome young Abhimanyu who followed him.

"Come, I will take you to my father the king. You can tell him how I defeated the bandits. I will tell him to offer you good pay."

Abhimanyu followed the prince as he entered the royal chambers. Inside the chambers, King Virat was relaxing and playing a game of dice with someone. Seeing the dice board, Abhimanyu was reminded of his uncle Yudhishtira and the terrible game of dice in Hastinapura.

Uttarakumar bowed before the king and said, "Father, I defeated the bandits today, and killed their chief and took him prisoner."

Virat looked at his son in surprise. He seemed to be astounded by his son's achievement. Probably the father knew what kind of a warrior his son was. He turned to Abhimanyu, who bowed low before him.

"Who is this?" asked the king suspiciously.

"Oh, he is an out-of-work soldier I met. I saved him from the bandits. He actually helped me fight the bandits. I am thinking of appointing him as my bodyguard."

King Virat looked at Abhimanyu carefully from head to toe.

"A handsome and strong young man. He reminds me of someone, but I am not able to figure out who. What do you say, Kanaka?" asked the king, addressing the man with whom he was playing dice. "Shall I appoint this young man as my son's bodyguard?"

Kanaka turned to look at Abhimanyu. He observed him closely. His eyes seemed to bore into Abhimanyu's soul, so intense was his stare. Abhimanyu felt his knees shake; his hands trembled and his lips quivered. He felt as though he would collapse but managed to stand straight.

Kanaka was none other than the former emperor of Indraprastha, the performer of the Rajasuya yagna, Dharmaraja Yudhishtira.

After staring at Abhimanyu, Yudhishtira turned away as though he was not interested. He said, "As you wish, my king. Anything you decide will be right."

Virat smiled and twirled his moustache and stroked his beard. He smiled at his son and said, "I am happy that you did something valorous today. Let this young man be your bodyguard. You can pay him the salary you want."

Abhimanyu bowed low before the king and stole a surreptitious glance at his uncle Yudhishtira, whose attention was on the game.

As Uttarakumar and Abhimanyu turned to leave, the king addressed the prince, "I have things to discuss with you. Our army has no commander, and I fear our enemies may take advantage of this. There is a lot of work to be done. Sit down! Kanaka is a wise man, let me take his suggestions and let us plan how to manage our army. I want to give you more responsibilities managing our army. Send your guard away." He dismissed Abhimanyu with a wave of his hand.

Uttarakumar sat down proudly next to his father and commanded Abhimanyu, "Go to the end of this corridor and turn right. You will find my chambers, wait for me there."

Abhimanyu bowed and left the room. His heart was thumping with excitement. He had found his uncle, and he was sure his father was somewhere nearby. He was unable to control his joy as he walked down the corridor. In his excitement, he turned left instead of right. Hearing the sound of dancing, he stopped.

He looked into the room ahead and heard a coarse voice that was strangely attractive. He looked all around him and peeped through the curtains. A dance seemed to be in progress. He heard a gruff voice keeping rhythm for the dance. Someone who seemed like a eunuch was seated on the floor and a girl was dancing.

He looked at the girl as she twirled gracefully. His heart skipped a beat and he looked at her again, his mouth hanging open. She was a young girl, probably a year younger than he was, and was exquisitely beautiful. For a moment, Abhimanyu wondered if he had come to Indra's palace and was seeing an apsara[10] perform.

As he looked at the girl dance, he experienced strange sensations in his heart. He kept staring at her. He had never seen a more beautiful girl. Actually, poor Abhimanyu had not seen any girl. So far, he had spent all his time practising warfare through the day. His friends were sons of princes and warriors with whom he roamed the countryside.

There were many pretty Yadava girls in Dwaraka. Having been singularly focused on mastering archery, he had never even looked twice at a girl. This was the

[10] Celestial dancer.

first time he was doing so closely, and his heart was racing. Her eyes were expressive, and they danced along with her. He looked at her beautiful face, at her lips which were curved in a smile as she danced.

He would probably have stood there watching her throughout the day, but the dance ended. The girl bowed before the eunuch and abruptly left. Abhimanyu stood there hoping to catch a glimpse of her again. He waited for a few moments, but it looked as though she would not return. He wondered who she was and sighed.

Just as he turned to go, the eunuch got up and stretched her hands. She turned, searching for something. Abhimanyu's heart seemed to stop. He felt as though a snake had glided down his spine. The hair on his hands stood straight and he gasped.

It was no eunuch who stood before him, it was his father Arjuna! Abhimanyu could not believe his eyes. He rubbed at them and looked again. Surely, he must be mistaken. Why was his father dressed as a eunuch? It had been nearly thirteen years since he had seen his father, but his father's face was etched in his mind.

The person before him was cleanshaven and dressed like a dancer with a saree. He could not forget those eyes and mouth. It was definitely his father. He had accomplished his mission. He had found Arjuna.

He wondered whether he should call out his father's name. But before he could do anything, a hand grabbed his shoulder, pulling him back. An angry palace guard stood glowering at him. Behind the guard was the beautiful girl.

She stood with her hands on her hips, glaring at him. Seeing her at such a close range made Abhimanyu's heart race. He felt his mouth go dry, looking at the exquisite beauty in front of him. The voice he heard next, though, was not beautiful. It was the guard.

"Who are you, rascal? How dare you come to the chambers of Princess Uttara?"

Abhimanyu opened his mouth to speak, but no words came out. He just gaped at the princess who was looking at him closely. He felt his face flush as the beautiful princess gazed at him, studying him carefully.

"Speak," said the guard, seizing Abhimanyu by his neck; he could have felled the guard in one blow but didn't. He stood still, watching the princess who looked at him wordlessly.

He heard a voice behind him, "Ah, there you are! I told you to turn right, why did you turn left? You seem to have little intelligence."

It was Uttarakumar. Hearing the commotion, he had come there and laughed on seeing Abhimanyu's plight, even as the guard released Abhimanyu and bowed to the prince. The lovely Uttara turned to her brother, and pointing at Abhimanyu, asked, "Who is this?"

"Oh, he is a soldier I met. He helped me defeat the bandits. I mean, I saved him from the bandits and made him my bodyguard."

"If you saved him, then why are you making him your bodyguard? It is the bodyguard who saves the prince and not the other way round, right?" asked the princess, her voice as sweet as that of a songbird.

Uttarakumar was flummoxed by the question and retorted angrily, "Go away, little girl! Go back to your dance class. Don't trouble me. I have work to do."

He motioned to Abhimanyu to follow him. Abhimanyu bowed to the princess and left. As he walked past her, she was so near that he felt like touching her cheeks, which seemed to be as soft as pink roses. As he walked off, he could feel her scanning him and, once again, he experienced strange emotions in his heart.

He spent a boring hour with Uttarakumar, who kept telling him tall tales of how brave he was. He kept nodding his head. Right now, his priority was to find his father and meet him. He didn't want to waste time listening to the useless prince.

Uttarakumar was soon tired. He told Abhimanyu, "I have many meetings with my father and the ministers. I will be busy all of today and tomorrow. Go to the garden and go beyond the lake. There you will find a room where my bodyguard who died today used to live. You can stay there. You will get all you need from the servants. Don't go anywhere. I will come for you tomorrow and train you on how to be a good warrior."

Abhimanyu quickly left, his intention being to search for his father who was surprisingly disguised as a eunuch. He was irritated when he observed a guard following him. It was one of the two guards whom he had saved during the fight with the bandits. The guard smiled at him and said, "You are a brave young man. The way you fought was incredible. Our cowardly prince took the credit for your hard work."

Abhimanyu smiled and waved his hand as though it didn't matter. The soldier said, "Come, I will take you to your rooms. I also stay there. Let us go together."

Abhimanyu realised that he could try to get information out of the soldier.

"The prince was saying that his uncle Keechaka died. How did that happen?"

"It was a surprise. Our commander was a powerful man. Enemies would shake before him. The one fault he had was that he lusted after women. Probably the husband of some woman killed him. He must have been a demon, as no human being could possibly kill the mighty Keechaka."

"Maybe some strangers have come to the city and they killed him."

"There are no strangers. The cook is the only new person here. He is a huge man. Who knows, maybe it was he who killed our commander. Other than that, there are two stable hands who are new. Then there is the beautiful maid to our queen who is new. The king's advisor is also new. Other than them, no other strangers are here."

"Er … I saw a eunuch in the palace."

The guard turned and glared at him, "Don't talk about that eunuch."

Little did the guard know that the new bodyguard wanted to talk only about the eunuch.

11

Abhimanyu Finds Love

Abhimanyu ran behind the guard, "Why do you say so? What happened to the eunuch?"

"The eunuch is Brihannala, Princess Uttara's dance teacher. She is new to this city. A very arrogant creature."

"Why? What did she do?"

"There is a beautiful maid working in the palace and I am trying to win her affections. The stupid maid likes another guard. I was arguing with her, caught her hand and tried to pull her. The horrible eunuch caught my hand and twisted it."

"Why?" asked Abhimanyu, though he knew the answer.

"What business is it of the eunuch? She said, don't you dare trouble any woman and touch her without her permission. I suspect the eunuch must be a man. Her grip was so tight that it left a mark on my hand. That eunuch has huge muscles on her hand. Now stop this nonsense, I am not interested in talking about the eunuch. This is your room, go stay there."

The guard walked away angrily.

Abhimanyu was now sure that his father was disguised as Brihannala. It was a brilliant disguise that none could penetrate. Abhimanyu had his food and rested for some time. He was determined to enter the palace at night and search for his father though he knew it was a risk. If the guards caught him, he would be jailed and this time Uttarakumar would not save him. He would have to fight his way out.

He waited until it became dark. The small dingy room was hot and full of mosquitoes. Abhimanyu was fed up sitting in the room and decided to take a walk. He came to the lake and stood behind a tree, making plans to enter the palace without being caught.

He had brought his bow and arrows with him and wanted to be prepared for all eventualities in case he was caught and needed to make an escape. He was still confused about how to get into the palace but was confident he could somehow enter it. Maybe he would say that the prince wanted him to guard his room. The problem was locating his father after that. He did not want to do anything to draw attention to himself.

As he stood thinking and watching the resplendent moon in the sky, he heard laughter. He looked from behind the tree. It was Princess Uttara! She was there for an evening walk with a friend.

He saw her as she stood next to the lake. Her reflection was visible in the lake along with the reflection of the moon and he found it difficult to decide which was more beautiful. Once again, he felt strange sensations in his heart. He knew all about love, having heard enough about the celebrated love life of his uncle Krishna. He had never given a thought about love in his life, having always been busy with his quest to become a warrior.

Looking at the beautiful Uttara, he understood why men fell in love. Abhimanyu felt he could stand there forever, looking at her beautiful face and listening to her sweet voice. He knew that it was not the time to think of love. He was here on a mission but the nymph-like princess before him was seriously disconcerting him.

The princess and her friend sat down under a peach tree. Uttara seemed faraway and her friend kept teasing her, asking why she was in this mood.

"Princess, I heard that there was a handsome young man near your quarters today. Why is it that you seem distracted after seeing him? What is the matter?" teased the friend.

Uttara blushed and the sight of her pink face turning red made Abhimanyu's heart leap. "No, no, it is nothing. I was thinking about something else."

"What, Princess, do tell me?" teased her friend.

Trying to change the topic, Uttara looked at the tree and exclaimed, "Look! There is such lovely fruit on this tree. It is ripe. How I wish I could eat them?"

"It is too high, Princess, else I would have got them for you. Maybe you can think of the handsome man you saw and make a wish. He may come and get the fruit for you."

"Shut up!" exclaimed Uttara, blushing again.

Her friend continued to tease her. She stood and spread the folds of her saree and looked up and said, "Oh handsome man who has won my princess's heart, come and get this tasty fruit for her."

Saying this, she looked at Uttara and smiled mischievously. She felt something hit her saree! A fruit from the tree had fallen into her outstretched dress.

Both the princess and her friend were astonished. They looked around but could not see anyone.

"Maybe the handsome man is a Gandharva. He must have come magically and thrown the fruit down for you."

Uttara was embarrassed. She was also irritated by her friend's constant teasing. She angrily told her friend to go away and leave her alone.

Her friend apologised for teasing her and left quickly, fearing that she might complain to the queen.

Uttara sat alone and ate the tasty fruit. She looked up at the tree. With a childish smile on her face, she spread the folds of her saree and looked up at the tree. She heard a whizzing sound and a fruit dropped into her lap. She was stunned. Slowly, she got up and looked around. There was no one.

She had heard a sound before the fruit fell and it heightened her curiosity. She cautiously walked towards a mango tree, stood under it and spread out her saree again. Within a second, a mango fell into her lap. This time she had seen what had happened. An arrow raced through the air and hit the fruit at its stalk, causing it to fall.

She ran quickly in the direction the arrow had come from.

"Who is it? Come out. I know someone is here," she said.

As she looked in anticipation, Abhimanyu stepped out from behind the tree.

Uttara looked at him, her mouth wide open in surprise.

He bowed before her and stood with an impish smile on his face. He had enjoyed her startled look when he had cut down the fruit with his arrow.

She looked at his bow and said, "You seem to be so skilled with the bow. Can you hit any target?"

Abhimanyu smiled and bowed, "Yes, Princess. For you, I can do anything in the world."

Uttara blushed and looked up. There was a tree full of flowers and she was standing directly under it. She looked at Abhimanyu and then at the tree. He got the message. He quickly fixed three arrows, bent down and released the arrows at the tree. His aim was accurate, and he hit the tree in the right places. A shower of flowers fell on the princess and she giggled joyfully.

Abhimanyu was delighted seeing the joy on the princess's face. He bowed before her and said, "Command me, Princess, what else should I do?"

Uttara put her finger to her chin and thought. She said, "I have heard of a great warrior called Arjuna, who could hit a target in the air by looking at its reflection in the water. Can you do that?"

"I can do anything for you, my princess."

Uttara blushed again. Her face had turned red like an apple. She looked at a mango tree near the lake. She told Abhimanyu, "Stand here and look into the water. You can see the reflection of the mango. Look at it and hit the mango and bring it down for me."

"Your word is my command," said Abhimanyu and walked towards the lake.

His heart was beating fast. He had heard of how his father had hit the fish on a rotating wheel by seeing its reflection. Abhimanyu had never tried something like this. He was determined to do it. He looked in the water and held his bow on his shoulder, aiming at the fruit.

He carefully observed the reflection and adjusted his aim. He said a prayer and released the arrow.

He closed his eyes, scared of failing before the pretty princess. He heard a merry exclamation. He looked at Uttara, who was standing with the mango in her hand and smiling at him.

Just then there was a thunderclap, and rain started pouring down from the skies.

The lovely princess was getting wet. Abhimanyu quickly started fixing arrows in his bow. Taking aim at the tree above him, he shot them continuously at the top of the tree. The first set of arrows were embedded in the tree. The next set stuck in the tail of the first set of arrows. He continued doing this until there was a dense canopy of arrows in the tree.

He bowed to the princess and motioned her to stand under the canopy. She stood under the awning of arrows, smiling at him, delighted by the brilliant exhibition of marksmanship, the likes of which she had never seen before.

"Why are you standing in the rain? Come under the tree," Uttara called out to Abhimanyu.

He took a few steps forward and smilingly said, "You are a princess and I am but an ordinary soldier. How can I stand next to the member of a royal family?"

Uttara laughed loudly and said, "You are no soldier. You must be a prince and that too from a very famous lineage trained under the best of teachers. No soldier can do what you have done. Now I understand—it is you who killed the bandits and saved my brother today."

Abhimanyu blushed and smiled. The alluring princess was very intelligent.

She stretched out her hand towards Abhimanyu. He took a few steps forward and held it gently. It was like touching the petals of a rose. She gently pulled him under the canopy to shade him from the rain.

They both stared at each other. Uttara was the first to speak, "Who are you? I am now sure you are a prince. Please tell me who you are."

Abhimanyu hesitated for a moment and then said, "I am here on a personal mission, Princess. I have not come with any evil intention. Forgive me, but I cannot tell you who I am. You guessed right though. I am a prince and I come from the greatest lineage ever."

Uttara looked into his eyes and said, "Hmm ... let me guess. The greatest lineage ever and amazing archery skills! You must be Arjuna, then? No, no, you can't be Arjuna. You are too young. Maybe his son?"

Abhimanyu was shocked at the way she had guessed his identity. He gaped at her in astonishment. He was amazed at her cleverness.

She giggled, seeing the expression on his face. Just then, a flash of lightning streaked through the sky, filling the entire garden with light. It was followed by a ferocious thunderclap that almost shook the ground. Uttara flinched at the sound and fell into Abhimanyu's arms.

He put his arms around her, holding her firmly. She placed her head on his chest and closed her eyes. He couldn't believe what was happening. The divine princess whose hair smelled of fragrant flowers, whose skin was soft as rose petals and who resembled an apsara in beauty was in his arms.

He sighed. He felt as though he was floating in the clouds. Probably this was love that affected even the gods and great kings. He held her wordlessly. Neither of them spoke as the rain lashed all around them.

After some time had passed, he touched her hair with a trembling hand. It was like silk. He caressed her head, moved his hand to her face and touched her cheeks. It was like touching velvet. She looked at him, smiled and touched his cheek in turn.

Neither of them had noticed that the rain had stopped. They had not even noticed the time fly by. It was pitch-black, and they only had eyes for each other in the moonlight. They heard a loud and angry voice.

"Princess!" cried out a woman.

They both turned. A woman was standing in the dark. She stepped forward. It was Draupadi!

Uttara gasped seeing her mother's maid Sairandhari. Without a word, she ran towards the palace. Abhimanyu stood awkwardly, not knowing what to say or do.

He cleared his throat and said, "Ah … good lady, it is not the princess's fault. It was raining … and … and…."

Draupadi lifted her hand, signalling him to stop talking. From behind a tree, a man stepped out towards him. It was Yudhishtira!

"Abhimanyu!" he said. "Why did you come here?"

12

Time for a Battle

Abhimanyu's face turned red. He was shocked that his identity was discovered.

"Uncle, you found out who I was?"

"Yes, I am not a fool, my child. I have been the emperor of a mighty kingdom. Can't I do something as simple as identifying my nephew?"

Draupadi smiled at him, "How can I not identify my dear child? Besides, you look just like your father."

"Where is Father? I came here in search of him and desperately want to meet him."

"No!" asserted Yudhishtira. "You will not meet him. Do you know how much of a problem you nearly caused? If Duryodhana's spies had seen you, they would have guessed we were here. We are hardly a few days away from finishing our thirteenth year in exile. You would have got us caught."

"I ... I ... I am sorry, Uncle. I just wanted to meet Father. I have been longing to meet him for so long. I did not intend to...."

Yudhishtira raised his hand, "Your intention doesn't matter. Every minute that you stay here will put us at risk. Your antics with the princess will put you in big trouble. Leave now!"

"Uncle, please allow me to meet my father once. I will just spend a few minutes with him. Then I will leave."

"Did you not hear me?" said Yudhishtira sternly. "I did not request you. This is my order. Go back to Dwaraka, now!"

With these words, Yudhishtira turned away and told Draupadi, "Send him off and return to the palace before the queen sends someone in search of you." He walked back to the palace.

Draupadi touched Abhimanyu's cheek affectionately. Tears rolled down Abhimanyu's eyes remembering his childhood and the affection Draupadi had shown towards him.

"I am sorry, Mother Draupadi. Forgive me."

"It is alright, my child. You must leave though. Even your father will be upset. The night is dark and so are the clouds. Go back to your room and leave tomorrow morning. Don't meet anyone. It is just a matter of a few days more. Our exile will be over and we will be back with you."

Abhimanyu bowed, touched her feet and took her blessing. He spent a sleepless night with thoughts of all that had transpired. He did not want to leave but dared not disobey his uncle.

The next morning, he got ready to leave and went to get his horse, wondering how he could avoid Uttarakumar who would probably summon him. He observed that all the soldiers were busy running around. Something seemed to be happening.

He did not care, took his horse and prepared to leave. As he turned to look one last time at the palace, he heard the sound of soft feet. Princess Uttara was running towards him. He looked at her in surprise. She seemed to be worried and he hoped that she had not got into trouble over what had happened the previous night.

She came running to him and he got down from his horse. She held his hand and said, "Prince, I need your help. I don't know who you are, but I know that you are a great warrior. My kingdom needs your help."

"What happened, Princess?"

"Our commander Keechaka is dead and our army is leaderless. My father never bothered about the army as my uncle would take care of it. My brother, as you know, is of no use. Last evening, thieves entered our kingdom to steal our cattle. My father thought it was a minor incident and ignored it. Today, the cattle thieves seemed to have assembled in huge numbers. My father fears they are not thieves but the mighty Trigartas who are our old enemies."

"Oh," said Abhimanyu. "So, your army is ready to fight them?"

"Yes, but I am worried because we don't have great warriors on our side. We depended too much on Uncle Keechaka and his brothers. My father is worried too. He has even drafted the cook to fight the war!"

She grasped both his arms tightly and looked deep in his eyes, "Please, Prince, fight alongside my father and save our kingdom. My father is not too experienced in battle. As I said, he depended too much on Uncle Keechaka. I am scared for him. Please be with him and protect him. Help him defeat the enemy."

Abhimanyu forgot his uncle's orders as he looked into Uttara's eyes. He could even defy the gods for her. He patted her hand and said, "Do not worry,

Princess. I will fight with your army. I promise that I will not allow the enemy to defeat your army. I will ensure that your father is unharmed."

He climbed on to his horse, fixed his quiver of arrows on his back, took out his bow and rode towards the Matsya army who were preparing to leave for battle. He joined the Matsya soldiers and rode towards the enemy. He observed King Virat at the head of the army. There was no sign of Uttarakumar.

Behind the king, he saw a huge man in armour with a bow in his hand. It was his uncle Bheema! To the left of King Virat was his uncle Yudhishtira. The king seemed to be planning an attack from three fronts. He directed Yudhishtira to take one division of the army and attack from the left, and summoned Bheema and directed him to attack from the right.

The king himself planned to attack from the centre. Abhimanyu rode his horse through the soldiers and stationed himself behind the king. The other soldiers glowered at him for his impertinence, but none objected. They all seemed to be apprehensive about the forthcoming battle without their commander.

Abhimanyu saw the huge Trigarta army before him. Their king, Susharma, was at the head of the army and the Trigartas were moving towards them. Bheema let out a huge roar and, leading his division from the right, charged at the Trigartas. Hearing the roar and seeing his confidence, the soldiers joined him. Yudhishtira's division then attacked from the left.

The king then charged into the battlefield with Abhimanyu behind him. Abhimanyu was full of confidence, but his heart was beating fast. This was the first battle he was fighting, and he was taking on the powerful Trigartas. He knew no fear, but he remembered that he not only had to fight the enemy but also protect the king.

The king may not have had much experience in battle but, unlike his son, he was brave. He charged at the enemy, shooting arrows at them. A fierce fight broke out between the Matsya and Trigarta armies. Abhimanyu encountered his first opponent, a Trigarta archer who took aim at him. Even before he could release the arrow, Abhimanyu's arrow had broken through his defence and hit him on the chest; he fell down dead.

It was Abhimanyu's first kill! He experienced a range of emotions. He was happy that what he had learnt from his teachers had helped him be a good warrior. Now, he could easily kill an opponent. The fact that he had taken someone's life caused him an odd feeling which he pushed aside. This was a battlefield, and the rule was clear—kill or be killed!

He charged at the enemy, making sure he was close to King Virat. He let loose a volley of arrows, causing enemy soldiers to be killed. Meanwhile, King Virat fought bravely. His kingdom was at stake and he slaughtered enemy soldiers. It looked like he did not need much help.

A soldier on an elephant charged towards the king. Abhimanyu immediately aimed a barbed arrow at the elephant's forehead and released the arrow with all the force he could command. The arrow hit the elephant's forehead and it tottered and fell dead, bringing down the warrior sitting on its back.

Meanwhile, to the far right, he could see his uncle Bheema massacring the Trigartas. He had broken through their ranks and ruined their carefully made formation. They were running all over the place as their warriors tried desperately to stop Bheema's ferocious attack.

Abhimanyu continued to attack the enemy, ruthlessly killing many of the enemy soldiers. He had hoped to fight alongside his father but he knew that his father was in the guise of a eunuch and obviously could not join the battle. He wondered what Uttara was doing. He would make her happy with his performance in the battle today.

Neither Abhimanyu nor anyone had any idea what was happening at the gates of Viratanagar. Susharma's attack was a ploy to draw away the Matsya army. Amassed in front of the gates of Viratanagar was the mighty Kaurava army led by Bheeshma. Drona, Karna and the crown prince Duryodhana were at the forefront. They were determined to take away the cattle and capture the kingdom.

There was consternation in the city as the guards ran to Uttarakumar and informed him of the enemy attack. He had no option but to take them on. He was the only warrior left in the city. Draupadi told him to take his sister's dance teacher with him. She said that Brihannala had once served as a charioteer with the great Arjuna and would bc of hclp.

Uttarakumar, full of bravado before the women, moved towards the enemy, as Arjuna rode the chariot in the guise of Brihannala. Uttarakumar panicked seeing the huge Kaurava army and was ready to flee when Brihannala stopped him. She took the chariot to the nearby woods and stopped before a Shami tree. She climbed up the tree and brought down what looked like a dead body wrapped in a shroud, as Uttarakumar looked on in surprise.

It was not a body but had many weapons, including a huge bow, the likes of which Uttarakumar had never seen before. Brihannala put on the armour and got ready for battle.

"Who are you? You are no dance teacher!" gasped Uttarakumar, astounded.

"I am Arjuna, son of Kunti. Come with me and I will teach you how to fight in a battle. Here, take the reins and ride the chariot into the battle."

Uttarakumar was thrilled by the fact that the great Arjuna was with him. He took the reins of the chariot and rode towards the Kauravas.

Duryodhana laughed loudly and addressed his warriors.

"Look there, a single chariot comes towards us and sitting in it is a eunuch."

Everyone laughed loudly, but their laughs turned into silence when the eunuch sitting in the chariot blew a conch. It shook the entire battlefield. The eunuch then shot a volley of arrows at the Kauravas killing many of the soldiers at the front instantly.

Bheeshma smiled and said, "That's no eunuch, only one man can fight like this. It is Arjuna!"

Duryodhana shouted in joy, "He has been discovered! Now, the Pandavas have to go twelve more years in exile."

Bheeshma shook his head and said, "No, Duryodhana. The thirteen years of exile were over just a few minutes ago. The calculation of time is complex and Arjuna has done it right, which is why he has come out."

Duryodhana was furious and shouted at his army, "Attack and kill him."

The Kaurava army charged at Arjuna and he slaughtered them, sending showers of arrows. Bheeshma, Karna, Kripa and Drona challenged Arjuna. He launched such a ferocious attack on them that they were beaten back. Seeing the arrows flying all over the place, Uttarakumar fainted.

Arjuna sat upright in the chariot and held the reins with his legs. Controlling the chariot with his legs, he charged at the Kauravas, showing them that he was the only warrior in the world who could take on an entire army singlehandedly.

He defeated Karna and forced him to flee from the battlefield. His arrows hit Bheeshma on the chest, causing him to fall into his chariot. He defeated Ashwathama and Kripa effortlessly. The angry Kauravas ganged up against him and attacked him.

The battle continued fiercely and Arjuna was hopelessly outnumbered. There were thousands of soldiers against one man. The situation called for the use of a powerful celestial weapon. Arjuna took out an arrow and touched it to his forehead. He chanted the hymn to invoke the powerful Sammohanastra.

He released the arrow at the Kauravas. The arrow leapt into the sky and released a thick smoke. Within seconds, it covered the entire Kaurava army and generated a noxious smell. The moment they smelt the smoke, the Kauravas collapsed unconscious.

Arjuna had defeated the entire Kaurava army effortlessly in the blink of an eye.

13

The Truth Is Revealed

Uttarakumar looked in awe at Arjuna's work and bowed before him in humility.

Arjuna smiled at him and said, "Go and cut pieces of the cloth that these brave warriors are wearing. Let's go back to the city, show the cloth pieces and claim that you defeated the entire Kaurava army yourself. You can then give the cloth pieces to Uttara to dress her dolls."

Uttarakumar smiled in glee and thanked Arjuna profusely.

Arjuna said, "Cut the clothes of all the warriors except my grandsire Bheeshma. If you dare to approach him, he may wake up and kill you instantly, so beware. Don't cut the clothes of Dronacharya, he is my teacher and I will not tolerate any insult to him."

Arjuna watched with a smile as Uttarakumar scurried around cutting pieces of clothes worn by the Kaurava greats.

Abhimanyu, on the other hand, had no idea of his father's recent achievements. He fought hard with the Trigartas, slaughtering their soldiers easily. Just then, a large chariot came before them. It was Susharma, the king of the Trigartas. He launched a ferocious attack on King Virat. Virat fought bravely but soon his bow was broken and Susharma fixed an arrow, aiming it at the throat of the king.

Even before Susharma could release the arrow, another arrow whizzed at him and broke his bow. He looked in surprise. It was a Matsya soldier seated on a horse. He was amazed and outraged. He picked up another bow and said, "Get out of my way, you foolish boy, how dare you take on me. I will kill your king today and claim his kingdom."

"You have to kill me first," said Abhimanyu with a smile on his face, standing between the king and Susharma. King Virat looked on in astonishment.

Susharma let loose a volley of arrows at Abhimanyu, who fought back ferociously. A fierce battle raged between them. Abhimanyu had found an opponent who could give him a proper fight. Some of Susharma's arrows hit his armour and hurt him. He was undaunted and fought fearlessly.

Soon Susharma's bow was broken and Abhimanyu's arrow pierced him in the chest, causing him to faint. His charioteer led him to safety as Abhimanyu sent him off with a volley of arrows, slaughtering his bodyguards.

Just then, news came of the battle near the main gate and the Kauravas' defeat. No sooner had the Trigarta army heard this than they fled from the spot. King Virat looked appreciatively at Abhimanyu and said, "Bravo young man, you are a brave warrior. I have never seen anyone fight so ferociously."

He looked behind Abhimanyu and said, "Come, Kanaka, this young lad has fought so bravely and saved my life. I hereby promote him to the rank of general."

Yudhishtira was next to Abhimanyu and glared at him, angry that Abhimanyu had disobeyed him. Abhimanyu could take on any army in the world but did not dare to stand in front of his furious uncle. Muttering words of gratitude and bowing before the king, he withdrew.

Not wishing to make Yudhishtira angry, he decided to leave for Dwaraka. As he was leaving, a huge figure blocked his way. It was Bheema!

Bheema looked at him angrily and said, "Draupadi told me about your arrival. When your uncle ordered you to leave, how dare you join the battle?"

Abhimanyu turned red and said, "Uncle ... I ... the princess ... the king...."

Bheema alighted from the chariot and charged towards Abhimanyu, who got down from his horse. It seemed like Bheema would hit him and Abhimanyu flinched, awaiting a blow from the terrible arms of Bheema.

To his surprise, Bheema hugged him warmly and kissed him affectionately on the forehead.

He said, "Bravo Abhimanyu, Arjuna will be proud of you. Your skill on the battlefield was exceptional. I am proud to call you my nephew."

Abhimanyu was thrilled hearing Bheema's words. Bheema asked him to return with the rest of the army and remain in his quarters without being seen. He promised him that he would allow him to meet Arjuna later in the night.

A happy Abhimanyu returned with the rest of the army. He was tempted to meet the princess but did not want to take the risk of running into Yudhishtira again. He went to the room allotted to him and stayed there until evening, coming out only to take a meal with the rest of the soldiers.

He was surprised hearing the news that Uttarakumar had singlehandedly defeated the Kaurava army.

One of the soldiers said, "Our coward prince defeated such a huge army, I just cannot believe it. He even cut pieces of their clothes to show his prowess. Unbelievable!"

Another soldier said, "I heard the eunuch who teaches dance to our princess was his charioteer."

Hearing this, a big smile appeared on Abhimanyu's face. He now knew what had happened. It was his father who had defeated the Kauravas and had graciously allowed the prince to take credit for it.

Meanwhile at the palace, Uttarakumar, surrounded by the women of the palace, was the centre of attention. He explained how he had, unaided, defeated the Kauravas as his mother, sister, mother's maid and other women listened to him in astonishment.

A little away, King Virat, satisfied with the battle and happy with his son's performance, was busy with his usual pastime—a game of dice with his advisor Kanaka.

"My son is so brave, I never knew he had such skills," announced the proud king.

"Yes, my king, but with Brihannala as his charioteer, this was expected."

"My son, unassisted, defeated the entire Kauravas."

"Yes, it was natural with Brihannala being his charioteer."

The king was irritated on hearing Kanaka's words. He continued to praise his son, "Such great warriors like Bheeshma, Drona, Karna and Duryodhana were in the Kaurava army yet my heroic son defeated them all by himself."

"Yes, my king, with Brihannala as his charioteer this was bound to happen."

Virat lost his temper. He shouted loudly, "How dare you give credit of my son's victory to a eunuch?"

In a fit of rage, he hurled the dice in his hands at Kanaka's face; it hit him on the nose and blood started dripping. The queen's maid Sairandhari came running and held out her hand to collect the drops of blood.

"What are you doing?" thundered the king.

"Oh, great King, Kanaka is a man of righteousness. Even if one drop of his blood falls on the ground, it will not be good for this kingdom."

Virat felt bad that he had hit his trusted advisor but was angry with the situation and walked away. Draupadi attended to her husband's wounds and treated them.

It was night and Abhimanyu waited eagerly. Bheema had asked him to come near a temple. He entered the Shiva temple and took the Lord's blessings. He stood there waiting for a long time. He heard the sound of anklets.

It was the eunuch Brihannala who was walking towards him. Abhimanyu's eyes filled with tears after seeing his father after so many years. He fell at his father's feet, and Arjuna blessed him and hugged him tightly. There were tears in his eyes on seeing his handsome son after so many years.

They sat down in the temple.

Arjuna said, "I know all that happened. I am proud of you, my son. I heard about your prowess on the battlefield. You are worthy of being a great warrior. I am thankful to Krishna for bringing you up to be such a fine young man with so much courage and skill."

Abhimanyu listened to his father's words happily. He was just happy being in front of his father and wanted nothing else. He had achieved his mission of being reunited with his father.

"I also heard of your prowess with the princess," said Arjuna, smiling at his son.

Abhimanyu blushed crimson.

Arjuna clapped him on his back and said, "Leave everything to me. Don't think about the princess now."

He held his son's hand and took him to his room in the palace. "Come and stay with me tonight. We have a lot to talk about. Tomorrow we will reveal our identity to the world. Our exile is over, and our family will be reunited."

Abhimanyu left happily with his father. Neither did he sleep nor allow Arjuna to sleep. Father and son spent the whole night conversing. It was Abhimanyu who talked as Arjuna wanted to know everything about his training, his life in Dwaraka and how his mother was faring.

It was the happiest moment in Abhimanyu's life. Finally, he fell asleep just before dawn as his father looked at him with a proud smile on his face.

The next day, the Pandavas were in their finest costumes. A grand dress was brought for Abhimanyu. They walked proudly into Virat's grand palace and sat down in the chairs reserved for visiting kings. Abhimanyu sat in a chair behind his father.

King Virat entered the assembly and sat on his throne. He was still feeling happy at the result of the battle. His son Uttarakumar sat next to him. He looked around the hall and was furious at seeing the Pandavas. He charged towards them, followed by his son.

"What is this, Kanaka? What is going on? You dare sit on the chair reserved for kings?" He looked in astonishment at everyone. "My wife's maid, the cook, the stable hands and the eunuch! How dare you do this, that too dressed in such finery?"

Uttarakumar held his father's hand and stopped him. "It is time you know the truth, Father."

"What truth?"

"It was not me who won the war. It was Brihannala who fought and defeated the Kauravas."

"What! A eunuch defeated the mighty Kaurava army?"

"Father, Brihannala is no eunuch. He is Arjuna, the greatest warrior on Earth. The son of Indra, the king of gods."

Hearing this, a shocked King Virat took few steps back stumbling and his son held on to him to prevent him from falling.

Draupadi got up and saluted the king, saying, "King Virat, I am not a maid. I am Draupadi, wife of the Pandavas and the daughter of King Drupada of Panchala. Your advisor Kanaka is none other than Yudhishtira, the former emperor of Indraprastha. The cook Vallabha is none other than the great Bheema, the son of Vayu. The stable hands you referred to are the brave Nakula and Sahadeva."

King Virat looked incredulous. He bowed towards Yudhishtira, and joining his hands, said, "Forgive me, Emperor, without knowing who you are I hurt you yesterday."

Yudhishtira got up, held Virat's hands in his and said, "My family is grateful to you. We had to spend a year of exile incognito and we chose your great kingdom. You sheltered my family for one year and our exile is now complete. Thank you for giving us shelter."

Virat bowed his hands to Arjuna and said, "Forgive me, great warrior. I insulted you without knowing who you are."

He turned to Yudhishtira and said, "With your permission, Emperor, I want to convert our friendship to a relationship. I offer my daughter's hand in marriage to the great warrior Arjuna."

Hearing these words Abhimanyu's heart sank; he stared at the king in horror.

Arjuna turned towards Abhimanyu and smiled. He said, "King Virat, Uttara was my student and is hence like my daughter. We have no daughter, and I will take her home as my daughter-in-law. She will be married to my son Abhimanyu."

With these words, he held Abhimanyu's hands and brought him forward.

King Virat embraced Abhimanyu and said, "I knew you must be a great warrior. I am proud to give my daughter to you in marriage."

A thrilled Abhimanyu looked around the hall in joy. On the upper floor, he saw Uttara and smiled at her. She smiled back shyly at him.

Virat raised his hands and announced, "Let the preparations commence for Uttara's wedding to Abhimanyu. This will the greatest wedding witnessed by mankind."

14

Abhimanyu Weds Uttara

Abhimanyu returned to Dwaraka in a royal cavalcade. He met his mother and uncle and informed them of all that had happened. They all got ready to leave for Viratanagar. The groom's procession left in a huge caravan with many chariots filled with gifts and gold. Abhimanyu, dressed as the groom, sat proudly with his mother.

Krishna, Balarama, Pradyumna, the queens Rukmini, Satyabhama and Revathi, Satyaki, Kritavarma and many others proceeded for the wedding in Matsya Kingdom. Abhimanyu was delighted at the turn of events. He had proved his skill in battle. He had reunited with his father. Now he was getting married to the most charming Uttara to whom he had lost his heart.

His uncle Krishna teased him continuously. He did not mind and looked forward to his wedding with the princess of Matsya Kingdom.

Meanwhile, the arrangements for the wedding were in full swing. A huge marriage hall was constructed and hundreds of people worked to decorate it as well as the palace. There was a huge hall to serve food to guests and hundreds of cooks prepared a variety of delicious foods. Prince Uttarakumar walked around accompanied by his younger brother Shweta, busily supervising the arrangements.

Queen Sudeshna prepared her daughter for the wedding. Uttara was decked up in the finest of dresses adorned with precious gems. She wore necklaces, bangles and rings of gold. She was thrilled that the handsome man she had lost her heart to would be her husband.

King Virat welcomed the guests to the wedding. Drupada, the king of Panchala, arrived with his son Dhrishtadyumna, as did other royals. All the guests were escorted to palaces and treated royally. Musicians played their instruments to welcome the guests. Poets composed lyrics praising the valour of the Pandavas and singers sang songs in their praise.

There was gaiety and celebration throughout the kingdom of Matsya, the people of which were happy to know that the great Pandavas had lived amidst them. They were even happier to learn that the heroic Abhimanyu was to be the son-in-law of their kingdom.

People came all the way from Dwaraka to see the wedding of Subhadra's son, who had grown in their land. People from Indraprastha came to see the wedding of the heir to their kingdom. They all prayed that Yudhishtira would return as emperor and there would be peace and prosperity again.

Thousands of guests had arrived, and excellent arrangements were made for all of them. King Virat had not made an idle boast when he had said that this would be the greatest wedding of the times. The ministers and citizens of Viratanagar happily joined in the wedding arrangements.

Abhimanyu was lodged in a special palace meant for the groom and his family. He spent an enjoyable time reuniting with his family. His thoughts dwelled on

Uttara and he yearned to meet her. He knew it would not be possible as she was inside another palace, busy with rituals and surrounded by her family members.

All the rituals of the wedding were carried out and preparations were done. On the night before the wedding, Arjuna came to Abhimanyu and said, "My son, I plan to give you special gifts for your wedding tomorrow morning. Finish your bath and the morning rituals. I will take you to the temple of Rudra and offer you gifts that will make you a truly exceptional warrior."

Abhimanyu wondered what his father would gift him. He was excited about his upcoming wedding and that he would be able to finally spend time with the lovely Uttara. He also hoped that since their exile was over, the Pandavas would get back Indraprastha. He knew in his heart that this might not happen, as the evil Duryodhana was unlikely to return the kingdom easily.

The next day, after finishing the ritual bath and other ceremonies, he went with his father to the temple of Lord Shiva and took his blessings. He sat before his father, who had come bearing gifts.

Arjuna picked up a mighty bow and gave it to Abhimanyu. "This, my son, is the Raudra. Use this great bow and you will find victory in battle."

He then picked up a coat of armour and gave it to his son. "This armour was gifted to me by the gods. It is almost impenetrable and will protect you from the weapons of your opponents in battle."

"Father, can no weapon affect this armour?"

"It is made of very strong metal and can withstand thousands of arrows. Of course, if someone keeps shooting arrows at it, then it is bound to be destroyed.

Such a situation is unlikely to happen as you will not stand there watching the enemy shooting weapons at you."

Abhimanyu bowed to his father and received the weapons.

"Now, my son, is the time to give you celestial weapons. I have obtained these astras from my guru Drona and the gods. I give them to you with the confidence that you will use them wisely. They are to be used only against opponents stronger than you or those equal in strength. Do not use the weapons in such a way that the gods become angry."

Arjuna then started teaching Abhimanyu the mantras or chants that would invoke the divine astras. Abhimanyu listened keenly, his heart swelling in pride that his father had presented him with celestial weapons. He would now be a great warrior whom none could defeat in battle.

"Remember, son, some of these astras can be used only once. So, use them with care. The potency of these weapons depends on the skills of the warrior. Never use the astras in anger but only when the situation demands it."

Just then Krishna walked in and smiled, seeing the gifts Arjuna had given his son.

"Everyone is searching for you. The wedding rituals will start soon. Come, Abhimanyu, it is time for you to get ready for your wedding ceremony."

"Uncle, my father has given me only a few celestial weapons. I am eagerly waiting for him to give the greatest of weapons like the Brahmastra and Pashupatastra."

Krishna said, "I already told you, Abhimanyu, that you are too young to receive these great weapons. You need to prove your worth on the battlefield and then you can make these weapons your own. These weapons can destroy the entire world. A sixteen-year-old cannot have these weapons."

Abhimanyu's face was downcast. Arjuna clapped him on the back and said, "Don't worry, son, there will soon be an occasion for you to prove yourself on the battlefield. When you do that, you can get all the weapons that I have. These are enough for now. Come now, let's go to the wedding."

Abhimanyu touched his father's feet and took his blessings. "I promise you, Father, I will prove to be a great warrior and make you proud of me."

Arjuna said, "The destiny of a warrior is in the battlefield, my son. That is where a warrior leaves his mark behind. The bravest warrior is not just the one who wins a battle. The one who gives up his life on the battlefield for his dharma, his country and his king is equally great. You have many years of your life ahead and will win many battles, I am confident of that."

"There is a lot I need to learn from you, Father. I still need to learn how to exit from the Chakravyuha battle formation."

Krishna said, "Forget the vyuha of battle, it is now time for you to enter the vyuha of marriage. Come, let's go."

Abhimanyu was decked up for the wedding. The finest garments had been selected for him, as were the best jewellery studded with precious gems. He looked resplendent and shone like the moon. Krishna led him to the marriage hall, with Arjuna and Subhadra following behind. Abhimanyu sat on the stage that had been constructed for the wedding, flanked by his proud parents.

The most revered sages in the land carried out all the ceremonies as per the scriptures, as King Virat looked on happily. Yudhishtira was seated on a huge throne with Krishna next to him, witnessing the ceremony with happiness in his heart.

Queen Sudeshna led her daughter to the stage. As she walked up gracefully, Abhimanyu looked at her, his heart leaping with joy. This most beautiful and intelligent princess would be his wife and his life would be one of eternal happiness.

Uttara looked like Goddess Lakshmi; Abhimanyu was no less and resembled Lord Narayana himself. The auspicious time arrived and Abhimanyu tied the sacred mangalasutra[11] around Uttara's neck, signifying them being united in wedlock.

Abhimanyu and Uttara were married in front of the sacred fire. The assembled king and guests showered their blessings on the couple even as the sages chanted mantras and poured ghee into the fire as offerings to the gods.

Abhimanyu and Uttara took the blessings of Arjuna and Subhadra, after which they were blessed by King Virat and his wife. The Pandavas and Draupadi blessed them with a long and happy married life.

Abhimanyu took Uttara to Lord Krishna and both of them fell at his feet, seeking his blessings. He hugged Abhimanyu in joy and blessed him. Putting his hand

[11] The mangalasutra is a sacred thread tied by the groom around the bride's neck at an auspicious time during the wedding ceremony.

on Uttara's head, he blessed her, saying, "May you give birth to the emperor of the world."

Everyone was pleased to hear Krishna's blessings. Subhadra wondered why his blessing was different. Everyone had blessed the couple with a long life together, but Krishna had given a different blessing. She was happy thinking that her son would soon be emperor and his son after him.

There were great celebrations in the city. Everyone had delicious food and drinks prepared from a variety of fruit. Guests received expensive gifts that were brought by Krishna from Dwaraka. King Virat gifted his son-in-law thousands of horses, hundreds of elephants and much gold. He bowed before Yudhishtira and said, "My kingdom is yours, great Emperor. I am at your service always."

Yudhishtira embraced Virat in joy. After a year of exile in Matsya Kingdom, they were now relatives and the Pandavas would stay here until Duryodhana returned their kingdom.

Thousands of common people were fed and given gifts. They all blessed the newly married couple. Celebrations went on for days in the kingdom. The Pandavas were happy and enjoyed the festivities. After thirteen years of hardship, they were now experiencing peace and happiness.

That night, Arjuna and Krishna led Abhimanyu to his palace where his wife was waiting for him. Krishna kept teasing Abhimanyu on the way, leaving him blushing.

Krishna remarked, "You are not going to battle, Abhimanyu. You are going to your wife. Don't handle her like you handle your bow. Handle her with love and care."

Abhimanyu's heart was dancing at the thought of finally getting to spend some time alone with his wife. Krishna gently pushed his nephew into the room and closed the door.

Abhimanyu walked in and saw Uttara seated on the bed, waiting for him. He went and sat next to her, his face glowing with happiness. She was sitting shyly, her head lowered. He lifted her chin, looking into her eyes, and saw love in them.

They sat there looking into each other's eyes for a long time before Abhimanyu caressed her cheek and gently embraced her. He kissed her tenderly and looked at her glowing face.

"I am truly blessed, Uttara, to have you as my wife. This is the happiest day of my life."

"Every girl would want a handsome and brave warrior like you as a husband. It is my fortune that you are my husband."

"Uttara, what do you think about my uncle Krishna?"

"They say he is the Lord Narayana himself, but why do you ask now?"

"Did you remember what he wished you?" asked Abhimanyu with a mischievous smile on his face.

Uttara blushed.

"We should respect his wishes," said Abhimanyu, smiling at Uttara. She smiled back at him coyly as he took her into his arms.

As Abhimanyu and Uttara became one, the rays of the moon showered blessings through the window.

15

Happiness! But a Dark Cloud Looms

Abhimanyu was experiencing the most pleasant time of his life. Having spent all of his youth training to be a warrior, the hardened prince now spent tender moments with his pretty wife. His family gave him the privacy he needed and allowed the couple to spend time together.

Abhimanyu felt blessed that he had the most beautiful and loving wife in the world. They spent time talking about many things and recollecting their first meeting.

"Uttara, I fell in love with you the moment I saw you. The time we spent in the garden that evening was memorable. At that time, I resolved that I would somehow make you my bride."

"I too was smitten by you the moment I saw you peeping into my chambers. At first, I was angry that a soldier dared peep into my room. But when I saw you, I felt strange feelings in my heart and knew that I was in love for the first time in my life. I never thought I would see you again, but then after what happened in the garden, I fell in love with you."

"How did you guess I was the son of Arjuna?"

"It was obvious, my dear husband. I have seen my uncle Keechaka, who was a great warrior, practise archery. Even he could not do all that you did so effortlessly. You must be a great archer. The only name in archery that comes to mind is Arjuna. Interestingly, it was your father himself who had told me everything about Arjuna."

"Oh, really, how did that happen?"

"I did not know that it was Arjuna who was teaching me dance. For me, he was Brihannala. I respected her because of her knowledge. She used to talk to me about so many things. She had told me about Arjuna."

"So, you decided that I must be Arjuna or his son?"

"Yes," giggled Uttara. "The guess was correct, and I impressed you, right?"

"Yes, I was already in love with you. I was besotted at your brilliance."

"How did the great Arjuna become a eunuch? He actually looked like a eunuch; it did not seem like a disguise. How was he so proficient in singing and dancing?"

"I know how this happened. Father has narrated it to me."

"I am curious to know, please tell me."

"When Father visited Indraloka[12], he had gone to the land of the Gandharvas, who, impressed with his bravery and knowledge, asked him to spend time with them. It was they who taught him singing and dancing."

"How did he become a eunuch?"

[12] The abode of Indra, the king of the gods.

"Once, the apsara Urvashi came to Father and tried to seduce him. When he said that he was not interested, she became angry and cursed him to become a eunuch. Indra used his powers and converted the curse to become a boon. Father could choose to become a eunuch any time he wanted. It suited him to become a eunuch to spend the year incognito."

"Their coming to our kingdom was a blessing from God. Had they not been here, you would not have come. I would not have met you and we would not be married."

"It is destiny that brought us together."

"Did you know, there was a proposal from Hastinapura for me?"

"What?"

"Yes, your uncle Duryodhana had sent a proposal asking my hand in marriage for his son Lakshmana. Fortunately, my father did not have a good opinion of the Kaurava prince and he refused, giving the excuse that I was too young. Had the Kaurava army defeated us, I would have been taken forcibly to Hastinapura."

"Yes, that's how Duryodhana married Lakshmana's mother. He carried her away forcibly. The Kauravas have no respect for women. My blood boils thinking of what they did to Mother Draupadi. We are all waiting for a chance to avenge that insult."

"Will there be a war, then?"

"I believe there will be a war. I know my uncle very well. He will not give us back our kingdom so easily. His heart is full of envy and hatred for my father and uncles. We may have to go to war to get back what is rightfully ours."

"You cannot go to war, my prince. You are too young. I fear for you."

"Don't fear, my sweet princess. You have seen what your husband can do. I am the son of Arjuna and nephew of Krishna. If there is a battle, I can handle myself very well. Don't fear for me. It is the wives of my opponents who should fear."

Uttara sighed, "I pray that good sense prevails and there is no war. I don't want anything to interrupt these precious moments we are enjoying."

Abhimanyu smiled and embraced his wife. He was spending the best moments of his life after his wedding and wished that life could be like this forever. It was not that he did not enjoy his training phase in Dwaraka, but this was blissful heaven.

It was an agreeable day, with the sun shining brightly. Abhimanyu and his wife were in the garden enjoying the pleasant environment. Birds of various kinds sang sweet songs and peacocks gracefully pranced all around the lake. It was an idyllic setting, the kind, a newly married couple would linger in. Faraway in the sky, however, dark clouds were moving slowly towards them.

These clouds were what worried the Pandavas. Their happiness would be cut short if the Kauravas refused to return their kingdom. They were prepared for war and not afraid for they wanted to get what rightfully belonged to them. After all, they had taken a lot of pain to build the city of Indraprastha and had governed it well.

It was not just them but the people of Indraprastha, who had lived happily under their rule, also wanted them back. All those who had assembled for Abhimanyu's wedding discussed how to handle this issue. Balarama upset the Pandavas by saying that it was entirely their fault that they gambled their kingdom and lost it. He asked them to go to Duryodhana with humility and beg him for their share of the kingdom.

Satyaki was furious hearing these words and criticised Balarama for supporting the vile Duryodhana. He said, "The Pandava kings are the greatest in the world. The mighty Bheema who can shake the ground is with them. Arjuna is the greatest warrior in the world and can decimate the Kaurava army in an instant. With the blessings of Shri Krishna, the Kauravas can be crushed easily. They better hand over the Pandavas' rightful share else be ready to face the consequences."

King Drupada intervened, "I agree that war has to be fought to get back what belongs to the Pandavas. However, we must give peace a chance. I propose sending an emissary to Hastinapura. I will send my chief priest on our behalf. He will try to convince the Kuru elders that having completed thirteen years of exile, the Pandavas should now be given back their kingdom."

Krishna concurred with Drupada and asked him to send the emissary. He asked all the assembled kings to simultaneously start preparations for war.

The Pandavas waited eagerly for Drupada's emissary to go to the Kauravas and return. Meanwhile, all arrangements for war had commenced. Arjuna and Krishna were discussing the prospects of war.

Arjuna said, "Krishna, with your divine Sudarshana Chakra and my celestial weapons, we can easily defeat the Kauravas. I am not worried about the war, only I don't want to kill my own family members."

Krishna said, "Arjuna, do not expect me to use the Sudarshana Chakra in the war. Similarly, I do not expect you to use the celestial weapons against the Kauravas."

Arjuna was shocked, "How can you say this, Krishna? I took so many pains to obtain the celestial weapons and you don't want me to use them. Why?"

Krishna said, "Arjuna, use your celestial weapons but remember that the three most powerful weapons—the Brahmastra, Narayanastra and Pashupatastra—are weapons of mass destruction. They do not just slay the enemy but, if not deployed properly, can destroy the entire land. Many innocents can die if you use these powerful weapons."

"So, how do we win the war?"

"Arjuna, you are the greatest warrior in the world. Do you not trust your skills? Do you not have other celestial weapons with you? Do you not have faith in Bheema, Satyaki, Drupada, Dhrishtadyumna and the others who support us?"

"I agree, Krishna. I must prove my abilities without using the almighty weapons in war."

Krishna held out his hand to Arjuna. "Promise me, Arjuna, that you will not use the weapons given by Brahma, Vishnu and Maheshwara in the forthcoming war and that you will fight using your own skills and showcase your greatness before the world."

Arjuna held Krishna's hand with both his own. "I promise you, Krishna, I will do as you say. I only ask you to be with me during the war."

Krishna just beamed at Arjuna.

Meanwhile, Drupada's messenger had met the Kauravas and delivered his message. There were deliberations on this message and King Dhritharashtra sent his trusted aide Sanjaya to meet the Pandavas and convey his reply.

Sanjaya arrived and delivered King Dhritharashtra's response, and the Pandavas were disappointed to learn that there was nothing concrete in it. He called for peace and harmony and appealed to the Pandavas not to go to war. His message was that the Pandavas would not gain anything by war and it would only lead to bloodshed.

Yudhishtira, after much discussion, sent a reply through Sanjaya saying that he did not want war but this did not mean that they were weak. He demanded that Indraprastha be returned to the Pandavas. Yudhishtira even offered to rule over a kingdom that was lesser in size than the Kauravas, if that would ensure peace.

Sanjaya returned and conveyed the message. He made it clear to Dhritharashtra and Bheeshma that if the Pandavas were not given back their kingdom, there would be war. There were lengthy discussions in the Kaurava kingdom and all the elders wanted peace. Duryodhana rejected all their views and refused to return Yudhishtira's kingdom. He was strongly supported by Karna and Shakuni.

Dhritharashtra sent a message to the Pandavas that he still preferred to pursue peace and was finding it difficult to convince his son to return the kingdom.

Yudhishtira called a meeting, where everyone was present and discussed what should be done.

Satyaki, supported by Arjuna and Bheema, strongly suggested that they go to war to claim what belonged to them. Abhimanyu also gave his opinion along with the other sons of the Pandavas and said that he supported Satyaki. The mood in the Pandava camp was staunchly in favour of war. They all looked at Yudhishtira to decipher what was in his mind.

Yudhishtira said, "I agree that we must get back what is ours. If we do not get it, we must fight to claim it. That is Kshatriya dharma. However, war will lead to thousands of deaths. We will be remembered forever for having killed our own family members for the sake of the kingdom. I believe that we must try for peace till the very end."

Draupadi said sadly, "My king, do you forget the humiliation I suffered? Will you, for the sake of peace, prevent Bheema's vow from being fulfilled?"

Yudhishtira tried to calm Draupadi down. Krishna stood up. "Yudhishtira, I am ready to go on your behalf to Hastinapura and make one last effort at peace."

Yudhishtira was delighted to hear Krishna's words. He bowed to Krishna. "Please leave for Hastinapura and negotiate on our behalf. I am sure the Kuru elders will heed your words and good sense will prevail. I trust that you will get us what we deserve."

Krishna left for Hastinapura. This was the last chance for peace, the final attempt to prevent a great war from taking place.

16

Preparations for War

The assembled Pandavas eagerly waited for Krishna to return. Everyone was gathered in the city of Upaplavya in Matsya Kingdom that King Virat had gifted for the exclusive use of the Pandavas. All the Pandavas wanted to know what had happened with Krishna's effort at brokering peace with the Kauravas.

Draupadi favoured war to ensure that her insult was avenged, and Bheema and Arjuna supported her. Abhimanyu and Draupadi's sons too were in favour of war. They believed that Duryodhana would try to humiliate them again in the name of peace, and they all trusted Krishna and knew that he would negotiate peace with their best interests in mind.

It had been nearly four days since Krishna had left for Hastinapura. He was expected back very soon. It was getting dark, and the Pandavas paced up and down the great hall that was built for their use. Soon they heard the sounds of a chariot. Krishna had returned!

They attentively awaited his entry. He entered the hall and the five Pandavas, their wives and children all stood up and bowed in obeisance before him. Yudhishtira led him to a throne in the centre of the hall.

Krishna sat down and everyone looked at him in anticipation.

"What happened, Krishna? Did Duryodhana agree to give back our kingdom? Did he heed your advice or the words of the Kuru elders?" asked Yudhishtira.

Krishna shook his head and Yudhishtira's heart sank. The hope of peace seemed to have been shattered.

"Duryodhana continues to show his arrogance. He refused to hand back the kingdom, saying you were discovered during the year of incognito travel. Bheeshma and Vidura objected, stating that the year of incognito exile was over when Arjuna was discovered. Duryodhana refused to see reason."

"You said you would offer an alternative plan if Duryodhana refused to hand over half the kingdom. What happened to that, Vaasudeva?" asked Arjuna.

"Yes, I addressed Dhritharashtra and made it clear that if you are not given what you deserve, there would be war; I pointed out the futility of it as well. I told him that he would have to see his own family members die, and then presented my alternative proposal."

"What was the alternative proposal, Krishna?" asked Draupadi.

"I suggested that they should give five villages to the five of you, as a compromise. Vidura was happy with this proposal. Duryodhana asked me the names of the five villages. I told him that I wanted Paniprastha, Indraprastha, Sonaprastha, Vrikshaprastha and Tilaprastha. He flatly refused to agree."

"Didn't the elders try to convince him, Krishna?" asked Yudhishtira.

"Everyone did their best to convince him. Bheeshma, Dhritharashtra, Vidura, Gandhari and Drona were all in favour of this proposal. They were happy with the alternative plan that would allow Duryodhana to still rule most of the country. Shakuni ruined the proposal by alerting Duryodhana to the fact that the five villages would be in the heart of the kingdom and would allow you to dominate. This made Duryodhana angry, and he walked out from the court after refusing to give up land that measured even the tip of a needle."

"So, it's war?" asked Bheema.

"Yes, there is no other alternative."

"Good," said Bheema. "Instead of begging, it is time we take what belongs to us by showing our valour on the battlefield. It will give me a chance to fulfil my vow to Draupadi by breaking Duryodhana's thigh and using Dushasana's blood to knot Draupadi's unkempt hair."

Abhimanyu was thrilled hearing these words. It was time for him to show the world what a brave warrior he was, time to make his father proud of his skill in warfare.

He stepped forward. "Uncle Krishna, bless me. I will join the battle with my father and uncles and teach the Kauravas a lesson."

"No!" shouted Subhadra and rushed forward to hold Abhimanyu's hand. "I will not allow you to join this war."

"I agree with you," said Draupadi. "He is just sixteen years old. How can we send a boy to war?"

"Mother Draupadi, my age may be sixteen, but I am as skilled and brave as an experienced warrior. You don't have to worry about me."

Subhadra hugged Abhimanyu and started crying, "No, son, I cannot live without you. Please don't go, you are too young to participate in a great war like this."

Abhimanyu smiled at his mother as he said, "Mother, what age was Skanda when he killed Taraka?[13] Age is not an issue, Mother. My skills give me the confidence to believe that I can defeat the enemy. I will come back safe after the war, having achieved great victories."

Arjuna stepped in, "No, Abhimanyu, I do not want to send you to war. It has hardly been a few days since you got married. Do you want to leave your young wife and go? She has just entered into married life. Spend more time with her and raise a family. Your time will come, son."

"Father, I am the son of the mighty Arjuna. My teachers are Krishna and Pradyumna. A warrior who can kill me is yet to be born," declared Abhimanyu, his chest swelling with pride.

"We will talk about this later," said Arjuna. "I suggest you talk to your wife before deciding."

Abhimanyu walked out sulking, determined to be a part of the war and prove his abilities.

Meanwhile, the Pandavas planned their next moves even as Krishna returned to Dwaraka. It was time to start building an army. King Virat and King Drupada, having given their daughters in marriage to their family, would fight with them. Shalya, the maternal uncle of Nakula and Sahadeva, was sure to be on

[13] Skanda (also known as Kartikeya or Subramanya), the son of Shiva and Parvati, was born to kill the demon Taraka. It is believed that he was just seven years old when he did so.

their side. There were many other kings who would ally with them.

Yudhishtira spent the next few days writing to potential allies and sending the letters by special emissaries. He invited them all to King Virat's palace, where they would meet and decide their strategy for war.

Arjuna had gone to Dwaraka to seek the support of Krishna and the Yadava army. Duryodhana arrived there at the same time. Krishna, who was asleep, saw Arjuna seated near his feet when he opened his eyes. Placing two options before him, he offered Arjuna the first choice. One option was to choose the Yadava army and the other was to choose Krishna, who made it clear that he would not personally fight in the war but would serve as a charioteer and advisor.

Arjuna did not need even a moment to decide. He chose Krishna. Duryodhana was happy as the large army of Dwaraka was at his disposal. Arjuna was, of course, happy that Krishna was with him.

As they met, the Pandavas expressed their happiness that they would have Krishna's blessings with them. They had invited all their allies and all of them had started arriving in Matsya Kingdom where King Virat played host.

Abhimanyu once again used the occasion to demand that he be allowed to join the war. He insisted on being given a chance to show his prowess in the battle.

Arjuna hugged his son. "I want to suggest something, son. I think you know Balarama has decided not to participate in the war."

"Oh! I didn't know that," said Abhimanyu.

"Yes, since Krishna is on our side, Balarama is reluctant to fight against him. He also did not want to disappoint Duryodhana by supporting us. Even Krishna's son Pradyumna has decided not to join the war. Both Balarama and Pradyumna are leaving on a pilgrimage to visit various holy sites. They will probably return after the war is over. I want you to join them, Abhimanyu."

"What! Father, are you serious? You want me, a sixteen-year-old, to go on a pilgrimage."

"I want you out of this war. Your mother and I love you a lot. I will never forgive myself if anything happens to you and neither will Subhadra. Think of Uttara before you choose to fight in the war."

"Don't worry, Father. I have mastered the art of archery. I have learnt the use of celestial weapons from you. I have even proved my skills in the battle with the Trigartas. In the name of Krishna of Dwaraka, I promise you that I will prove myself a worthy warrior in the war."

"Yes, Arjuna, I concur," said Bheema. "I have seen his skill in archery and must say it almost equals yours. He will be a big asset in this war, and in fact, I have a feeling that he will make a great contribution to this war. He will have my son Ghatotkacha to fight alongside him. Let him fight."

Arjuna hesitated for a moment. He sighed, "All right, my son, I will permit you to fight the war. May God bless you with success."

Abhimanyu touched his father's feet and took his blessings as well as his uncles'.

The strategy for the Great War was formulated the next day in the court of King Virat. All the Pandava allies were present. King Virat presided over the meeting as the host. King Drupada of Panchala, Satyaki, the Yadava warrior of the Vrishni clan and the five Pandavas were seated. Krishna's presence gave confidence to the kings, princes and generals.

Sahadeva, the king of Magadha, pledged support to the Pandavas. Dhristaketu, the king of Chedi, was present and offered his aid to Yudhishtira.

A lengthy discussion ensued as to who should head the Pandava army. It was known that Bheeshma would head the Kaurava army and they should prepare to face his might. They needed a strong commander who could rally their forces and lead them with confidence.

Many names were discussed including that of Virat, Drupada, his son Dhrishtadyumna and even Shikhandi. Finally, Yudhishtira requested Krishna to make the decision.

Krishna said, "Every one of these great kings and warriors here is invincible. Each one of them has the ability to defeat the Kauravas. I nominate the brave Dhrishtadyumna, who was born from the fire, to be the commander of the Pandava forces."

Everyone hailed Krishna's decision. The kings seated Dhrishtadyumna at the centre of the hall. Yudhishtira garlanded him and the assembled Pandavas and their allies showered petals on him, wishing him success.

Soon it was time to bid goodbye to the womenfolk and leave for the Kurukshetra battlefield where the Great War would be fought.

Abhimanyu went to Uttara, who was weeping with her face covered. He embraced her gently and said, "I understand your sorrow, my dear wife. Remember, you married me because I am a warrior and the son of Arjuna. Don't cry. Have confidence in my abilities."

"I have complete confidence in you, dear husband. Your valour is immense but you have to fight against the likes of Bheeshma, Drona, Duryodhana, Karna and so many other greats," said Uttara, looking at Abhimanyu with tears in her eyes.

Abhimanyu kissed her tenderly and held her in a tight embrace, saying, "Let the enemy have 10,000 heroic warriors. I am the son of Arjuna and the nephew of Krishna. None of them can stand before me. My sweet princess, be assured that your husband is going to terrorise the enemy. I will return a hero and make you proud."

Uttara smiled through her tears. "I am proud of you and I know you will live up to the expectations of being the son of the greatest archer in the world. But my heart still aches when I think of being away from you."

Abhimanyu kissed her on the forehead. "The next time you see me, I will be before you as the greatest warrior in this war and a supreme hero."

They embraced for one last time and Abhimanyu left to bid a tearful goodbye to his mother. It was time to leave for the Great War.

17

All Is Ready for the Great War

The Pandavas and their allies left for the Kurukshetra battlefield after bidding a tearful goodbye to the women. The Upapandavas and Abhimanyu also left for the war. All the women left behind prayed to the gods to bring back their family members safely.

The Pandavas reached the huge battlefield of Kurukshetra and set up camp at one end. At the other end, the Kauravas were already setting up camp. There were thousands of tents that had been set up by workers who had reached earlier.

There were tents for the soldiers, tents for the warriors, tents for the princes and kings, and a huge tent for the war council to meet in. Big tents were constructed for the armoury where soldiers worked non-stop to produce weapons, armours and shields for the soldiers. There were tents where cooks prepared nutritious food and drinks for the hungry and tired warriors.

A large number of physicians were available in special tents to tend to the wounded. They had all the herbs and medications to treat the injured and send them back to fight. Satyaki, the Vrishni warrior, was a physician himself and supervised the arrangements at the medical camp.

There were special teams of soldiers to transport the injured and dead back to the camp. There was a vast group of soldiers whose job was only to tend to the animals. Horses and elephants had separate enclosures with sufficient food and water and persons to take care of them. The animals would be decked with the finest jewellery and armour before the soldiers mounted them and led them to the battlefield.

Thousands of chariots were lined up, ready for the warriors to climb on them and take them to battle. Charioteers waited near the chariots for their masters to arrive. The atmosphere was one of hectic activity, with intense arrangements being made for the war.

The Pandavas had their council meeting under the leadership of their commander, Dhrishtadyumna. All the Pandavas, their allies and other warriors were present in the war-council tent as strategies for the war were made. Abhimanyu was seated proudly along with the other great warriors and kings, awaiting the instructions of his commander.

Dhrishtadyumna addressed the council, "Our army is now ready. We have seven akshauhinis (full divisions) with us for the war. Each akshauhini has 21,870 elephants and an equal number of chariots. There are 65,610 cavalry and 1,09,350 infantry soldiers in one akshauhini. Our seven akshauhinis come from King Virata, King Drupada, King Sahadeva, King Dhrishtaketu, King Kuntibhoja, King Malayadhwaja and the brave Satyaki."

"We have a great army assembled ready to take on the Kauravas," said Yudhishtira.

"Yes, my emperor," said Dhrishtadyumna. "However, we must note that the Kauravas have eleven akshauhinis. My spies have been busy collecting information. We must be ready to face an army that is larger than ours."

Krishna said, "We have warriors like Arjuna, Bheema and Satyaki on our side who themselves are equal to an akshauhini each. Abhimanyu, Ghatotkacha, Virata, Drupada—there are innumerable great warriors who can easily defeat the Kauravas."

Dhrishtadyumna said, "I agree, Lord Krishna, that we may be weaker in numbers, but I am also confident that we can match our opponents in skills and warfare. I have some more good news. Bheeshma has classified his warriors as maharathas, athirathas and rathas based on their abilities. I heard that he classified Karna as an ardha ratha, declaring that he is capable of fighting in a chariot only if he has another warrior with him."

"That's surprising! Why did the grandsire say so?" said Arjuna.

"Karna has given away his armour to a Brahmin who sought it. This has weakened him considerably. He has a curse on his head from his teacher Parashurama which, according to Bheeshma, has reduced his abilities. Anyway, Karna was so offended that he has taken a decision not to fight the war as long as Bheeshma heads the Kauravas."

"Ha," exclaimed Bheema, slapping his thigh. "Duryodhana's strength has been reduced by half, thanks to this decision."

"Yes," said Arjuna. "But I will miss the chance of defeating Karna in battle."

"You will get your chance, Arjuna, don't worry," assured Krishna.

Dhrishtadyumna planned the arrangements for the war and battle formations to counter the Kauravas. The mood in the Pandava camp was upbeat.

Yudhishtira got up to address the gathering, "My allies and warriors, I want to thank you for coming forward to support me and my brothers in this dharma yudh. This is not merely a war being fought for me to gain land. This is a war for righteousness. When we fight, let us fight in the right way."

"I agree, great king," concurred King Virat. "We are fighting on the side of dharma and must follow dharma."

"Let me list out the rules of war, which we must scrupulously follow. The first rule is that we start fighting after sunrise and stop at sunset. We shall wait for the commanders to sound the conch shells and commence the war."

Everyone nodded their heads.

"Many warriors must not attack a single warrior. A warrior must fight with one his equal. It is prohibited to kill a warrior who is unarmed or unconscious. It is also prohibited to kill someone who has surrendered. We will take prisoners and treat them with the respect they deserve. There is no question of attacking anyone from behind. We must fight face to face like true warriors. We must fight in equal combat with one who has the same weapons and is mounted on the same vehicle of war. I implore you to follow these rules."

"What if the enemy violates these rules, Brother?" asked Arjuna.

"Our adherence to rules does not depend on what our opponents do. We will fight with dharma and follow the rules of the war. If they do not follow the rules, they will have to face the consequences. I do not believe that Pitamaha Bheeshma will allow his army to break the rules."

Everyone nodded in agreement. Abhimanyu was in a high state of excitement, waiting for the war to commence.

As soon as the meeting was over, he proceeded to his chariot and visited the armoury. He loaded his chariot with weapons galore. He had his own bow that he had brought with him. The huge bow was made of strong wood and he personally fixed the bowstring, making sure to check its strength. The strings were made from the bark of the bamboo plant and were strong and flexible.

He pulled back the string, bending the bow to test its strength. His bow was almost 5 feet tall and was powerful. He had many such bows with him. There were hundreds of quivers of arrows in his chariot. Each of these huge quivers had a belt that he could wear around his shoulders to allow him to quickly reach out and draw an arrow.

Each quiver had hundreds of arrows made of iron and tightly packed together. In the centre of the quiver were special arrows, some of them gold with feathers, others with crescent arrowheads and still others in a serpentine shape. There were many barbed arrows that were sharper than the others.

He also had spears, swords and shields in his chariot, as well as the mace gifted to him by Balarama. His chariot was resplendent and drawn by four white horses. It had huge wheels that were firmly fixed to it, as well as Abhimanyu's standard, with a flag depicting a karnikara tree with golden leaves. The chariot had a golden canopy.

All the warriors checked and rechecked the arrangements for their vehicles before retiring for the night. Everyone was awake well before sunrise and assembled on the battlefield.

Dhrishtadyumna decided to arrange the army in the Vajra formation (Vajra vyuha) that resembled the mighty weapon of Lord Indra. Bheema led from the front, with Dhrishtadyumna and the other Pandavas behind him. Soldiers surrounded the formation in a box shape.

Abhimanyu was placed beside his cousin Ghatotkacha on one side and his brother Iravan, the son of Arjuna and the Naga princess Uloopi, on the other. He eagerly awaited the sunrise and the blowing of the conches to start the battle. To his surprise, he observed Krishna leading Arjuna away from the formation. His father alighted from the chariot.

The armies were surprised to see this. Abhimanyu was worried about his father putting down his weapons and climbing down from the chariot. He was tempted to go to him but controlled his curiosity; he was assigned a position and was determined to stand there and hold it.

Meanwhile, Arjuna, out of his chariot, was looking thoroughly dispirited. He addressed Krishna, "Oh Vaasudeva, look at the army in front of us. It is headed by Bheeshma, my grandfather. I am expected to kill him on the battlefield. How can I do it? To his right is

Drona, my teacher. If I am standing here regarded as a skilled warrior, it is only because of Drona. How can I kill my teacher, who the scriptures say is like God?"

Krishna did not say anything and just smiled.

"Everywhere I look, I see my relatives. My cousins may have harmed us, but they share our blood. How can I slaughter them? Are the skills I learnt meant to destroy my own family? I cannot fight, Krishna. Isn't it a sin to kill your own family? No, Krishna, for the sake of winning the war, I cannot kill my own blood."

Krishna twinkled and circled his hand. With one gesture, he had brought time to a standstill. All the others on the battlefield stood still. Neither did flags flutter in the wind nor did animals move. There was silence all around as both the armies were transfixed to their spots.

"My dear Arjuna," said Krishna, "are you worried that your loved ones will die? What is death? Is it that someone in front of you falls on the ground mortally injured? Is that person dead according to you?"

"Yes," said Arjuna.

"No," replied Krishna, "he is not dead. It is his body that is dead. The flesh, muscles and bones form the body, which has perished. The person does not perish. There is no death, Partha. I have lived forever, and so have you. So has Bheeshma, so has Duryodhana and everyone here."

"How, Krishna? I do not understand, please explain," asked Arjuna looking astonished at Krishna's statement.

"What is the difference between that stone and you? It sits silently without life, whereas you have life. What is life? It is nothing but the soul, the energy that has entered your physical body. You are not this body; Arjuna, you are the energy, the soul inside. The soul can never be destroyed, it is permanent in nature."

"What happens to the soul after the body dies?"

"Don't you throw your old clothes and wear new ones daily? In the same way, once the body is old or dead, the soul sheds the body and moves to a new body. The old body is of no use. It has no energy, which is why it is consumed in flames. The soul moves on incarnating again and again until it attains liberation. Then the soul becomes one with the Supreme Being."

Arjuna looked on in wonderment as he listened to Krishna's words of wisdom.

"You are born to do something in this life—that is your karma. Do it sincerely and don't worry about the results, leave it to me. You are fighting for the cause of righteousness. There is no sin attached when you kill an opponent on the battlefield. So shed your worries and thoughts aside and focus on your responsibilities."

With these words, Krishna revealed his true form. Arjuna was transported out of the world and looked on in awe at the magnificent Vishwaroopa[14] of Krishna.

[14] The omniversal form of God, which subsumes the entire universe.

18

The War Starts

Arjuna was in outer space. The planets and stars rotated and revolved around him. In front of him was Krishna; he was larger than all the planets and loomed over the entire universe. He was so effulgent that Arjuna found it difficult to keep his eyes open.

He could see a thousand arms with each one of them having a weapon. He saw the Sudarshana Chakra of Vishnu. He saw the trishula of Shiva. He saw the lotus of Brahma. When he looked up, he saw a hundred heads. He saw Shiva. He saw Vishnu. He saw Brahma, Parashurama, Indra, Durga, Lakshmi and many other gods and goddesses.

Arjuna gazed in awe at this divine form of Krishna. He felt that the secrets of the universe had been revealed to him and he now knew what he should do. He opened his eyes and saw that they were back on the battlefield. Krishna had restored time again, and Arjuna could hear the sounds of horses and elephants and observed everyone focused on him.

He bowed to Krishna and touched his feet. "I understand my duty, Janardhana[15], thank you for reminding me of it. I am grateful that you helped me

[15] This is yet another name of Krishna that translates to one who liberates his devotees (from the cycle of birth and death).

resolve my confusion and I am now ready to fight for dharma."

They got onto the chariot and Krishna led Arjuna back to the formation. The Pandavas, who were worried when Arjuna had left, were relieved to see him back. Krishna lifted his conch Panchajanya and blew it. Arjuna, Yudhishtira and all the other warriors blew their conches to signify the start of the war.

The ground vibrated because of the thundering sound of the conches. Bheeshma blew his conch and the battle was announced. Both the armies charged at each other, the ground shaking with the sound of chariots, elephants, horses and shoes.

Soldiers fell upon each other in combat. Abhimanyu charged into the battlefield. He lifted his great bow, fixed an arrow on it and awaited his first opponent. A warrior on a chariot confronted him and shot an arrow. Within an instant, Abhimanyu shot his own arrow, which cut his opponent's arrow into two.

Even before his opponent could release another arrow. Abhimanyu shot a razor-sharp arrow that rushed through the air and beheaded his opponent. His first victory on the battlefield enthused Abhimanyu, and he directed his charioteer to charge ahead into the ranks of the opposition.

Meanwhile, Arjuna took on Bheeshma and the battle was fierce. Bheema fought with Duryodhana and Satyaki with his fellow Yadava Kritavarma. Abhimanyu scythed through the battlefield, drawing his huge bow again and again and releasing a shower of arrows. He was soon leaving behind a trail of dead bodies.

He encountered Vrihadvala, the king of Kosala. Abhimanyu smilingly fixed an arrow on his bow; as he was about to release the arrow, a blazing arrow from Vrihadvala cut his bowstring. The next arrow broke his standard, causing his flag to fall. The next one killed Abhimanyu's charioteer and his chariot shook.

Abhimanyu had learnt a lesson, that of never underestimating his enemy. He moved quickly, picking up another bow and shot nine arrows consecutively. They were released so fast that it seemed that all of them came towards Vrihadvala at the same time. Abhimanyu's arrows shattered the Kosala king's bow. His standard was shattered, his charioteer killed and Vrihadvala himself was struck by arrows.

Vrihadvala grabbed the reins of his chariot and pulled his chariot away. He had no option but to leave the battlefield. Seeing their king humiliated, many soldiers of Kosala fled the battlefield in panic.

Abhimanyu, being a maharathi warrior had a reserve chariot behind him. He quickly descended from his old chariot, climbed on to the other chariot and continued his assault on the Kauravas. He killed hundreds of Kauravas, gaining strength and confidence.

He fixed an arrow to his bow, pulled the string to its maximum length and used the power of his great arms to release it. The arrow hurtled towards his opponent, killing him. Moving at top speed, Abhimanyu took out another arrow from his quiver, fixed it and shot. He moved so fast that it seemed he was shooting tens of arrows simultaneously.

Meanwhile, Bheeshma was demonstrating his might to the Pandava army. None could stand before him.

Arjuna fought long and hard but was beaten back by the furious attack of the Kaurava commander. Bheeshma seemed unstoppable as he attacked the Pandavas mercilessly, killing hundreds of Pandava soldiers.

He streaked past so that it seemed as if a gush of wind had rushed through, slaughtering everyone in its wake. The only thing visible was his shining golden standard with the flag of the palm tree fluttering on it.

Duryodhana had appointed Shalya, Kripa, Kritavarma, Durmukha and Vivinsati to act as Bheeshma's guards. The combined attack of these warriors made the Pandava army reel. When all looked bleak, someone swiftly blocked Bheeshma's way and challenged him. It was Abhimanyu!

Yudhishtira stared in awe as the sixteen-old-year boy, with the arrogance of his youth, challenged his great-grandfather who was more than five times his age. He was least bothered about the stature of his opponent and his experience and fearlessly attacked Bheeshma, sending a shower of arrows at him.

Bheeshma's guards counter-attacked Abhimanyu and he met their challenge head-on. Five arrows hit Shalya, causing him to fall back. One arrow hit Kritavarma on his armour, breaking it. He showered Bheeshma with nine arrows as though showing his respect for the Kuru elder though a garland of arrows.

One piercing arrow killed Durmukha's charioteer, while two well-aimed arrows cut off Kripa's bow and pierced his shoulder, injuring him. Bheeshma was furious that his well-planned attack had been taken apart by a boy. He charged at Abhimanyu, letting loose a volley of arrows. The whizzing arrows broke the standard of Abhimanyu's chariot and his charioteer was wounded.

Shalya, Kritavarma and Kripa joined Bheeshma, and the four of them shot a flurry of arrows at Abhimanyu. Without even flinching, he cut off all the arrows shot by his opponents. He took back the attack to the enemy. Swinging around, he released arrows in quick succession, forcing his opponents into a defensive mode.

He shot nine arrows at Bheeshma that broke through his defence. The arrows knocked off his standard, causing it to fall. The sight of the palm tree flag falling off the chariot shocked the Kauravas. The Pandavas were exultant at the way young Abhimanyu had delivered such a blow to the mighty Bheeshma.

A furious Bheeshma used an astra and shot a shower of a thousand arrows at Abhimanyu. Even before he could react, the entire Pandava army came to his support. Bheema swatted at the arrows with his mace, causing them to disperse. Virat, Drupada, Dhrishtadyumna, Yudhishtira and Satyaki joined the battle to support Abhimanyu. A fierce battle raged between the warriors.

Uttarakumara charged at Shalya and attacked him. He was mounted on an elephant and let loose many arrows at Shalya. The experienced Shalya was not perturbed, defending himself from Uttarakumara's attack by flinging a sharp spear. The spear raced through the air and struck the crown prince of Matsya in the heart. Uttarakumar died instantly.

Even as he was dying, his elephant attacked Shalya's chariot and killed his horses. Shalya quickly cut its trunk and killed it. Uttarakumara's younger brother

Shweta rushed at Shalya in anger. It did not take much time for Shalya to slay Shweta as well.

Abhimanyu was distraught at the brutal killing of his brothers-in-law. He furiously attacked Shalya, who was prepared and hurled missile after missile at Abhimanyu, who found it difficult to counter him. While the son was engaged in battle with Shalya, the father was busy fighting his guru Drona.

Bheema was engaged by Dushasana, Satyaki by Bhurishravas and Dhrishtadyumna by Ashwatthama. All this while, Bheeshma continued his merciless onslaught on the Pandavas, massacring their soldiers. He dominated the battlefield all day like a colossus.

The hapless Pandavas looked at the sun hopefully, waiting for it to set. Abhimanyu fought desperately to defeat Shalya and just as he was gaining the upper hand, Kripa joined Shalya and both attacked Abhimanyu, whose energy was beginning to drop.

The battle raged furiously and Bheeshma was mercilessly decimating the Pandava soldiers. In the midst of the battle, Bheeshma suddenly stopped, looked up and blew his conch. It was sunset and the battle had ended for the day. The Pandava soldiers sighed in relief.

The victorious Kauravas joyously celebrated as they returned to their camp. The Pandavas returned to theirs, shoulders slumped and heads bowed. They knew they had lost the first day. However, Krishna reminded them that this was only the first day, and the war had many days to go.

King Virat mourned the loss of both his sons. His piteous wailing was like a knife that struck Abhimanyu in the heart. It was the first time someone close to him had died and the experience was highly tragic. He deeply mourned the loss of Uttarakumar who had helped him meet Uttara, and wondered how afflicted Uttara would be.

He also understood the reason for his wife's and mother's fears and their reluctance to send him to battle. He vowed to himself to give his best and help in ending the war at the earliest so he could return home to his wife and mother.

The Pandavas slept with the hope that the next day would be a good one and would help them forget the humiliation they had suffered at the hands of Bheeshma.

The next day, the armies lined up before sunrise. Yudhishtira told Dhrishtadyumna how the great sage Brihaspathi had mentioned a bird battle formation. Accordingly, the Pandavas formed the Krauncha vyuha or the crane formation, which was arranged like a bird in flight. Arjuna was asked to head the army and stood at the tip of the beak.

Drupada commanded the region of the head of the crane; Kuntibhoja and Shaivya were its eyes; Nakula and Sahadeva commanded the two wings of the formation; Virat and Dhristaketu protected the formation's tail region. Seeing this formation, Bheeshma formed the Garuda vyuha or eagle formation to counter it.

The moment the sun rose, Bheeshma sounded the conch. Arjuna, Krishna and the rest of the Pandavas sounded their conches as well and the second day's battle commenced. The two armies hurled themselves at each other in deadly combat.

Like on the first day, Bheeshma charged at the Pandavas with the intention of destroying them in battle. In the same way as the previous day, he was challenged by the brave Abhimanyu, who attacked him fiercely.

Arjuna joined his son and launched a ferocious attack on Bheeshma, knowing that if Bheeshma was not checked, the Kauravas would once again win the battle. There was a fierce fight between the Kuru elder and the great archer. Their battle raged on through the day as both of them used all the weapons and skills they had, but could not defeat the other.

The Pandavas' plan had worked. With Arjuna leading the attack and keeping Bheeshma in control, it was Bheema's turn to avenge the defeat of the previous day. Bheema launched such a ferocious attack that it terrorised the Kauravas. He used his mighty mace and scattered the Kauravas as if they were chaff before the wind.

One after the other, the Kaurava warriors tried to block Bheema but had to suffer defeat as his mace destroyed each missile they hurled at him. He destroyed the chariots of many a Kaurava hero and wreaked havoc.

Meanwhile, Abhimanyu waged a fierce war with Duryodhana's son Lakshmana. Both of them were full of exuberance and determined to prove their worth in battle. They attacked each other with arrows of different types. Lakshmana proved to be a powerful opponent for Abhimanyu. As they fought, Lakshmana released a powerful missile that snapped Abhimanyu's bow into two. Then, he shot another barbed arrow that raced towards Abhimanyu, threatening to behead him.

19

Abhimanyu's Heroics

As Lakshmana's arrow came towards him, Abhimanyu cut it into two at lightning speed using a sword. In the blink of an eye, he picked up another bow and launched a powerful counter-attack against Lakshmana. Soon, he destroyed the standard of Lakshmana's chariot and broke his bow. Seeing his son in trouble, Duryodhana charged towards Abhimanyu.

Abhimanyu did not flinch on seeing the Kaurava leader attack him. He greeted Duryodhana with a flurry of arrows. Father and son fought with Abhimanyu fiercely. Other generals joined Duryodhana to attack Abhimanyu. He feared none, fixed five arrows at a time and swivelled, shooting arrows all around him.

Meanwhile, Arjuna's ferocious attack became stronger and soon he shattered Bheeshma's bow and his chariot. When Drona came to Bheeshma's defence, Arjuna destroyed Drona's chariot as well. The two leading heroes had no option but to leave the battlefield to get new chariots. Arjuna noted that his son was in trouble.

He charged at Duryodhana and launched a mighty attack, causing the Kaurava leader to flee. Abhimanyu joined his father in his charge against the Kauravas. Arjuna's archery skills and Bheema's raw vigour ensured that the Kauravas suffered a terrible defeat. As the conches sounded to end the day's battle, it was the

Pandavas turn to celebrate while the Kauravas returned dejected.

On the third day of the war, Bheeshma again formed the Garuda vyuha. He placed Drona and Kritavarma at the eyes of the eagle while Ashwatthama and Kripa were at the head. The Kalingas and Kosala armies were stationed at the two wings while the other warriors were stationed all over the formation.

In response, Dhrishtadyumna formed the Ardha Chandra or crescent formation, with Arjuna at the front. The army stood behind him in the form of a half-moon. Bheema was placed at one end, while Abhimanyu was stationed at the other end of the moon. Yudhishtira and Dhrishtadyumna were at the centre of the formation while Satyaki and Ghatotkacha formed the back of the crescent moon.

The battle commenced and the two armies hurled themselves at each other. The intensity of the fighting grew forceful with each passing day. Warriors of both the armies were determined to excel and give their best. The crescent formation was able to successfully counter the eagle.

Arjuna charged at the head of the formation, scattering the Kaurava army. The strongest of the Kauravas—Drona, Ashwatthama, Kripa and Kritavarma—were at the forefront of the Kaurava army and stationed there to hold back Arjuna. They could only watch as Arjuna tore apart the formation with his fierce attack.

Abhimanyu, at one end of the crescent formation, attacked the wings of the eagle formation. He took on the Kosala army and once again faced the Kosala king

Vrihadvala, whom he had previously defeated. The battle was fierce and this time Vrihadvala was well prepared and fought bravely. A fierce skirmish broke out, lasting hours.

In the meantime, Bheema's ferocious attack helped him break through the formation and reach Duryodhana. The two arch-enemies fought fiercely. Bheema drew his bowstring back until his ear and let loose a sharp arrow. The arrow dashed through Duryodhana's defence and landed on his chest.

The arrow severely impacted Duryodhana's armour, splintering it. Unable to bear the anguish, he swooned and collapsed. Seeing him fall, his charioteer quickly led him back to the camp.

The Kaurava army saw their crown prince fall and thought he was dead. A buzz spread through the battlefield and the panicky Kaurava army fled helter-skelter. Bheema charged through the Kaurava army, decimating it.

Seeing this, Bheeshma was furious. He charged into the battlefield, shooting hundreds of arrows and devastating the Pandava army. None could stand against his enraged assault. Great warriors like Satyaki, Abhimanyu and Dhrishtadyumna were beaten back.

Krishna addressed Arjuna, "Partha, you must defeat Bheeshma and kill him. He is in a ferocious form and none can defeat him except you. Slay him else your army will face defeat."

Arjuna agreed to Krishna's recommendation and challenged Bheeshma. A fierce duel began. Bheeshma's arrows were released with so much force that they scythed through Arjuna's defences, putting him on the defensive. As Arjuna struggled to take on Bheeshma, Krishna was angry.

He turned to Arjuna and lifted his finger. On his finger appeared the almighty Sudarshana Chakra. The wheel of Vishnu whirled around his finger, emitting sparks and glistening in the afternoon sun. Krishna told Arjuna, "Partha, if you can't slay Bheeshma, then I will kill him with my chakra and end this battle."

Arjuna at once held Krishna's hand and appealed to him, "No, Krishna, please don't attack. You have taken a vow not to fight, please don't break it. I promise you that I will defeat my grandsire and finish him."

Krishna was mollified with these words and made the Sudarshana Chakra disappear.

The entire Kaurava warrior force had rallied behind Bheeshma. Duryodhana had returned and with him were Drona, Dushasana, Kritavarma, Kripa, Bhurishravas, Jayadratha and Paurava. All of them rained a shower of arrows at the Pandavas.

Abhimanyu, Satyaki, Dhrishtadyumna and Ghatotkacha joined the battle to support Arjuna. They were overwhelmed by the combined might of the Kaurava warriors and found it difficult to handle the rain of missiles unleashed against them.

Arjuna was charged up when he saw his army on the defensive. Finding the shower of arrows unstoppable, he decided that this was the right time to use a divyastra. He closed his eyes and prayed to his divine father Indra; instantly, the Mahendrastra appeared before him. He bowed to the missile and with his mind directed it at the Kauravas.

Under Arjuna's expert guidance the Mahendrastra disappeared into the clouds, where it exploded. A huge ball of light appeared that stunned the Kauravas. As it broke up, thousands of missiles emerged from the sky and rained down on the Kauravas.

The horrified Kauravas could only watch haplessly as the iron missiles showered death and destruction. The chariots of most of the Kaurava warriors were crushed. Bheeshma and Drona picked up their bows to use divine weapons to deal with Arjuna's attack. The force with which the arrows fell destroyed their bows and chariots, compelling them to duck for cover.

The shower of death from the sky continued for a few minutes. The air was filled with dense arrows and blood flowed all over the battlefield as Kaurava soldiers were annihilated. When the air cleared, Bheeshma and Duryodhana gaped in horror.

Their chariots and weapons were crushed. Thousands of their soldiers lay dead. In just one instant, Arjuna had killed 10,000 soldiers and 700 elephants. The armies of the Kshudrika and Malava allies of the Kauravas were completely destroyed.

Arjuna charged ahead supported by Abhimanyu, Satyaki and the rest of the Pandava warriors. Seeing them advance, the Kauravas were forced to flee. Only Bheeshma and Drona tried to defend themselves but found it impossible to take on the charge of the Pandavas.

Abhimanyu swooped ahead, killing Kaurava generals and soldiers. A hundred elephant warriors charged at him but Abhimanyu did not flinch. Supported by his cousin, the mighty Ghatotkacha, he destroyed the enemy. Warriors went down as their great elephants collapsed killing hordes of infantry soldiers.

Bheeshma looked desperately up at the sky. He observed the sun setting in the west and quickly blew his conch, signifying the end of the battle. Yudhishtira blew his conch as well, followed by Arjuna and the others. The victorious Pandavas celebrated as they returned to their camp. They were exultant in their praise of Arjuna, who had singlehandedly saved the day for them.

The fourth day once again saw Arjuna lead the Pandava army against the Kauravas. Given the previous day, the Kauravas were terrorised just by the sight of Arjuna with Krishna sitting in front, a beatific smile on his face.

The battle raged on. Bheeshma once again unleashed a merciless attack on the Pandavas. Arjuna rode up to Bheeshma, determined to stop him. Seeing Bheeshma in trouble, Drona, Duryodhana, Ashwatthama, Chitrasena, Shalya and Shalaputra came to support him.

Abhimanyu briskly came up to support his father. His younger brother Shrutakarma, who was the son of Arjuna and Draupadi, joined him. Both the warriors joined their father and the three of them waged a savage battle against the best of the Kauravas.

Seeing the three of them take on so many of the Kauravas, Shalya, along with the Trigarta and Kekeya armies, attacked them. Dhrishtadyumna came to their defence and launched an aggressive attack on Shalya.

Soon Dhrishtadyumna killed the son of King Samyamani in battle. An enraged Samyamani joined hands with Shalya and attacked Dhrishtadyumna.

Their combined attack caused Dhrishtadyumna to go on the defensive. They broke his bow, and just as they were preparing to kill him, Abhimanyu, seeing his commander in trouble, stormed to his defence.

He let loose a deluge of keen arrows that broke Shalya's bow; three arrows pierced his body, causing him to fall. Seeing this, Duryodhana, along with ten of his brothers, attacked Abhimanyu and soon a brutal battle was underway. Nakula and Sahadeva, along with Draupadi's sons, joined Abhimanyu and a violent struggle raged for hours.

While Arjuna battled with Bheeshma and Satyaki with Drona, Bheema saw the fiendish combat between Duryodhana and the Pandava warriors. He rushed in, swinging his mighty mace and creating havoc. Elephants, chariots and soldiers on foot charged Bheema to allay him but he was unstoppable.

As the sun bore down mercilessly and the heat became intolerable, so did the conflict on the ground. Bheema spread terror amidst the elephant division of the Kaurava army, slaughtering elephants and the warriors on them without a second thought. The entire elephant division of King Samyamani was slaughtered.

King Samyamani, accompanied by Shalya, tore towards Bheema on his elephant. Both of them attacked Bheema pitilessly. Duryodhana joined the battle and shot a powerful arrow that struck Bheema on the chest, causing him to fall back in his chariot, holding his standard for support.

Abhimanyu, on seeing his uncle in difficulty, darted to defend him, shooting a flurry of arrows. His golden arrows with feathers struck Shalya, causing him to collapse in his chariot. Samyamani lunged at Abhimanyu on his huge elephant. The elephant seemed to be on the verge of smashing Abhimanyu's chariot when, without even flinching, Abhimanyu shot two arrows.

The first one, a serrated arrow, struck the elephant on its forehead and instantly killed it. The second one was a crescent-shaped arrow that struck King Samyamani on his neck and beheaded him. The bodies of the king and his elephant fell lifeless to the ground.

Bheema had recovered and he launched a furious counter-attack on Duryodhana. His brothers came to support him. In a wild mood, Bheema who himself resembled an elephant in a rut, brutally attacked the Kauravas. In front of Duryodhana, he slaughtered his brothers one by one.

Now ten of Duryodhana's brothers were dead and the other Kaurava princes fled in panic. Bhagadatta, the king of Pragjyotisha, charged at Bheema. He was stopped by Bheema's son Ghatotkacha, whose turn it was to wreak havoc.

The terrible attack of the Pandavas shook the Kauravas. Bheeshma observed that the sun was almost about to set. He declared that it was foolish to launch a new attack at this time, especially when Ghatotkacha was on the rampage; his demonic powers would increase tenfold as the sun set. Prudently, Bheeshma sounded the conch, announcing the retreat of the Kauravas. The day's battle had ended overwhelmingly in favour of the Pandavas, even as Duryodhana mourned the loss of his brothers.

20

Abhimanyu Proves Himself

It was a night of darkness and pain for Duryodhana. He met with Bheeshma and expressed his sadness and frustration.

"We have such great warriors on our side. You are the unconquerable and unparalleled warrior. Guru Drona is the one who taught the Pandavas to hold their bows and maces. Ashwatthama, Bhurishravas, Dushasana, Shakuni, Kritavarma are all mighty warriors. Yet we are losing so badly. Why is this happening? What strategy can help us win?"

Bheeshma got up and affectionately caressed Duryodhana's forehead. "My child, our warriors are, without a doubt, more powerful than anyone in the world. If we still lose, it is only because of one reason and that is Krishna!"

"What is so great about that magician? How do his illusions work so well?"

"You are mistaken, Duryodhana. Krishna is no magician. He is none other than Mahavishnu, the preserver of the world, the wielder of the Sudarshana Chakra. He has come to Earth with a mission and is aiding the forces of good against those of evil. Vidura and I told you very clearly not to fight this war and agree to Krishna's offer of negotiation. You were the one who chose the option of war. Now we must wait for the inevitable."

A dumbstruck Duryodhana walked away on hearing these words, refusing to accept that Krishna was God and would ensure their defeat. He dejectedly and desperately hoped for a miracle.

The next day, Bheeshma formed the crocodile or makara battle formation, to which the Pandavas responded with the hawk or syena formation. Bheema stood at the beak of the hawk, ready to crush the Kauravas; right behind him was Arjuna. The fearsome appearance of the two brothers caused the Kaurava army to quake with fear.

Yudhishtira was at the tail of the hawk and guarding him were Abhimanyu and the sons of Draupadi. The battle began with Bheema and Arjuna once again routing the Kaurava soldiers. It was again up to the old warhorse Bheeshma to counter them. Satyaki launched an attack on Bheeshma and Drona rushed to Bheeshma's help.

Both Drona and Bheeshma showered arrows on Satyaki, putting him in difficulty. Just then Bheema entered the battlefield, destroying the arrows shot by Drona. Abhimanyu came to Bheema's support and engaged with Drona. Arjuna charged at the Kauravas, firing hundreds of arrows and leaving behind a pile of dead bodies wherever he went.

Arjuna flew towards Bheeshma and attacked him. A fierce battle raged on through the day between the two armies. Yudhishtira charged at the elephant division of the Kauravas, killing hundreds. When Shalya attacked him, Satyaki and Abhimanyu came to his help. The scorching heat of the mid-day sun exhausted the warriors, but they battled on bravely with no time to rest.

A vicious duel broke out between Bheema and Bheeshma, with the war veteran emerging victorious. Another duel raged between Ashwatthama and Arjuna for a long time before Arjuna broke Ashwatthama's bows. Krishna, knowing that Ashwatthama was a chiranjeevi[16] and could not be killed, did not waste time and led Arjuna away.

Chitrasena, son of Dhritharashtra, attacked Abhimanyu and both fought valiantly. Chitrasena shot a golden arrow with feathers that broke through Abhimanyu's defences and struck him on the chest. He, totally unperturbed, counter-attacked and showered arrows on Chitrasena.

Duryodhana's son Lakshmana came to Chitrasena's help and attacked Abhimanyu. The two cousins fought for a long time. Lakshmana, full of energy and enthusiasm, took on the highly skilled Abhimanyu but ultimately could not counter Abhimanyu's fierce attack.

Abhimanyu shot six arrows, three of which killed Lakshmana's charioteer and his two horses. The other three arrows broke the wheels of the chariot, causing it to totter and shake. As Abhimanyu took aim to kill Lakshmana, Kripa raced in and took him to safety in his chariot. Abhimanyu pursued them but was blocked by the Kaurava army.

[16] It is believed that there are seven immortals who can never die and will live until the end of Earth. They are Vyasa, Hanuman, Parashurama, Vibhishana, Ashwatthama, Mahabali and Kripa.

He vented his anger on the Kaurava soldiers by firing arrows at will. His fingers moved at the speed of light and he unleashed hundreds of arrows, beheading Kaurava soldiers and destroying their chariots. Elephants charged at him, only to collapse dead as his stinging arrows tore into their foreheads.

Duryodhana sent in 20,000 charioteers to attack Arjuna. He effortlessly defended himself from them and counter-attacked so furiously that thousands of charioteers fell dead within minutes. Bhurishravas and Satyaki fought furiously, while Bheema took on Dushasana.

As the sun slowly started sinking, Arjuna's energy levels seemed to soar. He continued his offensive vigorously and of the 20,000 warriors who attacked him, hardly anyone remained. Bheeshma, stupefied by the carnage, admonished Duryodhana for his strategy that had turned out to be counterproductive.

As the Pandavas continued to slaughter the Kauravas, Bheeshma looked eagerly at the sun. The moment the sun started its descent, he blew his conch, marking the end of the day. The Pandavas stopped and blew their conches and the drummers played their drums victoriously.

It was yet another triumphant day for the Pandavas who day by day seemed to be getting stronger and stronger. Arjuna, Bheema, Satyaki and Abhimanyu were among the heroic warriors who slayed most of the enemy warriors, and they were praised by Yudhishtira for their heroism on the battlefield.

As an exhausted Abhimanyu returned to camp, he felt pride for being singled out for praise. He was happy that he was fighting along with his father and other illustrious warriors. Every night as he retired to bed, he looked forward to the next day to achieve greater glory.

The next day it was the Pandavas who formed the makara or crocodile formation, to which the Kauravas responded with the krauncha or heron formation. Bheema was placed at the head of the formation at the tip of the crocodile's snout with Arjuna behind him, and Abhimanyu was stationed in the middle.

As the battle started, Bheema set upon Drona while Arjuna engaged Bheeshma. A brutal scrimmage broke out between Bheema and Drona, with both the warriors shooting powerful arrows at each other. Drona's arrows hit Bheema, but he seemed not to care. His arrows slammed through Drona's defences and killed his charioteer.

Drona did not care; manoeuvring the chariot's reins with his feet, he laid into Bheema. Dhrishtadyumna joined the fray and attacked Drona, allowing Bheema to move ahead. Bheema charged at the Kaurava forces, scattering them.

Duryodhana directed his brothers to attack Bheema and many of them surrounded him and showered him with arrows. A furious Bheema grabbed his mighty mace, jumped out of the chariot and attacked the Kauravas. He swung his mace, smashing all the weapons hurled at him. Horses, elephants, chariots and soldiers collapsed as his mace came in contact with them.

He roared and charged at Duryodhana's brothers and they fled for their lives. He rushed into the midst of the Kaurava forces, wreaking havoc. Dhrishtadyumna, who had forced Drona to withdraw, went in search of Bheema and was flabbergasted to see his empty chariot. He thought something had happened to Bheema.

Looking ahead, he saw the line of bodies which, on following, took him to Bheema. He joined Bheema and both the warriors rained death on the Kaurava army. Bheema was given a chariot and he continued to wage war against the Kauravas.

Once again, the Kaurava princes and generals assembled, led by Duryodhana himself. They surrounded Bheema and Dhrishtadyumna. Arrows, spears, maces and clubs were hurled at the two warriors who grimly fought their enemies.

Duryodhana and Bheema hurled insults and weapons at each other. Bheema's savage attack stunned Duryodhana. Soon Bheema's sharp arrows killed Duryodhana's charioteer and injured him severely. His chariot standard was brought down, and his chariot collapsed. As Duryodhana swooned, Kripa came up, took him away in his chariot and tended to him.

The intensity of the attack on the two warriors increased. It was two against 2,000 and Dhrishtadyumna decided to use a celestial weapon. He invoked the Pramohanaastra and shot it at the Kauravas. The arrow flew up, exploding and releasing a thick, poisonous smoke that caused the Kauravas to lose consciousness.

Drona, on seeing the Kauravas keel over, rushed to the spot and invoked the Pragnaastra. The weapon released a fine mist of medicated water that dispelled the poisonous smoke. The shower revived the unconscious Kauravas and the battle continued with greater zeal. Duryodhana once again returned to the fray with his brothers and pounced on Bheema and Dhrishtadyumna.

Seeing the two trapped in between thousands of Kauravas, Yudhishtira summoned Abhimanyu and commanded him to lead a platoon of soldiers to help his uncles who were in trouble. Draupadi's sons joined Abhimanyu.

Abhimanyu swiftly organised his platoon and formed the Suchimukha vyuha or needle formation. With himself at the tip of the needle, he arranged his platoon in a line and charged at the Kauravas.

Bheema and Dhrishtadyumna were fighting valiantly and killing Kaurava soldiers. Many of them fled and ran into Abhimanyu's platoon, only to be massacred. Abhimanyu's platoon forced itself through the Kaurava warriors and launched a searing attack. The warriors in the chariots and elephants, whom Abhimanyu had brought with him, hurled themselves at the Kauravas.

Bheema had meanwhile climbed into the chariot of the Kekeya prince and had been taken away from the battle, while Dhrishtadyumna fought against Drona. Soon Dhrishtadyumna began to tire as Drona assaulted him, killed his charioteer and broke his chariot.

Abhimanyu bounded in and protected Dhrishtadyumna from Drona's arrows, pulling him into his chariot and taking him away to safety. Bheema, who had returned in another chariot, confronted Duryodhana and his brothers.

Abhimanyu had escorted Dhrishtadyumna to a new chariot. He rejoined the fray, assisting Bheema in attacking the Kaurava princes. Duryodhana's brothers Vikarna, Chitrasena and Durjaya launched a combined attack against Abhimanyu which he fearlessly countered with his arrows.

It did not take much time for Abhimanyu to dominate the three Kaurava princes. His ferocious shower of arrows sent Durjaya scurrying away. He killed Vikarna's charioteer and brought his chariot down. Vikarna climbed into Chitrasena's chariot and both the brothers attacked Abhimanyu together.

Abhimanyu brought out a snake-shaped missile and shot it at Vikarna. The arrow glided through the air and broke Vikarna's bow, stabbing him above the chest. Unable to tolerate the torment, Vikarna swooned and fell into the chariot; Chitrasena, scared, fled the battlefield to safety.

Abhimanyu continued his assault on the Kauravas. The Kaurava generals who had come to support their princes had to bear the brunt of his attack. He shot arrows nonstop, slaughtering the Kaurava army as his chariot darted through them.

The sun soon changed colour and became red as the sky turned from blue to orange. The two armies fought barbarously, with soldiers dying on both sides. Abhimanyu and the Upapandavas dashed through the Kaurava army, killing many of them.

Bheema defeated Duryodhana and fought with his brothers, and Arjuna was engaged with the Trigarta army. Seeing his forces in trouble, Bheeshma rallied them around and fought valiantly against the Pandavas. Soon the sky turned dark; the sun was setting. Both sides were tired after a hectic day of battle.

The conches were sounded and both armies withdrew to their camps. The Pandavas had dominated yet again.

Abhimanyu had once again shown his prowess on the battlefield and had proved to be a great warrior and an asset to the Pandavas. The Pandava brothers and Dhrishtadyumna praised the young man for his valour as they celebrated the day's win.

21

Abhimanyu Continues to Excel

On the seventh day of the war, the Kauravas arranged themselves in the form of the mandala or galaxy formation. Dhrishtadyumna responded with the Vajra vyuha where the Pandava army was organised in the form of a thunderbolt. As the battle began, the warriors engaged with each other furiously.

Duryodhana charged at Dhrishtadyumna while Yudhishtira battled the Kalinga forces. Shikhandi battled Ashwatthama. Nakula and Sahadeva fought against their uncle Shalya. Arjuna moved towards Bheeshma but was blocked and engaged by Susharma and his Trigarta army.

Vikarna, Chitrasena and Durmarshana confronted Abhimanyu. A fierce duel broke out between the leading warriors of the two armies. The Kauravas, who had suffered defeat every day after the first day, were determined to attain success. They gave their best and fought furiously with an iron resolve to defeat the Pandavas.

The Trigartas surrounded Arjuna and attacked him nonstop. It was an unfair and unequal battle, with more than a thousand warriors taking on one man. Arjuna did not even worry about the number of opponents he faced but attacked them all, shooting arrows one after the other. He was finding it very difficult to counter the attack of the Trigartas.

He invoked the Aindrastra and the weapon appeared before him. He guided it high in the sky and commanded it to attack the Trigartas. The Aindrastra exploded into thousands of flaming sparks, each spark becoming a searingly hot arrow. The hot shower of iron missiles fell on the Trigartas and devastated a thousand of them in an instant.

Susharma fled for his life and ran to Bheeshma for help. An enraged Bheeshma charged at his favourite grandson; Arjuna was prepared and countered the attack. Both warriors fought long and hard.

The Kaurava brothers put their heart into the battle and put up a good show, but they were no match for Abhimanyu. They found it difficult to cope with the missiles Abhimanyu shot at them. Soon they were on the defensive, desperately blocking his fiery arrows.

Abhimanyu let loose a volley of barbed arrows that busted through the defences of the Kaurava princes and broke their bows, killed their charioteers and horses, and brought down the standards of their chariots. The three princes cowered before Abhimanyu as he affixed three golden arrows to slay them.

Then Abhimanyu remembered Bheema's vow. He did not want to break it by killing the sons of Dhritharashtra. He turned his chariot away and attacked other Kaurava warriors. The three brothers were humiliated by the way a boy had defeated them and the fact that he spared their lives and moved away contemptuously.

Yudhishtira fought with Shutayush, the king of Kalinga. After a long-drawn-out battle, Yudhishtira was hit on his shoulders. The angry Pandava released arrows with alacrity and broke Shutayush's bow. Yudhishtira shattered his opponent's chariot after killing the charioteer. The king jumped from his broken chariot and ran for his life, not caring about the mortifying way he was fleeing the battlefield. His soldiers joined him in the flight.

Bheeshma fought with Yudhishtira and broke his chariot. He was saved by Nakula and returned to continue the battle. Drona defeated King Drupada, forcing him to fall back. Drona then attacked the soldiers of Panchala, massacring them mercilessly. Bheema fought with Duryodhana's brothers and destroyed their chariots.

Abhimanyu fought with the Kaurava princes. After their experience of the previous battle, they knew that Abhimanyu would not kill them, hence they targeted him mercilessly. Soon Bheeshma joined them to attack Abhimanyu.

Seeing Abhimanyu in trouble, Krishna urged Arjuna to support his son. An incensed Arjuna charged at Bheeshma. Father and son joined forces and rained thousands of arrows on Bheeshma and the Kaurava princes. As the two armies scrambled, the sun set behind the mountains. Bheeshma blew his conch, sounding the end of hostilities, and the armies returned to camp.

Arjuna was once again full of praise for his son's valour. Father and son rode back to camp, satisfied with the day's successes. The armies retired for the night, not knowing what the next day would bring. Soldiers and warriors alike went to sleep, wondering if this was their last night on Earth.

The eighth day saw Bheeshma form the Kurma vyuha or turtle formation, with the soldiers in the arrangement and Bheeshma standing at the head. To counter this formation, the Pandavas used the Trishula vyuha or the trident formation. The Pandava army lined up to form the staff of the trident with three spokes.

Bheema stood at the front of the formation with Arjuna, Yudhishtira and Dhrishtadyumna at the head of the trident's remaining spokes. Abhimanyu stood behind Arjuna along with his brother Iravan. On his other side was his cousin Ghatotkacha, looking ominous seated on his elephant.

The moment the war started, Bheema charged at the Kauravas. He drew arrows quickly, fixed them to his huge bow Vayavya, pulled the string hard and released the arrow, imparting maximum power through the muscles of his huge arms. The arrows blazed through the air, hitting their target with great intensity.

He attacked Bheeshma's charioteer, killing him instantly. He aimed his arrows at the horses, hitting them on their tails; the horses panicked and fled, taking Bheeshma away and exposing the Kauravas to Bheema's wrath.

Duryodhana's brother Sunabha targeted Bheema and had to face the brunt of his attack. His bow was shattered by one arrow and the next one cut his head off, killing him. Seeing him fall, his brothers Aparajitha, Kundhadhara, Panditaka, Vishalaksha, Mahodara, Adityaketu and Vahsavin shouted in anger and attacked Bheema.

Abhimanyu charged towards them to help his uncle, but Bheema did not need anyone's help. His arrows flew all around like lightning. Within moments, the bows and standards of the Kaurava princes' charioteers were smashed to smithereens. The arrows shot by Bheema hit Mahodara, Vahsavin and Panditaka on their chests so hard that their hearts ruptured, killing them instantly.

Bheema's blistering arrows beheaded the rest of the Kaurava princes brutally. Eight of Duryodhana's brothers lay dead in front of his eyes. Seeing their brothers fall, the rest of the Kauravas fled in panic even as Duryodhana shouted at them, asking them to return.

Bheema went in pursuit of the fleeing Kauravas, smashing the carefully organised formation. He charged through the army, attacking them relentlessly. The warriors on elephants and chariots ran amok, unable to withstand his attack. As they fled away from Bheema, they found Abhimanyu waiting for them with his deadly arrows.

Uncle and nephew slaughtered the Kauravas. At the other end, Arjuna attacked the Kaurava generals, killing them by the dozens. Bheema's clever strategy of killing Bheeshma's charioteer had taken Bheeshma out of the battlefield, allowing the Pandavas to dominate.

Ghatotkacha joined Abhimanyu and both of them terrorised the Kauravas. Duryodhana was outraged. He charged towards Abhimanyu in his chariot, shooting arrows at him. Abhimanyu quickly counter-attacked cutting down the missiles that Duryodhana hurled at him.

Duryodhana may have been a great warrior with the mace, but he was no match for Abhimanyu in archery; the latter broke his bow and brought his flag down. Duryodhana quickly picked up another bow and fixed an arrow. Abhimanyu's missile raced, breaking his bow again and piercing his armour causing the Kaurava prince to fall back in his chariot.

Five generals charged to defend Duryodhana and all of them lay dead within moments, Abhimanyu's arrows penetrating their hearts. Duryodhana was bewildered, expecting Abhimanyu to kill him next. He looked on in trepidation, awaiting death.

Abhimanyu moved towards him with a smile on his face and lowered his bow. He said, "Uncle, don't worry. I won't kill you. Your death is written at the hands of my uncle Bheema. He will take care of you. Go now, I spare your life, live to fight another day."

Duryodhana was chastened by the insult from this sixteen-year-old, to which he would have preferred death. Seeing Duryodhana in this situation, the Pragjyotisha king Bhagadatta charged at Abhimanyu on a huge black elephant that looked like death.

The elephant charged towards Abhimanyu with the intention of breaking his chariot. Abhimanyu pulled out a honed arrow and released it. As it whizzed into the elephant's forehead, it caused it to fall lifeless, with the result that Bhagadatta fell to the ground.

Bheeshma had returned to the battle in a new chariot. Drona, who received him, updated him on the situation. He saw Abhimanyu's prowess and sung his praises to Drona, "The son of Arjuna proves to be as great a warrior as his father. I understand none other than Krishna and his son trained him. It is no wonder his prowess is so great. Go, Drona, take our forces and challenge Abhimanyu. Stop him before he destroys our army."

The Kaurava princes rushed at Abhimanyu, surrounding and attacking him. He fought them bravely. Seeing him in trouble, Krishna took Arjuna towards Abhimanyu to defend him. Father and son caused a bloodbath in the Kaurava camp.

Meanwhile, Iravan and his Naga army slaughtered the Kauravas. He took on Shakuni and his Gandhara brothers and beheaded three of them effortlessly. Duryodhana, who was frustrated, decided that if Abhimanyu could not be slain, he would have to make do with another son of Arjuna.

He called the demon Alamvusha, who was the son of the sage Rishyashringa. Alamvusha was a rakshasa who possessed strange powers with which he magically defeated his enemies. Duryodhana asked Alamvusha to kill Iravan. Both Iravan and Alamvusha were skilled in illusion and magic, and they attacked each other fiercely.

Iravan created the illusion of a million snakes that attacked the Kauravas. Alamvusha countered it with a huge garuda (eagle) that caused the Nagas to panic and flee. As Iravan tried to stop his Naga army from fleeing, Alamvusha shot a hundred arrows at Iravan that beheaded him and he fell dead.

Bheema's fury was unabated. He charged through the Kaurava formation, killing their warriors and soldiers. Some of the Kaurava princes, who had fled, came back to challenge Bheema; he effortlessly took them on and they met the same fate as their brothers. Eight more Kaurava princes—Vivisvati, Virajas, Anadhatri, Suvahu, Deerghababu, Deerghalochana, Anadriti and Kanyakadhvaja—were killed by Bheema one after the other.

Duryodhana's sorrow and anger knew no bounds. Bheema had slaughtered sixteen of his brothers. Simultaneously, Arjuna mourned the loss of his son Iravan. There was a temporary cessation of hostilities as both sides mourned their dead.

Bheeshma reorganised his army like an ocean (oormi), with waves of soldiers lined one after the other. Dhrishtadyumna responded with a horned formation (shringhataka) to penetrate the ocean.

The battle resumed and both armies continued to attack each other. Abhimanyu and Ghatotkacha once again joined forces, causing bloodshed in the Kaurava camp. Bheeshma and Drona responded by attacking the Pandavas and killing their soldiers.

As the sunset hour approached, Ghatotkacha's magical powers increased. He created an illusion of a dead Duryodhana, causing the Kauravas to panic and scatter. Duryodhana had to run behind them to prove that he was alive and stop them from escaping.

The bloodshed continued until sunset. Rivers of crimson flowed through the battlefield and bodies piled up as the conches sounded to end the day's battle. Both sides wearily made their way back to camp. The Pandavas were happy with their achievements of the day but sad at the loss of Iravan.

The Kaurava camp was in distress. Duryodhana raged at Bheeshma, "Grandsire, I lost sixteen brothers and the arrogant son of Partha tells me to go and live.

It is all because you do not want to kill them. Step aside and let Karna take over, he will guide us to victory."

"Don't question my valour, Duryodhana. I told you how foolish it is to fight against an opponent who had Krishna's blessings. Anyway, tomorrow I will do my best to kill Arjuna. If I succeed, the war will be won."

Bheeshma thus consoled Duryodhana with these words before retiring for the night.

22

The Might of Bheeshma

It was the ninth day of the Great War, and the two armies again faced each other. Bheeshma had formed the Sarvatobhadra vyuha, which was to ensure safety on all sides. The army took up its position in the form of a square protected from all sides. At the corners of the square stood all the leading warriors of the Kauravas, with Bheeshma at the forefront.

The Pandavas, in turn, formed the Nakshathramandala vyuha, a star-shaped formation with five stars. The Pandava princes were at the forefront led by their commander Dhrishtadyumna. Shikandhi and Ghatotkacha held their positions at the sides. Abhimanyu and King Drupada were at the rear.

No sooner had the conches been blown than both the armies attacked each other in full fury. The star-shaped formation was able to break through the Kaurava formation and soon both the armies were engaged in fierce combat.

Abhimanyu, full of energy, charged at the Kaurava soldiers, slaughtering them with ease. From the rear of the formation, he charged to the front, breaking through the Kaurava ranks ruthlessly. He continuously shot arrows of different types that ravaged the Kauravas.

He shot serpent-shaped arrows that slithered through the air, finding their mark in the enemy's chest.

He shot barbed arrows at chariot warriors, slaying them instantly. The golden arrows with feathers were reserved for the elephant warriors, each of whom could only watch as an arrow glided towards them, penetrating their defences.

Kripa blocked Abhimanyu, who was scything through the Kaurava army. He took out five arrows and released them, causing Kripa's chariot to totter and forcing him back. Ashwatthama was the next and he released fifty arrows at Abhimanyu.

Abhimanyu responded with a shower of arrows of his own. The son of the teacher Drona and the son of his student Arjuna battled each other fiercely. Ashwatthama was a great warrior but even he found it difficult to match Abhimanyu's energy. It did not take much time for Abhimanyu to push back Ashwatthama. He knew that Ashwatthama was a chiranjeevi and could not be killed. He moved ahead to fight other warriors.

Abhimanyu continued his relentless charge from one end of the battlefield to the other. Drona charged at him, releasing powerful arrows. Abhimanyu was unstoppable and used the Agneyastra to create a flaming ball of fire that whooshed towards Drona, burning his soldiers. At the last minute, Drona summoned the Varunastra and managed to extinguish the fire.

Having reserved the celestial weapons for the general, he shot at the others, slaughtering them. He released three arrows at a time, killing three soldiers instantaneously. The Pandavas watched him in admiration and Yudhishtira was profuse in his praise for him.

At the other end, Arjuna was wreaking havoc. Father and son had sent the Kaurava army into a state of panic. A furious Duryodhana summoned Alamvusha. To counter him, the Pandavas used Ghatotkacha who, being the son of a rakshasi, could fight Alamvusha in the same way.

Duryodhana told Alamvusha, "Father and son are scattering my army like the wind. I need to stop this son of Subhadra immediately. Go and use all your skills, Alamvusha, and slay him. Let Arjuna suffer a tragedy today. Kill Abhimanyu just like you killed his brother Iravan."

Alamvusha charged towards the Pandavas, firing hundreds of missiles that slaughtered their soldiers. Draupadi's sons challenged him and he unleashed a wave of powerful weapons that they struggled to counter. Seeing his brothers in difficulty, Abhimanyu charged at Alamvusha shooting arrows and destroying his weapons.

Both the warriors were striking each other furiously. Alamvusha released magical arrows that came in the form of bloodsucking monsters towards Abhimanyu. Some of them found their mark, lacerating Abhimanyu. Furious at being hit, he shot a hundred arrows in a volley, at such speed that it seemed all were shot at the same time.

Alamvusha was inundated by this fiery shower of arrows and was forced to retreat. Enraged, he decided to use his demonic powers. He opened his mouth and a dark, dense cloud of fog emanated from it. Within moments, the fog had engulfed the battlefield, creating darkness. It was so dark that the soldiers could not even see their own hand.

Alamvusha laughed manically. His eyes turned red, emitting a ray of light, and he was able to see through the darkness. He charged towards Abhimanyu, slaughtering the soldiers who came in his way with his mighty sword. There was panic among the Pandava soldiers as they were being attacked in the dark; neither could they see what was happening nor could they defend themselves.

Abhimanyu took out an arrow and fixed it on his bow. He pressed it to his forehead and remembered Lord Surya, the dispeller of darkness. He chanted the divine mantra taught by his father and converted the arrow into the Jyotikshastra, the solar weapon. He did not even have to release the arrow, it shot high up into the air and exploded.

From the explosion were released thousands of rays that filled the air with brilliant light. It was as though the sun had dropped on Earth. The rays of light dispelled the cloud of darkness in an instant. Alamvusha, who revelled in darkness, closed his eyes, unable to tolerate the radiance of the solar weapon.

Alamvusha desperately hurled an array of weapons at Abhimanyu, all of which were burnt to cinders by the rays of the solar weapon. As the effect of the weapon subsided, Abhimanyu charged towards Alamvusha, continuously shooting arrows. Alamvusha tried to defend himself but could not face the onslaught.

Abhimanyu picked the sharpest arrows from his quiver which hit Alamvusha all over his body. The demon cried out in pain, and unable to face the assault, fled from the battlefield, trampling over his own soldiers in panic.

Seeing his troops being defeated, Bheeshma charged at Abhimanyu and a fierce fight broke out. Abhimanyu struggled to defend himself from Bheeshma's arrows. Soon Kripa, Drona and Jayadratha joined Bheeshma in showering arrows at Abhimanyu.

As Abhimanyu struggled to face their fierce attack, a shower of arrows whizzed from behind him and destroyed the enemy's arrows in an instant. Arjuna had rushed to defend his son and attacked Bheeshma. The battle was long and hard as warriors from both sides fought each other the whole day.

Bheeshma was unstoppable and caused devastation for the Pandavas. Yudhishtira appealed to Arjuna to stop Bheeshma's assault, fearing that he would destroy the entire Pandava army in a day. Arjuna challenged Bheeshma and attacked him. It was a duel between two of the greatest warriors.

Arjuna managed to breach Bheeshma's defences and shattered his bow. Bheeshma smiled in appreciation at Arjuna's skill and quickly picked up another bow to continue his attack. Bheeshma's attack was so furious that Arjuna was hit from all sides. Wounded and bleeding, he fought valiantly.

Seeing his father in trouble, Abhimanyu charged at Bheeshma but was repelled as the latter unleashed a fiery shower of arrows, destroying Abhimanyu's bow. Bheeshma picked up a razor-sharp arrow and shot at Arjuna, hitting him on his shoulder. The arrow entered deep into his flesh and blood gushed out.

Krishna was infuriated at this. He realised that Bheeshma was being ruthless while Arjuna was not giving his best out of respect for his grandfather. The sight of Arjuna in agony made Krishna angry. He knew that he had to do something else Bheeshma would take the war away from the Pandavas. He had taken a vow not to fight but decided to break this vow.

He let out a scream of rage that sounded like a tiger's roar; it shook the battlefield. He jumped from the chariot and rushed at Bheeshma. Seeing a fallen chariot wheel, he picked it up and fixed it on his finger like the Sudarshana Chakra. Charging at Bheeshma, he raised his finger to release the wheel from his hand.

In the normal course of battle, a charioteer attacking a great warrior will elicit laughs of derision. When the charioteer was none other than Krishna, everyone was aghast. No one had seen Krishna in such a wild fury—his nostrils were flared, his eyes were wide open and his index finger effortlessly rotated the wheel with the intention of beheading Bheeshma.

The entire Pandava and Kaurava armies were stunned. There was absolute silence as everyone stopped fighting and stood watching Krishna's rage. There was fear in the hearts of the Kauravas and shock amongst the Pandavas. Only one person smiled, and that was Bheeshma.

He threw his weapons and alighted from the chariot. He stopped in front of Krishna and kneeled, his arms folded in salutation.

Bheeshma said, "Come, my lord, come. Use the wheel and behead me. End my existence and let me find peace. My father's boon of immortality has been a curse to me. I have lived more than a hundred years, taking the onus of protecting this empire. Now I see my grandchildren fighting to kill each other. I am tired, O Krishna. End my existence and let me find peace."

Arjuna, who had been stunned by Krishna's aggression, recovered himself. Ignoring his bleeding wounds, he leapt from his chariot and rushed towards Krishna; he fell to the ground and grabbed Krishna's feet, touching his head to them.

"My Lord Vaasudeva, please don't do this. You have taken a vow not to fight, don't break the vow now. I do not want to be the sinner who caused you to break your vow. I promise I will fight to the best of my ability and not give you an occasion to come to my defence again. I beg you to return to the chariot."

Krishna's anger had subsided when he heard Bheeshma's anguished words. Arjuna's pleading helped him regain his composure. He now knew that his action had borne fruit. Arjuna would not hesitate to kill Bheeshma. He went back to his chariot and the battle resumed. Soon it was dark and the day's battle ended.

It had been Bheeshma's day. He had ravaged the Pandava army, slaughtering thousands. Corpses had piled up and vultures and jackals hung around, waiting to feast. The stench of blood and death was overwhelming. The Pandavas returned to their camp, despondent at their loss.

Gathered together, they went to Krishna, who told them that they had to kill Bheeshma else they were sure to be defeated. He advised them to meet Bheeshma secretly late in the night and take his blessings.

Following his advice, the Pandavas visited the Kaurava camp in secret, and avoiding the guards, entered Bheeshma's tent. He was awake as though waiting for them. He welcomed them and asked them to sit down. The Pandavas fell at his feet to take his blessings which he freely gave.

When Arjuna fell at his feet, he hugged him, saying, "May you find victory and achieve your goals."

"Pitamaha," said Arjuna. "How can I find victory when you lead the Kauravas?"

Bheeshma laughed loudly, "Kill me and you will find victory. Put Shikhandi in front of you and attack me. I will not fight Shikhandi and your arrows will deliver me the death I am eagerly awaiting. Dharma must prevail and for that, you must win. Do what I say."

The Pandavas bowed before Bheeshma and left, thinking about the big day that lay ahead when they had to do the unthinkable—kill their grandfather. Arjuna's heart was heavy, as he knew he would be the one to kill his grandfather who had brought him up with love and affection. Tears streamed down his cheeks, but he had given a promise to Krishna and he would fulfil it.

The Pandavas trudged back to their camp knowing that they would win the next day, but their hearts ached, realising the cost of the victory.

23

The Death of Bheeshma

On the tenth day of the battle, the two armies stood against each other. Arjuna did not sleep the whole night knowing what was expected of him. The next day he addressed Krishna as soon as he met him and asked, "Vaasudeva, today I have to do the unthinkable and kill my grandsire."

"Arjuna, you are not killing your grandsire, you are killing the leader of the enemy. What is first for you—your duty as a warrior for your country or your personal feelings?"

"I agree, Krishna, my duty comes first, but I feel bad that I have to stand behind Shikhandi and kill my grandfather in this heinous manner."

"It is his wish, Partha. No one stops him from attacking Shikhandi; he can kill Shikhandi with just one arrow, but it is his decision not to attack him. This does not mean that you should stand and watch. There is nothing wrong in killing Bheeshma if he himself refuses to fight. He desires death and only you can give it."

"Why does the great Bheeshma refuse to fight Shikhandi? Is it because Shikhandi is a eunuch?"

"There is a story behind it, Partha. Many years ago, Bheeshma was tasked by Queen Satyavathi to find a bride for her son Vichitryavirya. The king of Kashi was organising a swayamvara for his daughters Amba, Ambika and Ambalika. He did not invite Hastinapura. This made Bheeshma angry and he attacked Kashi and brought the three princesses to Hastinapura."

"What happened then?"

"Ambika and Ambalika were wedded to Vichitryavirya. Amba requested Bheeshma to leave her as she was in love with Shalva, the king of Saubala, and wanted to marry him. Bheeshma agreed to her request and allowed her to leave. However, Shalva, who was defeated by Bheeshma refused to marry her and turned her away."

"What did she do?"

"Amba went back to Bheeshma and asked him to marry her. He refused as he had taken a vow of remaining a bachelor. A furious Amba prayed to Parashurama[17], who went to Bheeshma and demanded that he marry Amba. When he refused, there was a ferocious battle between Bheeshma and Parashurama on this very battlefield."

"Who won that battle, Krishna?"

"Neither of them! They fought for twenty-three days without any result. On the last day, both hurled Brahmastras at each other. Lord Brahma himself intervened and asked them to stop as their weapons could destroy the entire Earth and lay it to waste. Brahma went to Amba who was meditating. She asked for a boon that she should be born as a man in her next life and cause Bheeshma's death; her boon was granted."

[17] Parashurama was the sixth incarnation of Vishnu. He killed twenty-one generations of Kshatriya kings to avenge the killing of his father by a Kshatriya king Kartaveeryarjuna.

"So Shikhandi is Amba?"

"Yes, he was born as a girl and adopted by your father-in-law King Drupada and then became a man. Shikhandi has been tagged as a eunuch by society. Bheeshma knows about Shikhandi's past and will not fight him."

"So, the die is cast today for my grandsire's death at my hands."

"Yes, Partha, do your job for your army and ensure the victory of dharma in this great war."

Just then the commanders sounded the alarm, indicating the commencement of the battle. Both the armies fell upon each other with the intention of wiping each other off the face of Earth.

There was an aggressive duel between the Pandavas and Bheeshma. Abhimanyu joined the rest of the Pandava warriors in attacking Bheeshma, but the veteran's mighty arrows just blew them away. None of the Pandavas could stand before his might and his blazing arrows put them on the defensive.

Arjuna charged in to defend his army and attacked Bheeshma, and Duryodhana rushed in with his army to protect Bheeshma. A vicious battle broke out, full of the sounds of clashing arrows. Bheeshma continued to blast through the Pandava formation, killing hundreds of soldiers. His arrows smote through the defences of all the Pandavas. Yudhishtira commanded Shikhandi to lead the Pandavas and stand in front as they attacked Bheeshma.

Seeing Shikhandi, Bheeshma ignored him and attacked the rest; Shikhandi's arrows did not bother Bheeshma as he continued his attack. Arjuna charged at Bheeshma and broke his bow, Bheeshma picked yet another one and Arjuna shattered it as well.

Shikhandi stood in front and attacked Bheeshma as Arjuna shot arrows from behind him. Arjuna's barbed arrows found their mark and Bheeshma was injured. He remarked to Dushasana, "Look at these arrows, they are not from Shikhandi's bow. The force with which these arrows are drawing away my life come from the mighty Gandiva of Arjuna."

Arjuna showered hundreds of arrows at Bheeshma while the rest of the Pandavas engaged the Kauravas, preventing them from coming to Bheeshma's defence. Arjuna's relentless attack finally worked and Bheeshma collapsed. As he fell, the arrows that protruded out of his body created a bed, allowing him to lay down on it.

The Pandavas quietly celebrated the fall of Bheeshma while the Kauravas mourned. Both sides stopped fighting and assembled in front of the fallen Kaurava commander. Arjuna was the hero who had ended the life of the most powerful warrior and had turned the war in favour of the Pandavas.

He was not proud of what he had done and was far from happy with the method used and rued that the death of his grandfather came at his hand. Abhimanyu stood next to his father in awe of his feat of killing the legendary Bheeshma.

Bheeshma observed the sun, which was in the Dakshinayana or southern route. He saw his divine mother, Goddess Ganga, in front of him. She told him to use his father's boon and not give up his life until the sun changed its path and moved into the Uttarayana (northern direction). She blessed him, saying that the moment he gave up his life would be known as the Uttarayana Punyakala and would be an auspicious day celebrated the world over.

Duryodhana rushed all his physicians to help Bheeshma but he sent them all back. He had decided to leave Earth and was waiting only for the right moment. He announced that he would lie on this bed until the moment came for him to quietly depart the world.

He lay on his bed of arrows in glory as the two armies stood before him with folded arms. His head, however, hung without any support. When he asked for a pillow, Duryodhana ordered many pillows to be brought. He rejected them all and requested a pillow that suited a hero dying on the battlefield.

Arjuna stepped forward and shot many arrows at the ground below Bheeshma's head. The arrows formed an iron pillow, and Bheeshma smiled at Arjuna in gratitude.

There was a hush as the two armies stood watching the Kuru elder on his bed of arrows. As the sun set, darkness descended but none of the warriors were ready to leave his side. It was a fitting tribute paid by the two armies to the greatest son of the Kuru race.

24

Advantage Pandavas

As Bheeshma lay on his bed of arrows awaiting the right time to exit the world, the Pandavas and Kauravas met him to take his blessings. Bheeshma summoned Arjuna and spoke to him in a low tone, "Arjuna, lying on this bed of arrows, my throat is parched. I am in need of water. Can you help me?"

Arjuna bowed to Bheeshma and circled his bed of arrows thrice in a gesture of respect. Standing in front of him, he fixed an arrow to his great bow. He chanted the Parjanya mantra that invokes water, and the arrow was charged with the power of the divine Parjanya[18]. Taking aim to the left of where Bheeshma lay, Arjuna shot the arrow into the ground.

The arrow penetrated deeply and created a channel, which went down to where the river flowed; through its power, it created a turbulent force that propelled the water up the channel. The water rushed up like a fountain. Arjuna had carefully selected the place to create the fountain so that the water would flow directly into Bheeshma's mouth.

The water brought up from the recesses of Earth was clear, sweet and tasted like nectar. Bheeshma drank his fill and was energised. Once he had finished, Arjuna

[18] The god of rain.

shot another arrow at the opening in the ground to close it and stop the stream of water. The assembled armies were astounded by Arjuna's feat.

Abhimanyu looked on in astonishment at his father's skills. He was proud of his father. His heart swelled with pride at the fact that having slain Bheeshma first for the sake of his army, Arjuna now nourished him with the respect he deserved as a grandfather.

Bheeshma was fulsome in his praise for Arjuna and appreciated his skills of archery and his knowledge of the divine weapons. Now he summoned Duryodhana before him.

"Duryodhana, did you not observe Arjuna's skill and mastery of archery? He is endowed with divine powers and with him is Lord Krishna, the incarnation of the preserver of the world Mahavishnu. It is not easy to defeat Arjuna in battle, my dear grandson. His affection for me prevented him from killing me all these days. It is a mistake to think that you can defeat the Pandavas."

Duryodhana was outraged by these words, and his heart sank. He stood there with his head bent.

"Listen to my advice, Duryodhana—let this war stop now. Let not brothers kill each other. There is still time. Give up half the kingdom to Yudhishtira, and you rule the other half. Let the Pandavas and Kauravas live in harmony. This will bring peace and prosperity."

Duryodhana, with his head bent low, said, "Forgive me, Grandfather, it is too late now. The decision has been taken. Let the war decide what will happen. He who wins the war will rule this country."

Bheeshma sighed, thinking of the mistake Duryodhana was making. "So be it then, may dharma and righteousness win. I pray to the gods to protect my family and bless the land of the Kurus."

One by one, the Kauravas and Pandavas came up to Bheeshma and took his blessings. Abhimanyu walked up to Bheeshma and saluted him—he circled him, touched his feet, went up to him and prostrated before him.

"Brave son of Arjuna, you are a true hero, a great warrior. You have all the skills and prowess that your father has along with the blessings of your uncle, the great Krishna. You will shine in battle and make a mark. I can foresee that one day you will show your prowess that none can defeat you in battle. I bless you with unlimited energy and strength."

So saying, Bheeshma blessed Abhimanyu by touching his head with his hands, and Abhimanyu sensed an energy course through his body. He left happily, grateful at having been blessed by the legendary warrior; he prayed that his words would come true and one day he would excel on the battlefield.

In the Kaurava camp, Duryodhana summoned a meeting of all the kings, princes and generals. He announced that Acharya[19] Drona would be the commander of the Kaurava army, and garlanded Drona and took his blessings. All the generals assembled applauded Duryodhana's decision and hailed Drona's appointment.

Drona asked everyone to be prepared to continue the war. He advised them to not be demoralised by Bheeshma's fall and asked them to focus on the task ahead, that of defeating the Pandavas. Then he

[19] Teacher.

summoned Karna and asked him, "King of Anga, I observed that you took the blessings of Bheeshma as we left."

"Yes, Acharya, the Kuru elder blessed me and regretted the way he had insulted me. I also apologised to him for not serving under him. I am now happy to inform you that I will be a part of the war from tomorrow and will strike terror in the hearts of the Pandavas."

Duryodhana was thrilled to hear Karna's decision and embraced him. The assembled Kauravas and allies who were distraught over Bheeshma's death were now jubilant that Karna had entered the war. They left for their respective tents, promising to fight with renewed vigour.

The next day, the two armies charged at each other. The commanders of both the armies—Drona and Dhrishtadyumna—were sworn enemies, and Dhrishtadyumna was hell-bent on defeating Drona and the Kauravas. The Kauravas, in turn, looked to Drona and Karna to give them victory. Both the armies fought cruelly, with soldiers falling on each other in mortal combat.

Drona, now the commander of the army, brought all his skills in warfare to the front. He charged at the Pandava army, scattering them as though they were flies. His chariot scythed through the Pandava ranks. His hands moved swiftly, releasing arrow after arrow that caused death and destruction. A number of soldiers and warriors tried to attack Drona but failed.

Drona's charge was so bloodthirsty that the Pandava soldiers broke rank and fled for their lives. He slew hundreds of soldiers within a few minutes of the battle. Dhrishtadyumna bravely rallied his troops, trying to reassemble them to take on Drona's might.

Abhimanyu had charged into battle, attacking the Kaurava soldiers and slaying them one by one. Now he charged through the Kaurava ranks attacking his opponents. He soon encountered King Paurava who attacked him with fiery arrows. Abhimanyu quickly destroyed the arrows and launched a counter-attack.

Their battle was grim, with the veteran king using his experience while the son of Arjuna used his skills, his youthful energy proving more useful. Paurava struggled to face Abhimanyu's ferocious assault. He let loose a flurry of arrows that destroyed Paurava's standard, bringing his flag down. His arrows killed Paurava's charioteer and shattered Paurava's bow.

Abhimanyu aimed an arrow at Paurava with the intention of ending his life. Just as he was about to release it, an arrow streaked at him from his left; it was shot by Shalya. His arrows hit Abhimanyu's bow, causing it to break in two. Shalya smiled at Abhimanyu but his smile was cut short and he faced an attack by none other than his nephew Nakula, who was furious with Shalya for attacking Abhimanyu stealthily.

As Nakula and Shalya feuded, Abhimanyu pulled out his sword from his scabbard and charged at a shaken Paurava with his shield in the other hand. He rushed at Paurava and boarded his chariot. Paurava pulled out his sword and tried to attack Abhimanyu. Within a second, Abhimanyu had broken the sword with a lunging swipe.

Abhimanyu grabbed Paurava by his hair and pulled him out of the chariot, hell-bent on executing him. Just as Paurava's journey on Earth seemed to have reached its end, the Sindhu king Jayadratha rushed to his defence. With his sword and shield in hand, he attacked Abhimanyu.

Abhimanyu let go of Paurava, who scurried away to safety. A cut-throat swordfight broke out between Abhimanyu and Jayadratha. Both the warriors were skilled and fought fiercely, and their swords clashed forcefully, generating sparks. Abhimanyu struck at his opponent's head but his sword found Jayadratha's shield.

Both the warriors used their swords and shields effectively to fight each other, and the battle continued for a long time with neither of them showing any weakness. The weapons clashed thunderously. Jayadratha used his shield to block Abhimanyu's attack, lifted his sword and brought it down in an arc towards Abhimanyu's neck.

Abhimanyu quickly used his huge shield to cover himself. He twisted the shield and Jayadratha's sword was caught in it. Jayadratha pulled hard but the sword refused to come out. As he prepared to pull the sword again, Abhimanyu pulled the shield back towards him and twisted it to his left. As Jayadratha pulled the sword hard, it snapped into two.

One half was stuck in Abhimanyu's shield and the other half was in Jayadratha's hand. Jayadratha threw away his broken sword and ran to his chariot. Abhimanyu quickly mounted his own chariot and asked his charioteer to charge at Jayadratha. Just then, Shalya came back into the battlefield and blocked Abhimanyu's way.

He aimed an iron arrow at Abhimanyu. Abhimanyu had thrown away his shield and was standing in his chariot with only his sword in his left hand. Shalya's arrow came charging towards him. Abhimanyu stood straight, his eyes focused on the missile Shalya had hurled. Just as it came near him, he reached out and grabbed the arrow with his bare hand.

As his huge hands held the arrow, its force was diminished. Abhimanyu's hand was smarting from contact with the missile. Without caring about the burn, he nonchalantly aimed the arrow back at Shalya. Thrusting his chest forward, he drew his hand back and flung the arrow with all his might, his muscles imparting energy to the arrow.

The arrow flung by Abhimanyu had the same force as though it were shot from a bow. Shalya did not expect this and stood stunned. The arrow killed his charioteer. The chariot shook and the panicked horses leapt causing Shalya to fall from his chariot.

Seeing the ease with which he defeated Shalya, his uncles Nakula and Bheema and his father-in-law Virat praised him for the prowess he displayed. Shalya picked up a huge mace and charged towards Abhimanyu, who picked up his own mace and was ready to alight from his chariot.

Just then, Bheema stopped Abhimanyu. "Leave him to me, nephew, he is mine. I will defeat him today."

Bheema charged at Shalya, and effortlessly defeated him, slugging his mace and causing him to flee.

Abhimanyu went in search of Jayadratha to continue his battle. On the way, he met many Kaurava warriors and engaged with them, emerging victorious each time.

Meanwhile, a brutish battle had broken out between Drona and Yudhishtira. The teacher and the student fought matchlessly, neither showing any weakness. Drona's experience and skills soon proved that he was the better of the two and he put Yudhishtira on the defensive. Just as he entertained hopes of defeating Yudhishtira, Arjuna charged into the battlefield.

He launched a fierce attack on Drona, which shocked him and pushed him back. Drona tried his best and used all his experience, but his favourite student Arjuna showed him why he was the greatest archer in the world. The day ended with a humiliating defeat for Drona at Arjuna's hands. Many Kaurava soldiers were killed and it was advantage Pandavas. The victorious Pandavas returned celebrating, while the Kauravas returned with long faces.

25

Drona's Frustration

Drona strode up and down the huge tent that the Kauravas used as their war council room. Duryodhana, Karna, Dushasana and the rest of the Kaurava princes and allies sat in a circle. Drona, being the commander, usually sat at the centre. However, today, he could not sit and seemed restless. The mood in the Kaurava camp was dark.

Drona was frustrated and vented it out on a servant who approached him with a glass of milk. He threw the glass away and pushed the servant out of his way.

"Why are you so angry, Acharya? Control your anger and sit down, let us discuss our strategy for tomorrow," said Karna.

"What strategy? There is no strategy that works. Any strategy we make fails because of Arjuna. I had subdued Yudhishtira yesterday. He was weakening and was not able to withstand my assault. In a few moments, I would have destroyed his weapons and chariot. But then, Arjuna came and ruined my plans."

"He killed Bheeshma by deceit and preens about the battlefield as though he is a great hero," said Karna angrily.

"It is all because of that cowherd Krishna. He uses his magical power to help Arjuna succeed," snapped Duryodhana.

"I don't think Krishna has used any magic till today, brother," said Duryodhana's brother Vikarna.

"He doesn't need to use magic. He hypnotises Arjuna's opponent from his charioteer's seat. Why do you think a great man like Krishna agreed to be a mere charioteer? That is their strategy. He uses his powers cunningly to weaken the opponent, allowing Arjuna to win every time."

"We must kill Krishna then," said Dushasana.

"Enough!" said Drona. "Let's not waste time with meaningless discussion. You cannot kill Krishna. The problem is not Krishna, it is Arjuna."

"Let us kill Arjuna then," said Dushasana.

"If that was so easy, my King Duryodhana would have done it long ago," said Karna.

"No, there is no use talking about killing Arjuna," said Drona. "We need to somehow keep him away from the battlefield. If he is not there, then defeating the rest of the Pandavas is easy."

"I agree, Acharya," said Karna. "Without Arjuna, the strength of the Pandavas gets reduced by half. It is time we dispatch one of the Pandavas to the other world."

"I know how to divert Arjuna," Duryodhana pronounced thoughtfully, stroking his moustache.

"How?" asked Drona and Karna in unison.

"Susharma will do it for us," said Duryodhana pointing to the Trigarta king. Susharma got up and walked towards where Drona stood and bowed to him.

"How? Explain," demanded Drona.

Duryodhana, looking at Susharma, said, "Susharma, his brothers and allies are sworn enemies of Arjuna. They are determined to kill him at any cost."

"Yes," asserted Susharma angrily, clenching his fist. "Arjuna defeated us and took away our kingdom when his brother performed the Rajasuya yagna. He and his brothers have humiliated us, defeating us not once but many times. For us, humiliation is worse than death. We have therefore taken a vow to defeat him."

"Interesting," said Karna. "What is your vow?"

"We are the Samshapatakas. We have taken a shapata (oath) to kill Arjuna. We will fight with Arjuna and kill him. If we fail, we will die happily. We are a suicide squad of 3,000 warriors and will give our lives to kill Arjuna."

Duryodhana got up and hugged Susharma, who was the cousin of his wife Bhanumathi.

"I salute your courage, Susharma, you are a brave man."

"Acharya," said Susharma to Drona, "give us a chance. We will help you get rid of Arjuna. In fact, we have decided that all of us will perform our own funeral rites tonight, preparing for our death. Tomorrow, we will take on Arjuna and kill him or we will die."

"Hmm," said Drona, massaging his beard thoughtfully, "I have a task for you then."

"Tell me, Acharya, I will do anything."

"Tomorrow morning, I want you to engage Arjuna and keep him busy the entire day. You have anyway decided to fight him to the finish. Do it tomorrow and keep him busy. Can you do it?"

"Yes," shouted Susharma joyfully. "We will do it. We will challenge Arjuna, surround him and attack him unceasingly. He has to kill all of us before he can escape from us. I promise you this, Acharya."

Drona patted Susharma on the back. "Good, keep him engaged and I will kill Yudhishtira tomorrow."

They then sat down and formulated their plans for the morrow.

The next day, as planned, Susharma came before Arjuna as soon as the day's battle started. "Arjuna, you claim to be a great warrior. I challenge you to defeat my brothers and me today. Come on and fight us if you are a man."

Hearing this, Arjuna laughed loudly, "Trigarta king, you forget my brothers and I have defeated you many times. You are no challenge to me."

An infuriated Susharma signalled to his seven brothers and all of them unleashed a barrage of arrows at Arjuna. He smilingly held up his shield and deflected them all in an instant and then picked up his bow, the great Gandiva, and shot a volley of arrows at the Trigarta kings.

A frenzied battle proceeded, with the Samshapatakas shooting arrow after arrow at Arjuna. He destroyed them all and took the attack back to them. Sudhanwan, one of the Trigarta kings, charged at Arjuna in his chariot.

Arjuna quickly fixed three arrows in his bow and released them. The first foiled the arrows that Sudhanwan had shot, the second shattered his bow and the third destroyed his flag. Arjuna then shot at Sudhanwan's chest; it pierced his heart and he fell dead.

Susharma was enraged on seeing his dead brother. He summoned the Samshapatakas and ordered them to attack Arjuna all at once. Three thousand warriors launched an attack on Arjuna raining arrows at him.

His hands moving like lightning, Arjuna unleashed an array of arrows to counter the attack. He fixed five arrows on his bow and shot them together at a time. Even before the arrows had left the bow, he had five more arrows ready.

His arrows destroyed the Samshapatakas' arrows. They did not stop and continued to shoot thousands of arrows at Arjuna who worked nonstop to counter their attack. Soon the sky was dark, filled with arrows from all sides.

Arjuna was now getting tired and the barrage of arrows, most of which fell before their chariot, was so dense that he was finding it difficult to see through it. Krishna turned to Arjuna and said, "Blow it all away, Partha." Then he smiled.

Arjuna got the message and decided to use a divyastra. He took out an arrow, touched it to his forehead and closed his eyes. He chanted the mantra that converted the arrow into the Vayavyastra, a divine weapon given to him by Lord Vayu, the wind god.

He shot the weapon into the air, and the astra transformed itself into a whirling cloud. As the cloud moved towards the Samshapatakas, it picked up speed and increased in size. It turned into a huge gale and struck Susharma and his warriors. Their chariots flew and all of them were knocked off and fell to the ground. Their weapons went flying in the air and were strewn all over.

The gale of wind that the Vayavyastra created brought with it a dust storm that enveloped the Samshapatakas, covering them with layers of dust. Arjuna had unleashed a storm that ravaged through Susharma's suicide squad.

Drona had watched as Susharma had challenged Arjuna in battle. He launched a vicious attack on the Pandavas, firing arrows of different types that sent the Pandava army scattering in all directions. As he searched for Yudhishtira, he unleashed death and devastation on the army, leaving a trail of corpses behind him.

Abhimanyu saw his father's teacher in this violent mode but was not scared. He decided to take him head-on. Abhimanyu was truly heroic. While the other Pandavas watched hesitantly, reluctant to take on Drona in this unbelievably aggressive mood, Abhimanyu, without a care, moved his chariot towards Drona.

Just as he neared Drona, he found his way blocked by his cousin Lakshmana.

"Get out of my way," said Abhimanyu contemptuously. "I have a battle to fight with your commander."

"Before you fight him, you need to first defeat me," said Lakshmana and shot three arrows at Abhimanyu. Two of the arrows struck Abhimanyu on his chest, his armour protected him but he felt insulted.

He shot three arrows back at Lakshmana that fractured his bow and fragmented his standard that had the Kaurava flag. An angry Lakshmana picked up another bow and aggressively shot arrows at Abhimanyu, who was startled by the ferity of the attack.

He defended himself from the arrows and attacked Lakshmana with his own. An intense duel took place between the two cousins. Lakshmana was no easy target and used all his skills to take on Abhimanyu.

Dhrishtadyumna led his soldiers to Drona and attacked him, keeping the Kaurava commander busy with his forces.

Duryodhana summoned his ally Bhagadatta, the king of Pragjyotisha.

"Bhagadatta, I need your help. I know what a great warrior you are, and it is now time to show your prowess. Unleash your power on the Pandavas. Arjuna and Krishna are not here. This is the time to vanquish the Pandavas. Do this for me."

"It is a pity that Arjuna and his charioteer are not here. I wanted a chance to kill them both in battle, especially that wily fox Krishna. No matter, I will show what I am today."

With these words, Bhagadatta mounted his white elephant Supratika—a divine elephant related to Airavata, Indra's elephant—and charged into the battlefield. Supratika was the largest elephant anyone had ever seen. Its towering presence was enough to make any soldier quake with fear. Its trumpet was like thunder and filled the enemy with dread.

Bhagadatta charged into the Pandava army and slaughtered them with his arrows and spears. His elephant trampled hundreds of soldiers to death. The Pandava soldiers with elephants charged at Bhagadatta but Supratika flung the elephants as though they were bamboo sticks and crushed them to death beneath its huge legs.

Bheema charged at Bhagadatta and attacked him with his mace. Even before the mace could hit him, the elephant caught it and cracked it into two. Bheema, wild with anger, went under the elephant; he knew the points where the vitality of the elephant originated and battered these with his bare hands.

The elephant roared in perturbation. It grabbed Bheema with its trunk and threw him on the ground. Bheema was dazed. The elephant raised its huge front leg to crush him. Displaying presence of mind, Bheema jumped between the elephant's legs and hid, confusing the elephant. He quietly escaped from the back and awaited the arrival of his elephant to take on the mighty Supratika.

Seeing Bheema disappear, Yudhishtira thought he was dead. He attacked Bhagadatta but struggled to face the onslaught of Bhagadatta and his wild elephant.

Meanwhile Arjuna, after blowing away the Samshapatakas, prepared to leave. A hundred more warriors surrounded and attacked him. He launched a pitiless attack on them and killed them in no time.

Krishna addressed Arjuna, "There seems to be a lot of commotion. I can see a white elephant creating ruin, it must be Bhagadatta's elephant. Let us go there, Arjuna."

Arjuna acquiesced and Krishna took the chariot towards Bhagadatta, who greeted them with a shower of sharp weapons. He destroyed all of Bhagadatta's missiles, and Bhagadatta in turn ordered his elephant to trample Arjuna's chariot. Krishna moved the chariot away post-haste.

Arjuna was now behind Bhagadatta and could have slain him and his elephant in an instant. He did not do so as it was unjust to attack from behind. He urged Krishna to take him face to face with Bhagadatta. A furious duel erupted.

Taking his aim, he sent a cascade of arrows. The first one shattered the armour of the elephant and the second broke the umbrella that shielded Bhagadatta. The furious king of Pragjyotisha hurled a lance that hit Arjuna's crown, causing it to topple.

Arjuna adjusted his crown and shot seventy-two arrows at Bhagadatta; they destroyed all his weapons, broke his crown and cut off his legs. Bhagadatta screamed in anguish. With no weapons left, he grabbed the elephant hook and chanted the mantra that invoked the Vaishnavastra. The elephant hook glowed and emitted sparkles.

He flung the Vaishnavastra at Arjuna and screamed, "Die, Arjuna! This was the weapon given by Vishnu to my father. No one can destroy this weapon nor survive it. Die, Arjuna, die!"

The collective of warriors watched on in horror as the Vaishnavastra blazed towards Arjuna with the intention of decapitating him.

26

The Kauravas Are Desperate

Arjuna, confounded, was unable to lift his bow as the Vaishnavastra hurtled towards him. Yudhishtira closed his eyes, fearing the worst.

Just as the divine weapon was about to touch Arjuna, Krishna stood up and blocked the path of the astra as the Pandavas gasped.

The Vaishnavastra that was intent on hitting its target and decimating it, hit Krishna on the neck. Having encountered its creator and master, the astra turned into a garland of fragrant flowers and adorned Krishna.

Arjuna complained to Krishna, "Vaasudeva, please allow me to fight my battles. Don't expose yourself to this risk."

Krishna smilingly replied, "Partha, the Vaishnavastra was given by Vishnu to Bhoomidevi for her son Naraka, whom I killed as punishment for his evil acts. He passed it on to his son Bhagadatta. No one can stop this astra. Had I not intervened you would be dead. Now focus on the task and finish off Bhagadatta, and let's go tackle Drona."

Arjuna shifted his attention to Bhagadatta and released a deluge of arrows on the elephant Supratika. Its head split and it fell, causing a minor Earthquake. As Bhagadatta was going down, he reached for a spear to attack Arjuna, who cut it down with an arrow. Arjuna next took out a crescent-shaped arrow and shot it at Bhagadatta, piercing him in the chest.

Bhagadatta collapsed, dead. Shakuni's brothers Achala and Vrishaka attacked Arjuna and he killed them both with a single arrow. He looked ahead and saw Abhimanyu engaged in a furious fight with Lakshmana; he considered his son's prowess in archery admiringly. Abhimanyu destroyed Lakshmana's chariot, causing him to flee.

Arjuna said proudly, "Look, Krishna, my son has proved to be a great warrior in battle. His skill in archery equals mine."

Krishna said, "He now challenges Drona, who is in a ferocious mood. He needs your help now, Partha. Let's go and fight Drona."

Even as Abhimanyu supported Bheema and Dhrishtadyumna in attacking Drona, Arjuna moved to join them. He challenged his teacher, who gladly accepted and unleashed a drizzle of missiles at Arjuna.

Arjuna made short work of all the weapons. He launched a hail of arrows at Drona, putting him on the defensive. Seeing Drona under attack, Karna charged at Arjuna. A rigorous duel erupted between Arjuna and Karna.

Despite Karna's skills in archery, he found it difficult to match Arjuna, who hit Karna with many arrows, injuring him. He cut off Karna's bow, forcing him to duck inside his chariot. It was now Abhimanyu's turn to admire his father's skills—he watched his father in action to understand the nuances of archery warfare.

Duryodhana and Shakuni came to Karna's help and attacked Arjuna. A harsh battle erupted between both sides, causing severe casualties. Thousands of soldiers lay dead. Arjuna, Bheema, Abhimanyu, Dhrishtadyumna and Satyaki led the battle from the Pandava side. Drona, Duryodhana, Karna, Shakuni and Bhurishravas countered them.

Drona's plans of defeating Yudhishtira had failed and he was now fighting a losing battle against the onslaught of the Pandavas. The Kauravas were overwhelmed by the inhuman attack by the Pandavas. Just then, the sun disappeared behind the horizon as though tired of watching the bloodshed. This signalled the end of the twelfth day's battle and both sides left for their respective camps.

There were celebrations in the Pandava camp. Everyone congratulated Arjuna for his valour and the way he fended off the attack of the Samshapatakas and finished off Bhagadatta.

Arjuna praised the skills of Abhimanyu, filling his chest with pride. Abhimanyu, in turn, praised the fierce prowess of Arjuna. All the Pandavas relaxed and enjoyed their food and drink, remembering the events of a successful day.

The Kaurava camp's mood was diametrically opposite—it betokened a sense of desperation. Their carefully made plans lay in tatters yet again. Duryodhana was incensed and vented his frustration on everyone, not even sparing Drona.

"Acharya, what happened to your plans? We failed yet again. I am tired of failure. How long will it take before we can taste the fruit of victory?"

"Patience, my prince, victory will be ours, we have to wait," said Drona.

"Let us keep waiting. Meanwhile, the Pandavas will wipe out our army and we will be left with nothing but the dust from the battlefield. You promised to defeat Yudhishtira and kill him. What happened? Why did your plan fail? Or is it that you have no intention of defeating your favourite Pandavas?" thundered Duryodhana.

"Calm down, Duryodhana," said Drona. "You saw how we were doing well. Just as we reached the door of victory, Arjuna came and shut it down."

"Arjuna, Arjuna! I am sick of hearing your adoration for Arjuna. I am beginning to suspect you want him to succeed."

"Don't say that, Prince. I am hurt by your words. I am the commander of this army and will be loyal until my last breath."

"Duryodhana, please do not doubt my father," said Ashwatthama. "He fought courageously against Arjuna but he seems to be indomitable."

"You, father and son, stop giving me excuses. Acharya, don't you have the celestial weapons given to you by the gods? Why didn't you use them against Arjuna?"

Ashwatthama tried to calm down Duryodhana even as Drona sat dejectedly. "Prince, the weapons given by the gods cannot be used so easily, there are rules and conduct governing their action."

"Don't tell me about rules and conduct! I suppose it was fair conduct to ask Ekalavya to cut off his thumb so that he would not overshadow your favourite Arjuna?" Duryodhana taunted Drona.

Drona got up and said, "Duryodhana, certain astras cannot be used against soldiers; if not used properly, we will lose the use of these astras and they may even turn against us."

"Stop it!" screamed Duryodhana. "Don't you have the Brahmastra, the greatest weapon of all? I am not asking you to use it against soldiers. Use it and kill Arjuna. Does the prospect of killing your favourite hurt you?"

"It is your words that are hurting me," said Drona sadly. "Arjuna also has the Brahmastra, he has every celestial weapon and anything I use, he can counter it. He has the Pashupatastra given to him personally by Lord Shiva, which I don't even have. If he had used it today, our entire army would have been wiped out and the war would be over. Such weapons are not to be used lightly."

"Alright, so you cannot defeat Arjuna. You cannot defeat Yudhishtira. Shall we go and surrender? Let us do it right now, brave warriors. Let us fall at the feet of the Pandavas and hand over everything to them and walk away and jump into the sea," remarked Duryodhana sarcastically.

Drona was terribly upset on hearing these words and sat with his head bowed. He got up and walked over to Duryodhana.

"Duryodhana, I promise you that tomorrow the course of the war will change. Let us make a new strategy. I have a plan."

"What is it, Acharya?" asked Karna.

"We were planning to defeat Yudhishtira and kill him. This will not help. It will make Arjuna and Bheema angrier. I have a better solution. Let us capture

Yudhishtira and take him prisoner. With Yudhishtira in our custody, the Pandavas will not fight, they will come to us to negotiate his surrender. We can end the war easily."

"Excellent idea, Acharya," said Karna.

Duryodhana was still in an inflammatory mood. "Oh yes, you will capture him like you did today, right?"

"Every day is a new day. Tomorrow I will launch an attack that will be remembered forever, as long as this Earth exists. I will organise a battle formation that is unbeatable and that will destroy the enemy. I will devise the Chakravyuha, the wheel formation."

"I have heard of it," said Karna. "It is supposed to be virtually impossible to breach."

"With this formation, we will be invincible," said Drona. "The wheel will move forward, destroying everything in its wake. Yudhishtira cannot escape tomorrow. But...."

"But what?" asked Duryodhana who seemed to have calmed down after hearing the new plan.

"There are only three people here who can breach the Chakravyuha. I am one of them. The other two are Arjuna and Krishna."

"So what use is your plan when Arjuna will ruin it again?"

"Wait, I have a solution for that. Susharma and his warriors held off Arjuna for some time, but he saw what was happening and came back. We have to take him away from the battlefield."

Susharma stepped forward, "Tell us what to do, Acharya. My warriors and I are ready to die with a smile on our face. All we want is to kill Arjuna."

"Then listen to me. Tomorrow, take all your warriors and challenge Arjuna. I know him well, he will not refuse. He will also be overconfident after today's win. What you have to do is to take him away from the battlefield. This is very important. Keep moving while you fight so that he has to chase you. Take him to the southernmost end of the battlefield. From there, he would not be able to see or hear the Chakravyuha.

"Excellent!" exclaimed Duryodhana, slapping his thigh, "This will work! Arjuna will be out for the rest of the day and we will use your Chakravyuha to capture Yudhishtira. Go, Susharma, and rest now. Make sure you engage Arjuna throughout the day. He must not return until the sun sets."

"I promise you that I will give my life if necessary," said Susharma, and left after bowing to Drona.

"Acharya, explain the Chakravyuha. How does it work?" asked Karna.

Drona explained the Chakravyuha battle formation as everyone looked on with great interest.

"It is the greatest battle formation and the most difficult one. We need perfect synchronisation amongst all the soldiers and that will be my responsibility. The Chakravyuha is a wheel formation. There are seven circles formed like a spiral. In each circle, there will be soldiers tightly packed together, leaving no gap for the enemy to enter. At the outermost ring will be the infantry soldiers. The next ring will have charioteers, the next will have warriors on elephants and the inner rings will have all our most powerful warriors."

Drona took a stick and drew the formation in the mud.

"This is the mouth of the Chakravyuha. Enemies think this is the way to enter the vyuha and that is the biggest mistake they will commit."

"Why?" asked Karna.

"The vyuha will be rotating ceaselessly to confuse the enemy. It will also revolve so that the entire formation moves forward. Drummers will keep sending signals to our soldiers as to how to move ahead."

"The first soldier will make a move to the left. The soldier next to him will move to fill his place and this will continue as a chain reaction. The vyuha thus will not be stationary but will keep moving forward. While the first ring will move in one direction, the second ring will move in another direction. This will totally confuse the enemy."

Duryodhana laughed in glee, "Excellent, Acharya, this formation will be tough to beat."

"Let us see what happens if someone tries to enter the vyuha. Our strongest soldiers at the mouth will decimate him. If he manages to enter, the vyuha will keep moving and he will automatically be sucked inside it. Even if he stands still, the vyuha will engulf him. This is how we will bring Yudhishtira inside and capture him."

"What if someone tries to enter from the sides?"

"Let us assume that someone kills a soldier. The next soldier will immediately move into his place so that no gap is created. The opponent will find it difficult to create a gap. Remember that the soldiers in the other rings will keep attacking. Assuming he somehow enters the first ring, the moment he enters, soldiers in the outer and inner rings will surround him and he will be attacked from both sides."

"What if he manages to enter?"

"Even if he reaches the inner circle, he will find our strongest warriors there and will be cut down easily. Each ring of our vyuha will have a top warrior commanding it who can easily coordinate the attack against the enemy. This is the spiral of death, it will keep moving forward and the enemy cannot stand still, they have to attack. If they attack, they will face an attack from all sides. If they stand still, the formation will come to them and engulf them. There is no escape."

Duryodhana bowed to Drona. "I apologise for my harsh words earlier, Acharya. Your plan is amazing. I am confident we will achieve success tomorrow. The moment the vyuha reaches Yudhishtira, we will pull him inside and take him prisoner and that is the end of the war."

Drona smiled, "Yes, now all of you rest. We have a busy day tomorrow. I need to build the formation first thing in the morning. Be prepared early."

The mood in the Kaurava camp had changed. The desperation and vexation had been replaced with confidence. The warriors left for their tents to retire for the night as Drona planned his arrangements for the big day.

CHAKRAVYUHA

1 Outermost ring of infantry commanded by Jayadratha

2 Ring containing cavalry commanded by Karna

3 Ring containing war elephants commanded by Ashwatthama

4 Ring containing chariots commanded by Dushasana

5 Ring containing war elephants commanded by Shalya

6 Ring containing chariots commanded by Kripa

7 Innermost ring comprising all types of divisions with Duryodhana at the centre

0 Drona at the entrance of the formation

27

Chakravyuha—the Spiral of Death

Abhimanyu and Uttara were in a beautiful forest, surrounded by waterfalls. It was a blissful place and Uttara teased Abhimanyu, making him chase after her through the forest. He watched his lovely wife run amongst the trees as he sprinted behind her, laughing. She skipped towards the waterfall even as the mist from the water sprayed over both of them.

She challenged him to catch her amid the waterfall. Abhimanyu was now worried. He called out to her and attempted to run behind her. She went inside the waterfall and vanished as he watched on in bewilderment. There was a shower of blood from the waterfall. Shouting her name, he leapt in to save Uttara. He had failed to notice a whirlpool in the waters that sucked him away. Shouting Uttara's name, he cried out in anguish and woke up in his bed.

Abhimanyu was shaken with the horrible nightmare and was sweating profusely. He took deep breaths to compose himself. The nightmare had worried him but had also made him more determined to finish the war and return to his sweet life. It was time to prepare for the day.

Drona had awoken early and was on the battlefield even before the first soldier arrived. He arranged his soldiers meticulously, giving directions on where they should stand. Slowly and surely, he formed each ring of the vyuha. He instructed the soldiers on how to move. He gave instructions to the drummers on the signals to be given. The Kaurava warriors arrived and he assigned responsibilities to everyone.

"Jayadratha, you must manage the first ring. Patrol it so that if someone breaches it from the sides, you can take them on."

Jayadratha, the brother-in-law of Duryodhana, bowed before Drona and left to assume his place.

"Karna, you monitor the second ring. Ashwatthama will be in the third ring. Dushasana will take the fourth ring, Shalya the fifth and Kripa the sixth. Prince Duryodhana, you will be at the centre of the vyuha. I will position myself near the entrance so that I can capture Yudhishtira."

All the warriors bowed before Drona and moved to their positions.

From faraway, Yudhishtira watched Drona make the formation. The Chakravyuha could only be seen from the top. From the front, it was difficult to make out the formation.

Yudhishtira remarked, "Acharya seems to be creating a vyuha to take us on."

Bheema laughed, "Let him do what he wants. We have Arjuna who can breach any vyuha. I will not be found wanting and we will once again crush the Kauravas today."

The moment Arjuna entered the battlefield, Susharma challenged him.

"Arjuna," called out Susharma, "yesterday you somehow managed to trick us. Today is a different day and my warriors are waiting for you. Come on, I challenge you to a fight to the death. Either we will live or you."

As Drona expected, Arjuna accepted the challenge. He waited for the commanders from both sides to blow their conches, signifying the start of the thirteenth day's battle. The moment the conches were blown, Arjuna charged towards the Samshapatakas. They immediately moved back as Arjuna neared them.

"Don't run cowards, stand and fight," demanded Arjuna.

Susharma responded by unleashing a storm of arrows. Even as Arjuna responded, the Samshapatakas moved back. Very soon, they had drawn him towards the end of the battlefield in the south. Nothing could be seen from there other than dust.

Susharma shouted at his warriors, "We must not allow Arjuna to leave at any cost! Let us keep him engaged in battle the entire day, even if all of us have to die."

His warriors responded by blowing their conches. A terrible duel started. Arjuna attacked Susharma's army and they responded with all their might.

Even as Arjuna fought the Samshapatakas, the Pandavas charged towards Drona's formation. Drona's arrows ruthlessly cut down the soldiers who tried to enter the formation through its mouth. The Pandavas were attacked from all directions and from multiple rings of the vyuha.

The constant movement of the soldiers within the rings confused the Pandavas. To their surprise, they found the enemy advancing towards them, doggedly destroying all the soldiers in their wake.

Yudhishtira exclaimed, "Oh! This is the Chakravyuha! It is one of the most complex and dangerous battle formations and there is no formation to counter it."

Bheema said, "Nothing is impossible for the mighty Pandavas."

"No, Bheema, don't underestimate the Chakravyuha. It is composed of rings of warriors who will attack you together. The formation will keep charging at you. I can see Guru Drona at the head of the formation in his most ferocious form. I fear the worst."

Abhimanyu listened with interest to this conversation. He got onto his chariot and instructed his charioteer. The charioteer took him to the left of the formation and moved away. Yudhishtira noticed the movement and was surprised. Abhimanyu seemed to be circling the formation and Yudhishtira wondered why.

Meanwhile, Arjuna continued battling the Samshapatakas. He was perplexed as they kept charging at him one after the other, then in twos, threes and fours. They yelled curses at him, threatening to kill him firing arrows and throwing their spears.

He effortlessly undercut their weapons and slew them with ease, but they never stopped coming and were persistent. While some were highly skilled and managed to engage with Arjuna for some time, the unskilled ones died within moments of charging.

While their prowess in warfare varied, their bravery was consistent. None of the soldiers even as much as flinched as Arjuna's sizzling arrows came at them. They seemed willing to face death without fear in their eyes.

Arjuna asked Krishna, "Why are these warriors so willing to brave death, Krishna? They come at me one after the other like moths hurl themselves onto the fire!"

"They have taken a vow to kill you, Arjuna. The aim of Susharma's army is to kill you or die."

"Is it? Then I will help them achieve their aim by dispatching them to the god of death straightaway." So saying, he shot down three more of their soldiers. Soon he was bored.

"Krishna, I am tired of this role of sending the soldiers to the other world. I want to go back and see what Drona is up to. My brothers may need my help."

"Finish this battle Arjuna, then we will go."

"I am tempted to use the Brahmastra, Krishna. Shall I use it and finish this battle now?"

Krishna smiled, "You know very well the rules of war. The Brahmastra is not meant to be used on ordinary warriors but on someone equal to you in expertise and status. Remember your promise to me to not use the most powerful of weapons!"

Arjuna concurred and continued his neverending task of killing the Samshapatakas one by one.

At the other end, Yudhishtira watched in dismay as the Pandava soldiers were butchered by Drona's formation. Bheema was itching to charge at Drona but Yudhishtira had restrained him. Dhrishtadyumna led the Pandava army bravely and tried to penetrate Drona's formation but could not.

A mass of soldiers charged at the mouth of the formation and Drona ruthlessly massacred them. Soldiers on foot hurled spears, killing the Pandavas' elephants. Warriors on elephants and horses from the inner rings of the vyuha shot a torrent of arrows, cutting down the Pandava soldiers even before they could reach the formation. Drona killed all who managed to enter the formation in an instant.

Dhrishtadyumna tried to break the Chakravyuha from the sides, hoping to enter through the gap created by killing a soldier. The moment a soldier fell, the next one moved in its place, closing the gap instantaneously. If anyone got close to the formation, soldiers from all sides attacked them.

One soldier managed to sneak in. Even before he could move to the second ring, he was felled by a wave of arrows. Truly, the Chakravyuha was unbreachable!

A frustrated Dhrishtadyumna charged at Drona, who shot a barrage of arrows, destroying his bow; he had no option but to retreat. Yudhishtira was worried as the vyuha slowly but surely kept advancing towards them.

Drona's vyuha seemed unbeatable. It looked as though the Pandavas were going to face a mortifying defeat that day.

Bheema said, "Brother, I have been observing the formation and it is moving towards you. When you shifted your position, Drona changed the direction of the movement. Very clearly, he wants to bring the formation to you. I think he intends to trap you within the vyuha."

"I will fight bravely, Bheema. Let us not fear. Dharma is on our side. We will do our duty."

"Brother, if Drona captures you, we are finished. The war will be over," sighed Bheema in anguish. "There is no option for us but to break this formation."

"If only Arjuna were here," said Yudhishtira. "None of us know how to break this formation."

"I know how!" said a voice to Yudhishtira's right. It was Abhimanyu.

"Abhimanyu! What are you saying? Where had you gone?"

"Uncle, I had gone on a round to observe the formation. I have examined it minutely and identified the weak spots. I can break the formation and enter it."

"How do you know that?" asked Bheema.

"When I was in my mother's womb, Uncle Krishna had explained how to breach the Chakravyuha. The lessons imparted in the womb are fresh in my mind, but…."

"But what?"

"There is a problem. My mother fell asleep before Uncle Krishna could explain how to exit the Chakravyuha. I never got a chance to learn it later. I can enter the Chakravyuha but don't know the strategy to exit it."

Bheema was excited on hearing Abhimanyu's words "Bravo, nephew, do this for us. Breach the vyuha and enter it. We will help you exit."

"Yes," said Yudhishtira. "We will lead our army behind you. Breach this formidable defence and open a gap for us. Enter through the gap. We will follow you and slaughter the Kaurava soldiers. We will break their formation and display our mastery in battle today. With our entire army inside the vyuha, exiting won't be a problem."

"Lead us, Abhimanyu, today we will follow you. Let us break this formation and give a death blow to Drona's plans," said Bheema.

"How are you planning to enter?" asked Dhrishtadyumna. "Do you have a plan to defeat Drona?"

"No, don't even think of defeating Drona. Entering through the mouth of the vyuha is not possible. You will be trapped. The secret is to enter through the sides and from the weak flanks. That is why I made a detailed survey of the formation. I know now where the weak flanks are and can enter from there; within seconds, I can penetrate two rings and go in. After that I have to face the brunt of the Kaurava attack."

"Don't worry, Abhimanyu," assured Yudhishtira "we will be close behind you. Just let us enter through and we will back you."

"Then let's go," said Abhimanyu, turning his chariot and moving towards the left of the formation. The Pandava princes signalled to their soldiers and all of them followed Abhimanyu.

Jayadratha, who was in charge of protecting the outermost circle, observed their movement. He moved along with them within the formation to see what they were planning.

Abhimanyu reached his target. He turned to the Pandava king and asked, "Are you ready, Sire?"

"Yes," said Yudhishtira, fixing an arrow on his bow. "Lead us into the vyuha."

Abhimanyu stood far from the outermost ring so that the soldiers could not attack him, waiting for the right moment when the formation moved. The soldiers, guided by the continuous beating of drums, kept shuffling to their left while moving forward.

Abhimanyu stopped in front of one soldier. Drawing three arrows, he released them at the soldier in front and also at the ones to his left and right. The power with which he released the arrows broke their armour and penetrated their chests, killing them immediately. As they fell, the other soldiers kept moving, following the rhythm of the drumbeats.

In an instant, Abhimanyu repeated the same exercise, this time targeting three soldiers in the second ring who were positioned right in front of where he stood.

Meanwhile, the soldiers in the first ring kept moving. There were dead soldiers who did not move, and their places were empty. This created a gap in the first ring and Abhimanyu shouted at his charioteer, "Charge!"

The charioteer drove the chariot at top speed and entered through the gap. Abhimanyu had broken through the Chakravyuha!

As he entered the vyuha, the dead soldiers had created a gap in the second ring as well and he effortlessly went through, reaching the third ring while pouring arrows at the Kaurava army. The stupefied Kaurava soldiers and warriors screamed at him to stop as their impenetrable formation was breached.

Jayadratha, who was guarding the outer ring of the vyuha, was amazed to see Abhimanyu break through it. In his inner mind, he appreciated the skill of Arjuna's son in breaking this impenetrable formation. He also realised that the Pandavas would now use the same gap to enter the formation. As the general responsible for the outer ring, he could not allow this to happen.

He charged into the outer ring and closed the gap, signalling to the drummers to stop; the movement of soldiers too stopped. Just as Yudhishtira and the Pandava princes were about to enter the Chakravyuha, they saw Jayadratha blocking their way.

"Jayadratha, get out of our way! Have you forgotten how we defeated and humiliated you when you had kidnapped Draupadi? We will give you the same treatment now," said Bheema, charging at Jayadratha.

Jayadratha laughed, "Yes, I remember. After that humiliation, I prayed for many years to Lord Shiva and have obtained a boon from him. The boon was to defeat you Pandavas in battle. I will use the boon today. You will not pass me and enter the Chakravyuha."

Jayadratha took out an arrow, chanted a mantra and released the arrow. That one arrow split into thousand arrows and formed a barrier in front of the charging Bheema, forcing him to stop.

As the Pandavas used their weapons desperately at the barrier, Jayadratha shouted at them, "My strength today is increased tenfold with the blessings of Lord Rudra. Without Arjuna, none of you can defeat me today."

Yudhishtira watched in dismay as the entry to the Chakravyuha was closed, leaving Abhimanyu alone and unassisted inside the deadly vyuha.

28

Trapped in the Chakravyuha

Abhimanyu was now inside the Chakravyuha. He charged ahead and shouted at his charioteer Sumitra, "Come on, take me to Drona. Let me see his expertise in battle. Today, I will teach Drona a lesson and destroy his arrogance."

The charioteer said, "My prince, Drona is a veteran in battle while this is your first experience in such a great arena. He is your father's teacher. You have led a life of luxury while Drona is battle-hardened. Do not risk your life, I beg of you."

Abhimanyu laughed loudly, "Sumitra, who is this Drona? He stands on the side of adharma and supports the evil Kauravas and I am supposed to respect him? No Drona can challenge me. I am the son of the greatest warrior on Earth, Arjuna. My guru is none other than my uncle Krishna, who is the Lord Incarnate. No Drona or Duryodhana can stand before me."

"Please, my prince, don't underestimate the strength of the Kauravas. They may be evil, but they are adept and dangerous."

"Ha, do you think I care for any of them? Let me see if they can face me in battle. Today, I lead the Pandavas into battle. I am replete with energy and have the blessings of Arjuna and Krishna. Even Indra cannot defeat me today. How can these puny Kauravas defeat me?"

"My lord, you are just a sixteen-year-old boy. They are all much older than you and are more experienced in warfare. Reconsider your decision and do not challenge Drona."

"Enough, Sumitra! Don't waste my time with such cowardly talk. So what if I am sixteen? My youth gives me the power and strength to destroy the entire Kaurava army. I am so pumped up today that even if Lord Rudra comes before me, I can defeat him in battle. Move fast and stop talking."

The charioteer shook his head sadly but decided to obey his master. He charged into the vyuha towards Drona. Soldiers tried to block Abhimanyu but he let loose a flood of arrows, killing whoever came into his path.

The Kauravas princes were furious that Abhimanyu had broken through the vyuha as they had expected none to break through it. Abhimanyu's rapid entry into the Chakravyuha had shaken them up creating disarray as the soldiers had stopped moving inside the formation and were in a state of confusion.

They did not know whether to guard the perimeter against further attacks or to tackle Abhimanyu. The Kaurava princes launched themselves against Abhimanyu and urged their soldiers to attack him. The soldiers responded and started attacking him with arrows and spears.

Abhimanyu glided through the Chakravyuha, destroying all the weapons hurled at him effortlessly. He seemed to be vibrant with energy and eager to take on the entire Kaurava army. He remembered how his father had defeated the Kauravas singlehandedly when they had attacked the Matsya Kingdom. This inspired him and he was now ready to take on the entire Kaurava army by himself.

His hands moved at the speed of light, reaching into his quiver and drawing three arrows at a time. He fixed the arrows on the bowstring and, with a quick pull, released the arrows with maximum force, causing a twanging sound from his bow.

The arrows whizzed towards the opponents at an unexpected speed. The three arrows he released at a time not only destroyed the weapons that the enemy hurled at him but also penetrated the enemy's defence, knocking him down. No sooner had he released one set of arrows than his fingers automatically moved to the next.

Anyone who wished to learn the skill of archery could educate himself from the attack Abhimanyu mounted on the Kauravas. He was a student of Pradyumna, who was none other Kamadeva, the god whose arrows had struck the heart of mighty Shiva. Abhimanyu had learnt from Krishna, the Lord Incarnate, and then, he had honed his skills from the greatest archer in the world, his father Arjuna.

All the lessons he had learnt were being put to practice. His teachers would have been proud of him today. Sumitra, who a few moments back had warned him about his lack of experience, was ecstatic watching this unbelievable exhibition of warfare.

Abhimanyu twirled around shooting arrows in all directions as his chariot raced ahead, breaking through the Kaurava ranks. His arrows found their mark each time, killing Kaurava soldiers. After the first wave of attacks, the Kauravas were in a state of shock at seeing Abhimanyu's skill and prowess.

The princes and warriors seemed stupefied and the soldiers were now in panic mode. Abhimanyu attacked soldiers on foot, warriors on chariots and on elephants. As his chariot moved ahead, he left in his wake the bodies of all those he had vanquished.

Seeing the trail of destruction, the Kaurava soldiers were in a total state of panic. There was a stampede as horses and elephants ran around trying to escape the shower of deadly arrows that Abhimanyu let loose on them. The soldiers did not try to control their animals. They seemed eager to escape Abhimanyu, whose savage attack was causing bloodshed.

With every passing minute, his vitality seemed to increase and his attack became fiercer. He used the sharpest arrows to behead his opponents. The horses and elephants carrying the headless corpses of their masters ran helter-skelter, colliding with each other. Severed heads lay all over the ground and the stench of death was all-pervading.

Even as Abhimanyu effortlessly sailed through the Chakravyuha, destroying his opponents, the Pandava princes struggled desperately to defeat Jayadratha. They let loose all their weapons on the barrier he had created, only to see a fresh barrier of arrows block their arrows. The boon given by Lord Shiva had made Jayadratha unbeatable today and the Pandavas were running out of ideas.

Bheema charged at the barrier with his mighty mace and thwacked it open, and a new one emerged almost miraculously. He furiously broke through it and charged at Jayadratha, roaring. Jayadratha shot yet another astra that came at Bheema emitting flames. Bheema struck at the missile with his mace and was flabbergasted when his weapon shattered. He had no option but to retreat to his chariot to search for a new weapon.

Yudhishtira, Dhrishtadyumna, Satyaki, Nakula, Sahadeva and the other Pandava princes and allies rained arrows and lances on the barrier but found it insurmountable. Yudhishtira was getting disheartened now. He had sent Abhimanyu inside the Chakravyuha, promising to follow him, but he was still stuck outside.

The boy was now alone in the Chakravyuha and did not know how to exit. He had charged in bravely with the confidence that his uncles would follow him and join him in the battle. Yudhishtira's heart sank with the realisation that thousands of enemy soldiers would have surrounded Abhimanyu. He prayed that they somehow defeat Jayadratha, join Abhimanyu and help him.

Yudhishtira had no idea what was happening inside the Chakravyuha. While Jayadratha held the outer ring of the vyuha intact, the inner rings had all but disintegrated thanks to the turmoil created by Abhimanyu's attack. No one knew what to do. Drona, who was at the mouth of the vyuha, had just heard about Abhimanyu's attack and was making arrangements to protect the entry point.

The other Kauravas seemed helpless. They just stood and watched Abhimanyu slaughter their army singlehandedly. It seemed as though he would decimate the Kauravas all by himself. On seeing the mayhem,

Duryodhana came out from the centre of the vyuha and was outraged to see Arjuna's son.

He was astounded that Abhimanyu had entered the carefully crafted formation, and was even more shocked to see the death and destruction he had left behind. His rage increased when he saw how his brothers and other generals stood silently watching the destruction. Screaming, he charged at Abhimanyu.

But Abhimanyu cut down all his arrows. He smiled at Duryodhana and said, "Be prepared to face defeat. Today, I will avenge the humiliation of Mother Draupadi."

Even before Duryodhana could shoot an arrow, ten arrows were rushing at him. He bent to avoid the arrows that destroyed his flag and hit his chariot, shaking it up. Duryodhana counter-attacked but Abhimanyu swiftly knocked down his arrows and shot more missiles that hit Duryodhana on the chest, sticking into his armour.

Drona, who had just reached the scene, realised that Abhimanyu would probably defeat Duryodhana. He shouted at his warriors, "Ashwatthama, Karna, Kripa, Shakuni, Bhurishravas, Paurava, what are you doing? Aren't you ashamed of yourself? Your prince is in danger and you are watching? Go and save him!"

Drona's words broke the spell that the Kaurava princes seemed to be under. They all charged at Abhimanyu and blocked his chariot, covering Duryodhana and protecting him from Abhimanyu's onslaught. They drew their weapons and covered Abhimanyu with arrows.

Their protecting Duryodhana enraged Abhimanyu. He deftly avoided their arrows and released his own, now appearing to be possessed. His fingers moved like lightning. Drawing five arrows at a time, he kept spinning as he released arrows in all directions. All the Kaurava princes found themselves under attack almost simultaneously.

As he noted Abhimanyu's prowess, Drona understood why the Kaurava warriors had been stupefied. This kind of attack was unprecedented by a single warrior. In his long and illustrious career, Drona had only seen this skill in warfare once.

That was when Arjuna had attacked the Kauravas in Matsya Kingdom and defeated them unassisted. Abhimanyu's attack seemed even more ferocious. Drona was furious that his carefully designed plan had been ruined by Abhimanyu. Instead of trying to capture Yudhishtira, his army's focus was now on saving itself from this young prince.

His anger was mixed with admiration for he was, after all, a guru, a teacher. He knew that Abhimanyu had learnt archery from none other than Krishna and his son Pradyumna and had to admit that Abhimanyu equalled Arjuna in valour and skill. He thanked his fortune that Arjuna was not there. Had both father and son joined hands, they would have probably vanquished his army and ended the war that day.

In parallel, Arjuna continued his fight against Susharma's army. They led him on a merry chase, attacking him and then moving back, forcing him to chase them. He was now at the very end of the Kurukshetra battlefield; when he turned, all was a blur. He wondered what Drona had planned and what his brothers were doing to counter Drona.

For a moment, he contemplated turning back and returning to the main battlefield. Maybe his brothers needed his help. But he could never consider turning his back to the enemy; it would be supreme embarrassment for a great warrior like him. Further, he knew that Krishna would never agree to it. So he concentrated on the enemy and attacked them with more vigour.

He was determined to wipe out the Samshapatakas today. If they wanted to die, then he would oblige them. He would kill them all as fast as possible and return to his army at the earliest. He wondered what his son was doing. Arjuna was worried about Abhimanyu; he had not wanted his son to fight the war for he was far too young.

However, his biggest concern now was his son's exuberance and overconfidence. He hoped that Abhimanyu stayed close to his uncles and did not take any risks. He was confident in his son's abilities but not in the Kauravas' adherence to the rules of war.

Little did Arjuna know that his son was trapped alone amidst thousands of enemy soldiers under a merciless attack from all the Kaurava warriors. Trapped in the Chakravyuha with no support, Abhimanyu was waging a solitary battle.

29

The Kauravas Are Humiliated

Abhimanyu was not the least bit worried that he was fighting a lone battle and was unaware that his uncles had been unable to follow him; he had assumed they were behind him, smashing apart the vyuha. He was so engrossed in his ferocious battle with the Kaurava warriors that he had no time to think of other things. Like his father Arjuna, he had single-minded determination and focus; his target was the Kauravas in front of him and he focused on them.

The Kaurava heroes were taken aback by his attack and struggled to face his ferocious onslaught. They were desperate for a strategy to counter his attack; with no answers forthcoming, their strategy at this time was to save their lives and the life of their crown prince Duryodhana.

The warriors regrouped and decided to launch a simultaneous counter-attack. The entire Kaurava warrior line-up formed an arch surrounding Abhimanyu. Karna, Kripa, Ashwatthama, Shakuni, Paurava, Vrishasena, Bhurishravas, Shalya, Kritavarma and Lakshmana shot simultaneously at Abhimanyu.

From launching an attack on the Kauravas, now Abhimanyu had been put on the defensive. He countered the deluge of arrows with his own, but more arrows kept coming at him. But thanks to the impenetrable armour given to him by Arjuna, they made no impact on him.

The attack of the Kauravas became more ferocious. They had now come out of their initial disbelief and were outraged at the way a sixteen-year-old boy had ruined their strategy; they were determined to finish him off. Abhimanyu found it difficult to counter the continuing flood of arrows, which made it harder for him to fight back.

One of the rules of war was—more than one warrior could not target an enemy. But this rule had long been broken in this war. This type of violation of the code of conduct had never occurred. There were literally a hundred warriors and soldiers targeting one boy. It was against all ethics.

A learned teacher like Drona could never allow such immoral warfare. Yet he stood silently watching all his top warriors attack a single opponent.

Abhimanyu decided the situation was ripe to use the divyastras he had obtained from his father. While divine weapons were to be used against an equal only, he decided that with a hundred men against him, there was nothing wrong in utilising them.

He decided to use the Aindrastra, the weapon of his grandfather Indra, the king of gods. He picked up an arrow and aimed it at the sky. Touching his bow and arrow to his head, he closed his eyes and recited the secret hymn his father had taught him. The hymn invoked the blessings of Indra whose power came surging into the arrow, causing it to sparkle and glow.

Abhimanyu released the arrow, and it went high into the sky and turned into a shimmering ball of heat. The ball exploded into thousands of particles, each turning into an arrow. Arrows rained down on the battlefield in front of Abhimanyu, and the weapons the Kauravas were hurling at Abhimanyu were pulverised in an instant.

The Kauravas were taken by surprise as death rained down on them. The arrows pierced their chariots, resulting in holes; they even fell on their horses and charioteers, who bore the brunt of this rude awakening.

Drona grasped what had happened and howled at his warriors, "It is the Aindrasta! Retreat or else you will all be slain by the shower of arrows. We have no option but to wait until the shower stops."

Hearing Drona's words, the Kaurava braves scurried away to safety but many of the soldiers and warriors who were not quick enough had to face the iron missiles. The brunt of the attack was borne by the infantry soldiers, who were cut down mercilessly, the razor-sharp missiles tearing into their helmets and armour.

Within minutes, there was a pile of corpses and broken chariots. Warriors on chariots who had lost their horses and charioteers scrambled to safety. The advantage was now with Abhimanyu. Instead of defending himself, he now took the battle to the Kauravas. The combined attack of arrows from the front as well as from the sky caused panic in the Kaurava camp.

The hot-blooded son of the king of Asmaka charged at Abhimanyu and attacked him once the arrows from the sky had stopped. Ten of his arrows struck Abhimanyu on his armour. He shook them off as though they were feathers that had fallen from a bird flying in the sky. Fixing five arrows in his bow, he shot twice releasing a total of ten arrows.

The arrows ripped into the son of Asmaka. One arrow killed his charioteer, the second and third killed his horses, and the fourth destroyed his standard and brought it down to the ground. The fifth and sixth severed his arms. The seventh and eighth pierced his legs, causing him to collapse. The ninth took off his crown and it flew into the air.

As he cried out piteously, the tenth arrow ended his misery, severing his head; the head landed on the ground with a thud, even as his chariot crumbled and fell apart. Seeing their leader fall, the Asmaka army fled for their lives, increasing the agitation in the Kaurava ranks.

Now Karna stepped in to attack Abhimanyu and unleashed a fiery shower of arrows at him. Abhimanyu countered them all calmly, stopping them midway and causing them to fall harmlessly onto the ground. An angry Karna used the Agneyastra—his arrow burst into flames and the missile charged at Abhimanyu, emitting smoke and fire.

Abhimanyu chanted the mantra for the Varunastra and released it. The tip of his arrow broke and water gushed out, extinguishing the fire from Karna's missile. Both the arrows fell harmlessly to the ground.

Karna launched more arrows at Abhimanyu. The speed at which the skilled archer released the arrows caused them to break through Abhimanyu's defences. Some of them pierced his armour and drew blood. An exasperated Abhimanyu launched a counter-attack with a fusillade of arrows at Karna, which Karna found difficult to counter.

An arrow splintered his bow into two, and Karna had to use his shield to defend himself from Abhimanyu's attack. Seeing the plight of his master, Karna's charioteer took him away to safety. Karna felt disgraced for having to flee from battle.

Abhimanyu, who was charged up from the encounter, went on an offensive at the Kauravas. He encountered the Kaurava warrior Sushena, who bravely tried to attack him. Abhimanyu made short work of Sushena, giving him an easy and painless death by way of an arrow that hit Sushena on his forehead rupturing it and shattering his brain.

Next, it was the turn of the warrior Drigalochana. He put up a heroic fight, throwing spears at Abhimanyu, which the latter fractured with his flaming arrows. He cut off Drigalochana's hand, stopping the spear attack. The next arrow wrecked Drigalochana's armour and entered his chest. Two more arrows tore into his heart, killing him.

Another brave Kaurava warrior, Kundavedhin, who had the blood of many Pandava soldiers on his hands, attacked Abhimanyu, who nonchalantly dealt with his attack. He fragmented Kundavedhin's bow and severed his head. The bravest of the Kaurava warriors and princes were being defeated and killed effortlessly by Abhimanyu.

The Kauravas were now desperate. Karna joined hands with Ashwatthama and Kritavarma and all three of the great Kaurava warriors attacked Abhimanyu simultaneously. The three warriors stood to the left, centre and right of Abhimanyu and shot iron missiles at him.

Abhimanyu spun around, releasing arrows in all directions. It was an unparalleled exhibition of archery. The speed at which he moved made it appear as though he had three sets of hands firing arrows at all the three Kaurava warriors. A fierce duel broke out between the son of Arjuna, with the three warriors ganging up on him.

With the benefit of youth, Abhimanyu was charged with so much vitality that it seemed impossible to defeat him. His arrows penetrated the defences of the Kaurava braves, putting them on the defensive, and his armour soon had arrows from the bows of Ashwatthama and Karna in it. He ignored these arrows and carried on with his assault nonstop.

Soon he was able to break through Ashwatthama's defences and hit his armour with sharp missiles, causing him to fall back. He broke Kritavarma's bow with well-aimed arrows. Karna had to face humiliation yet again having been beaten back by Abhimanyu's ferocious onslaught.

As the three warriors fell back, Abhimanyu let out a ferocious roar like a lion prompting his charioteer to charge ahead, deep into the vyuha. His charge was so aggressive than many Kaurava princes retreated. As his chariot scythed through the enemy defences, he kept showering his enemy with arrows, slaying soldiers and beating back warriors. The Kaurava warriors kept trying to stop him but were unsuccessful.

The brother of the Madra king Shalya charged at Abhimanyu in a display of bravado. He had a quiver of golden arrows that he emptied on Abhimanyu; they pierced his armour and stuck out of it. None of the arrows though was able to break the powerful armour gifted by Arjuna.

He shone brilliantly with the golden arrows sticking out of him. Never had the Kauravas seen such a sight. He turned his anger on Shalya's brother and let loose five arrows at him. The first arrow destroyed his standard, bringing down his flag. The second killed his charioteer, and the third and fourth broke his chariot's wheels, causing his chariot to wobble.

The fifth arrow, delivered with precision, beheaded him and his head flew into the air and landed with a thud on the ground in front of Shalya, who cried out in anguish at the sight of his beloved decapitated brother.

Even before Shalya could think of revenge, he saw Abhimanyu charge towards him. He ducked to avoid the arrows but could not escape a blazing one that landed on his crown. His crown protected him else it would have torn into his forehead. The impact of the arrow caused Shalya to swoon. His charioteer quickly took him away to safety. Seeing their king faint, many of his soldiers followed him out of the battlefield.

Every successful encounter with the enemy seemed to make Abhimanyu more energised. Instead of being tired by his efforts, he seemed to grow in vitality. He charged through the enemy ranks causing mayhem, and the Kaurava soldiers fled in panic.

Drona looked at him admiringly and turned to Kripa who stood next to him. "Kripa, look at Arjuna's son—today the son excels the father. This is archery warfare of the highest order that will make even the gods proud. Today Abhimanyu stands out as the greatest warrior in this battlefield. Even I cannot defeat him if he continues to battle like this."

Drona did not know that Duryodhana was right behind him and heard every word he said, each word making him puff up with fury.

30

The Greatest Warrior on Earth

Drona would have never praised Abhimanyu had he known Duryodhana was behind him. His praise for Arjuna had made him the target of Duryodhana's anger many a time. Duryodhana had been jealous of Arjuna right from the time they started training under Drona as youths. Arjuna was far more skilled than any of the Pandava or Kaurava princes. This was why Drona gave him special attention. Drona's intention was to make Arjuna a master archer who would be the best warrior in the world. While he succeeded in doing this, it made Duryodhana jealous and resentful of Arjuna. Bheema's prowess with the mace was also another reason for Duryodhana's jealousy.

Hearing his commander Drona praising his arch-enemy Arjuna's son made Duryodhana wild with anger. He turned to his brother Dushasana and addressed him, "Did you hear our teacher? He is fulsome in praise for the son of Arjuna. Being the commander of our forces, it is his responsibility to win the war for us. He has to protect our forces and do everything to destroy the enemy. Instead, he now openly praises the son of Arjuna who is ravaging our army."

"He has always been biased, Brother," said Dushasana sadly.

"It is my misfortune, Brother, that all the elders, whether Bheeshma, Drona or Vidura, always side with the Pandavas. Their open favouritism is what has led to this situation. Had they treated all of us equally, we would never be fighting this war. Their bias is solely responsible for creating a rift between us cousins," spat out Duryodhana bitterly.

"I know, how can we kill Arjuna's son when our commander refuses to take him on?"

"We cannot rely on Drona. We have to do the job ourselves."

"I agree, Brother. I promise you, I will slay Abhimanyu and bring his head to you," said Dushasana. Drawing his bow and arrow, he asked his charioteer to take him towards the rampaging Abhimanyu.

Dushasana let loose a hail of arrows at Abhimanyu, attacking him from the side instead of facing him from the front. The arrows injured Abhimanyu's upper arms, but it didn't bother him. He stopped his attack on the hapless Kaurava army and turned to Dushasana.

He counter-attacked and a bitter fight erupted between the two warriors, with the twanging of the bowstrings, the whizzing of arrows and the clashing of metal. What Dushasana lacked in skill, he made up for in effort. For the first time that day, Abhimanyu faced a challenging situation as Dushasana aggressively matched Abhimanyu arrow for arrow.

Having put Abhimanyu on the defensive, Dushasana got overconfident. "Hey, son of Arjuna," he hollered. "Hope your father saw your face this morning. It is the last time he would have seen you alive. You are not going back today for I will cut you into pieces with my arrows."

The stinging wounds on Abhimanyu's arms and the words of Dushasana infuriated him but granted him greater energy; he now shot arrows with greater accuracy and intensity. His arrows came faster at Dushasana than he had expected. Now it was Dushasana's turn to be on the defensive.

"Listen, O Kaurava," taunted Abhimanyu. "This is not your palace where you rule and you can get away with anything. Your blind king may have closed his eyes to how your despicable brother and uncle cheated us during the game of dice. That day you could do anything, and you violated the modesty of Mother Draupadi by daring to touch her. Today is different, you foolish man. This is a battlefield, not your palace. Here I rule, not your blind father who allows you to do what you want."

Abhimanyu was able to breach Dushasana's defences and struck him on his armour, splitting it with a mighty crack. While Dushasana struggled to defend himself, Abhimanyu jeered at him unforgivingly, "You got away with the most shameless behaviour that day, Dushasana. Today I am going to hold you to account. Every insult you heaped on my family will be avenged. I will teach you a lesson you won't forget."

Abhimanyu's words stung Dushasana more than his arrows. He was determined to prove Abhimanyu wrong and was dead set on defeating him. With renewed strength, he bombarded Abhimanyu with arrows, many of which hit him. Abhimanyu was hurt, but he ignored his gashes and focused on his goal—that of teaching a lesson to the man who had insulted his family.

The warriors injured each other but kept going, determined to bring glory to their side. Abhimanyu had actually expected a tempestuous duel with Karna but had been surprised at the ease with which he had defeated him.

Now that Dushasana was giving him a tough fight, he felt that here was a warrior who equalled him. He had a special arrow in his arsenal made from the toughest iron. Its edge was so sharp that it could go through a wall. The arrow blazed through the air, cutting Dushasana's into two midway.

The arrow also fragmented Dushasana's bow and landed on the chest. He was fortunate that most of the arrow's force had been expended and it did not go deep into his chest.

Abhimanyu affixed another barbed arrow to his bow, planning to kill Dushasana. Then he remembered his uncle Bheema's request to leave the sons of Dhritharashtra to him and decided to honour his uncle's wishes; he put down his arrow. Dushasana was severely injured by Abhimanyu's arrow. He tried to stand firm and reached for another bow but stumbled and collapsed, losing consciousness.

Seeing his master fall, Dushasana's loyal charioteer fled from the scene, taking his master to safety, as Abhimanyu laughed loudly. The sight of his brother fleeing from the battlefield and Abhimanyu's laughter had Duryodhana seeing red. He summoned Karna, "Teach him a lesson, King of Anga. Defeat him in battle and avenge my brother's humiliation."

Karna, who had been beaten twice by Abhimanyu that day, was wary of challenging him again. But he had no option now as he had to respect his friend's words.

For a warrior, avoiding a fight was akin to surrender. Karna once again challenged Abhimanyu to battle, shooting missile after missile at him.

Abhimanyu countered them all effortlessly. The sight of his father's arch-enemy electrified him. He had heard a lot about Karna's valour and was intent on crushing him yet again. Every arrow Karna released saw Abhimanyu counter it with two. The air reverberated with clashing arrows, sparks falling everywhere.

Soon Abhimanyu put Karna on the defensive, launching a vicious attack. He released a shower of seventy-three arrows at Karna from all sides, damaging his chariot and hitting him repeatedly. Karna was injured.

He no longer had his legendary armour that could protect him from even the wrath of the gods. Without his divine armour, he found it difficult to face Abhimanyu's assault. Abhimanyu's arrows penetrated his armour repeatedly, causing him many lacerations. Karna was weakened.

Abhimanyu pulled out his sharpest arrow and released it, fracturing Karna's bow and causing him to fall back. He aimed another arrow and destroyed Karna's standard so that his flag fell. He debated whether to kill Karna or leave him for his father to kill. Even as he thought about it, Karna's brother charged at him.

He came in front of Karna's chariot to protect his brother and shot a barrage of arrows, hitting Abhimanyu's chariot's umbrella and flag, tilting the chariot. Seeing this, Duryodhana shrieked in delight. Abhimanyu did not flinch. He fixed an arrow, pulled back the string to its maximum length and released the arrow.

The missile breached through the defences of Karna's brother like lightning, hitting him on the neck. The force at which the arrow was released severed his head. The headless body of Karna's brother toppled on the ground, causing despondency in the Kaurava camp.

The fall of Karna's brother exposed Karna to Abhimanyu's attack yet again. Grieving over the loss of his brother, Karna was in no condition to take on the intense attack mounted by Abhimanyu. His repeated onslaught forced Karna to go on the defensive, and he had to once again retreat from the battle.

Karna's son Vrishasena took his place. He was provoked at seeing the way his father had been repeatedly defeated by Abhimanyu. He charged at Abhimanyu, but this did not bother Abhimanyu in the least. Responding aggressively, within moments Abhimanyu had cut off his bow. He shot a volley of arrows that killed his charioteer and brought down his flag. The moment the charioteer died, Vrishasena's horses took him away to safety, galloping away from the battlefield.

It was, without doubt, the most forgettable day for the Kauravas. Duryodhana seethed in anger as he helplessly watched Abhimanyu run amok, slaughtering his army. The most reliable Karna had been defeated over and over again. His brother was embarrassed and hundreds of his warriors slain in combat. His own defeat at the hands of Arjuna's son rankled him and prevented him from taking him on.

The Kaurava warriors looked on in amazement as Abhimanyu's chariot raced through the Chakravyuha, causing devastation. The losses the Kauravas were suffering every minute were unimaginable. Even Arjuna had never created this kind of pandemonium in the Kaurava ranks. It was absolute turmoil.

Vasitaya, a warrior who was the leader of a division of chariots, blocked Abhimanyu's way. Even though his legs were shaking after seeing how Abhimanyu had decimated his division, he displayed bravado by attacking Abhimanyu and shouting at him.

"You will not move ahead, Abhimanyu! Today I will kill you or die tryin—"

Even before he could complete his statement, he saw a sharp arrow whooshing towards him at an unbelievable speed. He desperately tried to hit the arrow with one of his own but had not even lifted his bow when Abhimanyu's arrow breached his defence and wounded him on the chest. It tore into his armour and went straight into his heart, killing him instantly.

Abhimanyu was shining on the battlefield with a lustre that made him glow. He looked like the full moon at night in his brilliance. Many of the enemy soldiers were awestruck just seeing him rush towards them. Brave warriors who had come to the battlefield ready to die for their crown prince ran away, losing their courage on witnessing Abhimanyu's charge.

He looked like no sixteen-year-old but resembled the destroyer, Lord Rudra, himself. Just as Rudra would charge seated on Nandi and decimate his enemies, Abhimanyu on his chariot burst through Drona's formation, massacring the enemy. It seemed as though he was on a mission to relieve Bhoomidevi of the burden of evil that had troubled her for so long.

Oblivious to his son's astonishing deeds, Arjuna, far off on the other side of the battlefield, continued to kill the Samshapatakas who charged at him one after the other. Arjuna would have been proud to know how his son had proved to be the greatest warrior on Earth, dealing death and destruction to his enemies, like the destroyer Lord Shiva.

31

The Destroyer Personified

The Kaurava princes and their allies felt that Abhimanyu was the destroyer personified who seemed to have resolved on concluding the war that day. The Kaurava princes and the great warriors in their army seemed to be made of stone as they watched the destroyer at work. All of them appeared to be helpless, not knowing what to do. A great warrior like Karna had been humiliated, the powerful Dushasana had barely got away with his life and Shalya was taken out of the battlefield injured.

Arjuna's young son had defeated the crown prince Duryodhana as well. The Kaurava commander Drona stood awestruck, admiring the heroism of his favourite student's offspring. Duryodhana seethed, shouting orders to his soldiers to attack Abhimanyu, knowing that he was sending them to their death.

Rukmaratha, the son of Shalya, approached Duryodhana, "Prince, I want to take on Abhimanyu. He has injured my father in battle and defeated him. I want to avenge his defeat."

Duryodhana nodded, sending Rukmaratha on a mission that he knew was likely to end badly. Shalya's army re-entered the battlefield along with Rukmaratha, having been assured that their king was safe. They now stood watching their prince take on the indefatigable Abhimanyu.

Rukmaratha shouted at his army, "Be ready to celebrate, my brave soldiers, I will now crush this son of Arjuna."

He charged towards Abhimanyu and shot nine arrows at him one after the other. Three arrows hit Abhimanyu in the left arm, three in the right arm and three in the chest. For Abhimanyu, these arrows were like pinpricks and he was barely perturbed. He turned his attention to Rukmaratha and said, "Being a cousin of my uncles Nakula and Sahadeva, you and your army fight for the Kaurava sinners? You will regret your mistake."

In a moment, Abhimanyu fixed three arrows simultaneously and shot them at Rukmaratha, severing his left arm, ripping off his right arm and finally, with the third, crescent-shaped arrow, chopping off his head that flew and fell in front of his army.

Seeing their prince's head, Shalya's army was outraged. They had been ashamed of how their king had been disgraced by a young boy. Now the boy had killed their prince. The general of their army blared, "Soldiers of Madra, we are Kshatriyas—warriors who were born to fight wars. It is our duty to fight for our king and our motherland. Today we fight for the respect of our rulers. Let us teach this arrogant son of Arjuna a lesson. Let us all charge at him together. We will send him to where our prince has gone."

Shalya's entire army, motivated by their general's words, charged at Abhimanyu from all sides. Armed with bows and arrows, maces, swords and spears, they hurtled towards him, committed to finishing him off. Even as Drona and Duryodhana watched, hundreds of soldiers charged at one boy with murderous intent.

King Shalya's army was committing a cardinal sin. One of the rules of war was that a warrior cannot be attacked by more than one opponent but now a mass of soldiers was ready to wage war on a single warrior. The Kaurava commander and princes should have stopped this but they watched silently, hoping that Abhimanyu would be killed at least now.

Seeing the horde of angry soldiers charging at him, Abhimanyu realised that he was moments away from death. This sort of situation called for exceptional measures, which was the use of the divyastra. He decided not to kill all the soldiers at one go but to defeat them one by one to showcase his prowess.

For this, the right weapon was the Gandharvastra. This was yet another powerful weapon given to him by his father. When Arjuna was in exile, Indra had invited him to the world of the gods. There he stayed for some time with the Gandharvas, the heavenly beings who practised magic and illusions. The Gandharva Tumvuru had taught Arjuna music and dance that had helped him become a dance teacher at King Virat's palace.

Pleased with Arjuna's dedication, Tumvuru had gifted him the divine weapon Gandharvastra that was capable of creating illusions that Arjuna had, in turn, passed on to Abhimanyu. It was this weapon that Abhimanyu planned to use and now he invoked it.

No sooner had he chanted the mantra than its effects were seen. The Madra army was charging towards Abhimanyu and was just about to pounce on him when suddenly he seemed to shimmer before them, bloating and spreading. They watched on, dumbstruck, as he split into two Abhimanyus.

Two Abhimanyus turned into four and then four into eight and so on. Within the twinkling of an eye, there were more than a hundred Abhimanyus before the army. They were unable to believe their eyes. They had heard of such a thing in tales told by their grandmothers but had never seen it in real life.

Rubbing their eyes in disbelief, the general and commanders thought it was the effect of the somras[20] they had consumed the previous night. They hoped it would go away but Abhimanyu kept multiplying in front of their eyes. Soon there were as many Abhimanyus as there were soldiers of the Madra army.

One Abhimanyu was difficult for the Kauravas to defeat; how could they even hope to defeat hundreds of him? As the soldiers watched in horror, the hundreds of Abhimanyus charged at them. It was an unequal battle as each of the Abhimanyus fought with one enemy soldier. The battle was over within moments, with hundreds of Madra soldiers being killed.

In reality, there was only one Abhimanyu. He moved his chariot so quickly that it appeared he was there at all places at once. It was the illusion created by the weapon of the Gandharvas. To the onlookers, it seemed as though there were hundreds of Abhimanyus fighting the enemy.

Shalya's army was nearly decimated and the remaining soldiers fled in terror. Drona and the rest of

[20] A drink that is believed to produce an alcohol-like effect.

the Kauravas were incredulous as multiple Abhimanyus ravaged them. They stood transfixed, witnessing the massacre in front of their eyes.

Soon the illusion created by the divine weapon wore off and they saw a victorious Abhimanyu standing before a mountain of corpses. Duryodhana was the first to recover from the effect of the illusion. He roared as he rushed towards Abhimanyu, shooting arrows at him which hit his armour, not making much of an impact.

Abhimanyu turned towards Duryodhana and ridiculed him, "Ha, welcome, leader of the Kauravas, the brave man who cheated at the game of dice. Welcome! Did you see how I dealt with your brother Dushasana? It is your turn now to meet the same fate."

A raging battle developed between the son of Arjuna and the crown prince of the Kauravas. Duryodhana could not face Abhimanyu. In this destroyer mode, Abhimanyu was virtually unbeatable and destroyed all the arrows that Duryodhana shot at him.

A furious Duryodhana threw his bow aside, picked up a spear and hurled it at Abhimanyu. In response, Abhimanyu picked up his shield in his left hand and blocked the spear, causing it to fall down harmlessly.

Duryodhana picked up his mace and asked his charioteer to charge towards Abhimanyu. With a smile on his face, Abhimanyu picked up a special arrow—a golden one decorated with feathers—that he had reserved for a particular opponent. Drawing back his bowstring with great force, he released it. The arrow propelled towards Duryodhana, looking like a golden missile with wings.

Duryodhana desperately tried to destroy the arrow with his mace but failed. It was too fast. It shattered the tip of Duryodhana's mace, rushed through his defences and hit him on his chest. The potency of the arrow had been reduced because of its contact with the mace and, thus, it did not hit Duryodhana with full force.

However, the impact with which it hit him did cause Duryodhana to fall back in his chariot. He was humiliated to be defeated yet again by Arjuna's son. Seeing Duryodhana in danger, Drona, who had stood silently all this while, was moved to action.

He shouted at the others to join him and charged towards Abhimanyu. He released arrow after arrow, compelling Abhimanyu to move back and putting him on the defence. Kripa and Kritavarma joined Drona and the three great warriors attacked Abhimanyu together.

Abhimanyu quickly cut down the arrows the three of them shot at him. He picked up multiple arrows, fixed them on his bow and shot them in quick succession launching a blistering attack on the Kaurava leaders. He shot eighty arrows at Kritavarma, destroying his bow and piercing him all over his body, necessitating his retreat.

He shot sixty arrows at Kripa, causing his chariot to shake with the effect. He then turned his attention to the commander of the Kauravas. Having destroyed the blazing arrows that Drona shot at him, he let loose fifty arrows at Drona, piercing his armour at many places and causing his bow to fall. Drona had no option but to pull back.

Ashwatthama, Karna and Vrihadvala charged at Abhimanyu. There was no stopping the heroic youth. He let loose a fusillade of ten arrows at Ashwatthama, injuring him and stopping his attack. He shot a sharp arrow at Karna. Seeing the arrows come rushing at his head, Karna tried to duck. Fortunately for him, the arrow missed his head but hit his left ear, causing it to bleed.

Abhimanyu had already defeated Vrihadvala, the king of Kosala, once during the early days of the war. Vrihadvala was itching for revenge and got his chance now. He shot fifty arrows at Abhimanyu, making him go on the defensive. He shot a knifelike arrow that breached Abhimanyu's defences and hit him on the chest. This enraged Abhimanyu and he thundered in distress.

He fixed a barbed arrow on his bow and shot it at the Kosala king. Even before he could retort, Abhimanyu's missile hurtled at him at top speed and ripped his chest open, stabbing his heart. Vrihadvala collapsed, instantly dead.

The Kosala army was a huge one. Vrihadvala, a loyal ally of Duryodhana, had brought with him an akshauhini that comprised more than 2,00,000 soldiers. There were 10,000 left by the thirteenth day. Seeing their king fall, all of them fled the battlefield for the safety of their city.

Duryodhana's son Lakshmana helped his injured father to recuperate and moved him to safety. He was terribly upset about the way Abhimanyu was humiliating the great Kaurava warriors. He had faced

Abhimanyu in battle before and had fought him well. Lakshmana was confident that he could defeat him.

"Abhimanyu," he bellowed, "I challenge you to fight me. It is time someone put an end to your arrogance. I will be the one who will wipe the arrogant smile off your face and dispatch you to hell."

With these words he charged at Abhimanyu, shooting arrows at him.

32

Intense Warfare

Lakshmana was an expert in warfare. His teacher was none other than Dronacharya. He had the ability to shoot arrows at lightning speed and considered himself an equal match for Abhimanyu. High on confidence, he attacked Abhimanyu knowing that his opponent would have been exhausted fighting all through the day.

While Lakshmana had skill and confidence on his side, what he lacked was experience. The intense battle that Abhimanyu had fought from the morning onwards had granted him the experience of a lifetime. It was as though he had fought a hundred wars successfully. Such was his faith in his ability to defeat the enemy.

Abhimanyu was born with a powerful body with broad shoulders and a huge chest, which made him very strong, and his training had helped him build his muscles. His strength gave him the ability to wage war relentlessly. Even though he had been fighting for hours, he was not at all tired and was eager to do more battle. He welcomed Lakshmana's challenge and countered him with his own arrows.

The two young warriors, scions of their races, one heir to the Pandavas and the other heir to the Kauravas, fought an intense battle. Abhimanyu's prowess was matched by Lakshmana's youthful exuberance. It was an equal battle for some time. After a while, Lakshmana's inexperience started to affect him.

Abhimanyu knew how to get through his rival's defences. He regularly breached Lakshmana's defences, hitting him on all parts of his body. This distracted Lakshmana and he was forced to go on the defensive, trying to save himself from Abhimanyu's attack.

"Look around you, Lakshmana," called out Abhimanyu, "look at this beautiful world. Look at the blue sky and the greenery beyond. Look at your family and friends behind you. Look carefully, for this is the last time you will be seeing this world. Goodbye, Cousin Lakshmana."

With these words, Abhimanyu picked up a special arrow shaped like a snake. It undulated surprisingly quickly in the air like an actual reptile. Lakshmana shot an arrow, hoping to break the serpentine missile coming at him, but failed.

Abhimanyu's arrow came at scorching speed and cut Lakshmana's neck; his head toppled into his chariot. Seeing his son's headless body from afar, Duryodhana wailed in sorrow, "Oh God! What a terrible day, I am forced to witness the death of my son. What will I do without you, my son? What will I tell your mother?"

Karna and Drona came to Duryodhana to console him. He furiously brushed them away and said, "Avenge my son if you can. By the end of this day, Arjuna must shed tears in the same way as I did. Go and destroy Abhimanyu. Don't stand before me. Go!"

Hearing his friend's words, Karna once again decided to attack Abhimanyu. It had been a terrible day in the battlefield for him. It was not once or twice but many times that Abhimanyu had beaten him. He had killed his brother and nearly killed his son. He had even injured him on his ear. Karna was unwilling to attack but had to do it. He was a brave warrior and did not fear death.

Meanwhile, Abhimanyu continuing his ruthless attack on the Kauravas, continuing to dispatch their soldiers to the other world. Vrindaraka was a strong and brave soldier who was the favourite of many of the Kauravas. He was one of the most powerful members of the infantry in the Kaurava ranks and was feared and respected by his opponents.

Infantry soldiers did not usually attack their opponents on horses. This was an exceptional day and Vrindaraka decided to attack Abhimanyu on foot. He was confident of his skill with his spear. He had planned to use his spear to kill Abhimanyu's horses, topple his chariot and forthwith defeat him in straight combat.

Even as Vrindaraka charged towards Abhimanyu's horses, Abhimanyu saw him. He lowered his bow, took out a spear of his own and flung it at Vrindaraka. The spear scythed through the air and lammed Vrindaraka's spear. It struck him on his chest, killing him immediately.

Abhimanyu suddenly felt a rush of air; looking up, he saw arrows whizzing at top speed towards him. He ducked to avoid them, and they barely missed his head. He grabbed his bow and turned to see who was shooting at him. It was Karna!

Abhimanyu sneered at Karna, "So, you are back again? I have defeated you so many times, yet you return for more?"

As he said this, he kept deflecting the arrows Karna shot at him.

Abhimanyu kept taunting Karna, "When I can defeat you so easily, imagine your fate when my father takes you on. You are no match for us, King of Anga."

An apoplectic Karna let loose three arrows that hit Abhimanyu on his arms and chest, drawing blood. For the first time that day, Abhimanyu felt unbearable pain from the arrows that struck him. Further, the multiple arrows shot at him had begun to weaken his armour. He focused to ignore the agony and concentrated on Karna.

More arrows breached Abhimanyu's defence, striking him on his hands. Karna seemed to have understood the strength of Abhimanyu's armour and targeted the parts of his huge arms that were not covered by it. His arrows were well directed and found their target. Abhimanyu's arrogant words motivated Karna to launch a fierce attack on him.

After suffering repeated injuries, it was now Abhimanyu's turn to attack. He picked up a special arrow that had multiple barbs on it and shot it at Karna. It crashed through his defences and hit him on his shoulders. The skin cut open and blood started streaming. Karna ignored his injury and focused on defeating Abhimanyu.

An intense fight developed between the two great warriors. Both of them were determined to win this battle. The whizzing sounds of arrows punctuated the air. Soon both of them were hurt and bleeding but neither was ready to give up. Karna was a powerful warrior, and Abhimanyu had a vitality that was seemingly inexhaustible.

They unleashed a barrage of arrows at each other. So intense were the sparks that their charioteers had to close their eyes. Gradually Karna's energy seemed to sap, while Abhimanyu's seemed to increase.

Abhimanyu's arrows were now coming at greater speed, and Karna struggled to defend himself. Abhimanyu had no intention of killing Karna; he wanted to leave that honour to his father. His sole intention was to defeat him again. As Karna defended himself from the flurry of arrows unleashed at him, Abhimanyu decided to target his chariot.

He shot powerful arrows at the chariot's wheels, destroying them and causing the wheels to shake; one wheel collapsed. Karna's chariot toppled to one side and he quickly jumped out of it.

Abhimanyu smiled at him, "I will not kill you when you are down. Repair your chariot quickly. It should not be difficult for you since you are the son of a charioteer."

Abhimanyu's insulting words hurt Karna, and he continued to attack him on foot. Karna's six trusted aides rushed to help their master. Abhimanyu affixed six arrows and shot them. They streaked through the air and found their mark. All six of his aides lay dead.

As Karna watched the carnage in shock, Abhimanyu ignored him and moved on. The son of Jayatsena of Magadha challenged him and shot many arrows at him. The arrows hit him on his armour and protruded from it. There were many such arrows on his body now. Abhimanyu quickly pulled them out and threw them on the ground.

Some of the arrows had found their mark, and they tormented him when he pulled them out but he did not flinch. He turned his attention to his opponent and released a sharp arrow at great speed. The arrow found its mark and beheaded him. Ashwakethu, the son of the Gandhara king, was the next to take him on.

When a great warrior like Karna could not face Abhimanyu, the fate of the others could be imagined! Anyone attacking Abhimanyu on this day was gambling with his life. It was virtually a suicide mission as warrior after warrior attacked Abhimanyu, only to be killed.

Ashwakethu's fate was the same. It hardly took Abhimanyu a minute to defeat him. His glowing arrows destroyed Ashwakethu's bow, shattered his crown and severed his head. The prince of Martikavata then charged at Abhimanyu.

Abhimanyu sighed, just as his father had done when the Samshapatakas came at him one by one, only to die. Abhimanyu thought aloud, "Why are these Kaurava princes so desperate to die? When their generals and kings cannot defeat me, why do they even try?"

It took just one arrow to kill the prince of Martikavata. As the princes of various kingdoms fell dead, it caused nervousness among their soldiers, who were part of the Kaurava army. Soldiers belonging to the kingdoms of vanquished princes fled from the battlefield.

Shalya, who had been rendered unconscious, had been taken to his camp. A physician had treated him, and his health was restored. He returned to the battlefield and was shocked to see his soldiers scattering in panic.

He stopped them and hollered, "Shame on you, cowards. Stop and fight for your country."

The soldiers said, "My lord, your son Rukmaratha was slain mercilessly by Abhimanyu. He killed all our commanders. We have no one to lead us."

Shalya was infuriated to hear this, "As long as I am alive, none of you shall leave the battlefield. Come with me, I will avenge my son's death. I will not rest until Abhimanyu is dead."

Shalya led his reluctant soldiers back to the battlefield, even as soldiers of other kingdoms ran away in fear. The chaos caused by Abhimanyu was unimaginable. It was only because Jayadratha held the outer ring intact that this panic had not led to a rout.

Jayadratha singlehandedly held off the Pandava army with his celestial weapons, preventing them from entering the Chakravyuha. While there was panic inside the Chakravyuha and the formation was broken, he still held the outer layer intact and prevented anyone from entering. Had he not done this, the Pandava army would have joined Abhimanyu and would have probably ended the war.

Abhimanyu continued his unabated massacre of the Kauravas. Warriors and soldiers were being slaughtered as bodies piled up. His progress was impeded with the bodies of those slain by him. He kept charging, his intention being to wipe out the Kaurava army.

A seething Duryodhana shouted at his army and encouraged them, "Come on, brave Kauravas, we cannot allow one boy to defeat the mighty Kauravas. Fight and show your prowess today."

Duryodhana's words motivated the Kaurava army and it hurled themselves on Abhimanyu, only to be slaughtered. Five of the top commanders of the

Kaurava army decided to challenge him. Shatrunjaya, Chandraketu, Mahamegha, Suryabasa and Suvarchas were accomplished warriors who had many victories against their names.

They rushed towards Abhimanyu, determination in their eyes. Abhimanyu watched them come, and his hands seemed to move at the speed of light. He shot five arrows so fast that it seemed he had shot a single magical arrow that split into five. The five arrows went at a scorching pace towards the five Kaurava commanders. Even before they could lift their weapons, the arrows hit their chest.

All five warriors fell dead one after the other as Abhimanyu looked on in satisfaction. Just then, an arrow whizzed past his head, and as he turned, another one almost knocked off his crown. He turned back to see who was shooting at him.

It was Durmasana, the son of Dushasana. He drew his bow and arrow and challenged Abhimanyu, "Abhimanyu, the creator Brahma has fixed today as your last day on this Earth. It is written in your destiny that I will be the one who will end your life today. Abhimanyu, be prepared for death."

So saying, the son of Dushasana shot a barbed arrow that came rushing towards Abhimanyu's neck at top speed. Abhimanyu saw death hurtling towards him.

33

The Death of Righteousness

Abhimanyu watched as the barbed arrow raced towards him with the intention of severing his neck. Just as it seemed that the arrow would hit its target, Abhimanyu deftly moved to his right. The arrow passed him and he could feel the heat of the arrow less than an inch from his neck. He turned to look at Dushasana's son.

Both the warriors studied each other. Durmasana had youth and strength on his side, while Abhimanyu had unlimited energy and skill on his. Both warriors let loose a volley of arrows. Soon the air was full of arrows clashing with each other. Dushasana's son shot arrows that hit Abhimanyu's chariot, causing it to shake. Durmasana's arrow hit the charioteer who cried out in distress.

Abhimanyu counter-attacked with his arrows. It did not take much time for him to prove his superiority. He cut off his opponent's standard, toppling his flag to the ground. He then released two arrows one after the other. The first one shattered his opponent's bow, causing it to break into many pieces. The second was a crescent-shaped arrow whose sharp blade gleamed in the light of the afternoon sun.

This arrow raced towards Dushasana's son as he looked on in horror. Just as he thought it would decapitate him, another arrow intercepted

Abhimanyu's, causing it to fall harmlessly on the ground. It was Drona! He had released a powerful arrow to save Dushasana's son.

Abhimanyu turned towards Drona in rage. Just as he was about to unleash a fierce attack on Drona, there was a commotion. Shalya charged into the battlefield, screaming and hurling abuses at Abhimanyu. Shalya was furious with Abhimanyu for killing his son. He shot a sharp missile that struck Abhimanyu square on the chest.

His impenetrable armour saved Abhimanyu yet again. He attacked Shalya, who had been already defeated. Shalya fought back valiantly but stood no chance against Abhimanyu's fierce display of archery warfare. Shalya's bow snapped into two, and Abhimanyu's arrow killed his charioteer. Shalya had no option but to flee again to save his life.

Abhimanyu then saw Shakuni in front of him. He remembered the humiliation that Draupadi had faced. He knew that it was this man who was squarely responsible for it. He charged at Shakuni with the intention of avenging the humiliation of his family; he attacked Shakuni with a shower of arrows, forcing him to push back. Abhimanyu kept shooting arrows one after the other.

Abhimanyu's attack was so intense that Shakuni could not withstand the assault. He tried desperately to fight but Abhimanyu's arrows scorched the air, destroying every arrow Shakuni shot. Abhimanyu's arrow hit his bowstring, cutting it, and hit him on the hand injuring him. He looked at Abhimanyu who fixed an arrow on his bow, his intention clearly to kill him.

Shakuni ducked and hid inside his chariot, ordering his charioteer to take him to safety even as Abhimanyu mocked him, "Come back and face me like a man. Don't run away like a coward."

The soldiers of Gandhara charged at Abhimanyu and blocked his attack on Shakuni. It was their turn to face the fury of Abhimanyu as he took them on, cutting them down one by one.

Duryodhana was seething. He could not control his anger and vented all his frustration on Drona.

"Acharya, you are the commander of this force. Why can't you kill this son of Arjuna? He is toying with our army and we are unable to do anything. Do you hesitate to kill him because he is the son of your favourite?"

Duryodhana's stinging words caused Drona to flinch.

"No, my prince. He is unbeatable. He seems to be possessed."

"Use your divine weapons and kill him, Acharya," screamed Duryodhana.

"Didn't you see how he has divine weapons of his own? He will counter whatever missile we hurl at him."

"Use the Brahmastra at him and destroy him."

"Duryodhana, I have told you this before. The Brahmastra is a weapon of mass destruction. It cannot be used in this situation."

"Then do something," roared Duryodhana. "If you can't do anything then tell me, let's fall at his feet and surrender. You take his left foot, I will take his right."

Duryodhana's sarcasm hurt Drona more than his inability to come up with a strategy to defeat Abhimanyu.

Just then, Shakuni approached him. Enraged at his mortification, he addressed Duryodhana.

"Prince, we can defeat Abhimanyu. I have a plan."

"Fast, let me know what it is," ordered Duryodhana.

"It is not possible for one or two of us warriors to defeat the son of Arjuna. He seems to have used some magic to become so powerful. Let all of us attack him at the same time. That's the only way to defeat him."

"Haven't we done that already?" asked Drona. "Even though the code of conduct prohibits it, we attacked him together and were sent packing."

"Yes, that was from the front, face to face," said Shakuni, an evil smile blooming on his face.

"What do you mean?" asked Drona and Duryodhana at the same time.

"Let's attack him from all sides, including from behind," said Shakuni, leering at Drona.

Duryodhana looked warily at Drona, expecting him to reject this idea.

Drona stroked his beard, thought for a few moments and said, "Maybe Shakuni's idea is right. Conventional tactics failed us. Maybe we need to look at unconventional tactics to defeat him."

Duryodhana was pleasantly surprised by Drona's response. He looked at Shakuni and smiled. Shakuni winked at him and gestured to Duryodhana to put the plan into progress.

"Alright, Acharya, let us do as Shakuni suggested. Lead the attack, we will come with you."

"This is adharma! How can the righteous Kuru race commit such a vile act?"

Hearing this objection, Duryodhana turned back angrily to see who it was. It was his younger brother Vikarna.

"Keep out of this, Vikarna. Warriors are formulating war strategies. Stay away."

"Brother Duryodhana, Acharya Drona! Do you even realise what you are doing? This is adharma. This is completely wrong and against the righteous path that the Kuru elders wanted future generations to follow. How can you even think of attacking a warrior from behind? Please, I appeal to you, don't do this."

"Vikarna, you are unfit to be a warrior. You are a coward. During the game of dice too, you treacherously supported the Pandavas and Draupadi, all because you are scared of Bheema. I made a mistake allowing a treacherous coward like you to fight for me. Like our father's illegal son Yuyutsu, you too should have gone over to the Pandavas," growled Duryodhana.

"Brother, don't question my loyalty. I remain loyal to you and to Hastinapura. Right or wrong, I am a soldier. I will do what you command. What you are planning to do is not just against the conduct of war, it is a cardinal sin. It is like murdering a man by stabbing him in the back. Remember, the gods are watching us," pleaded Vikarna.

Duryodhana turned away from him in contempt. Vikarna then approached Drona.

"Acharya, if you do this today, it will become a precedent that will be the death of righteousness. Don't kill dharma. What we do today, we have to reap tomorrow. Imagine if Arjuna adopts the same tactics against us! Will anyone of us survive? Please don't sully the good name of Bheeshma, our King Dhritharashtra and the Kuru race, I beg of you," appealed Vikarna.

Drona closed his eyes and did not respond.

"Enough, Vikarna! Don't waste our time. I do not need lectures from you. Our army is being slaughtered. It is our job to defeat the enemy on the battlefield and we are doing this. If you are scared, run away, go and hide somewhere. I order you, get out of here," shouted Duryodhana.

Vikarna knew that no one was in a mood to listen to him. He turned and withdrew from the place.

The moment he left, Shakuni quickly appealed to Drona, "Acharya, let us not waste our time. Let us go ahead quickly and stop this massacre of our soldiers."

"Yes, Acharya, make your strategy, let's finish this quickly," commanded Duryodhana.

Drona spoke in a soft tone, causing everyone to come close to listen to him, "We will attack him from all sides. The most skilled among all of you is Karna. He has to go behind Abhimanyu and cut his bowstring. The moment he does that, we will destroy his chariot and bring him to the ground. We will then take him prisoner."

"He will not surrender, we will kill him and bring this unlucky day's battle to an end," said Shakuni.

Duryodhana let out a screech of joy and slapped his thigh, "Excellent, Commander Drona! I knew you would do something to help us win today's battle. Come on, then, let's get started."

Shakuni and Duryodhana grinned at each other. Their plan had succeeded. They were now ready to kill Abhimanyu. The death of righteousness was nigh.

34

The Warrior Prince's Destiny

Drona closed his eyes for a moment as though praying to the gods to forgive him for what he was about to do. He knew that what he was doing was unpardonable, but he had no option but to heed Duryodhana's words. He knew that had he not agreed to this, he would once again be accused of being partial to his favourite Arjuna's son. He was worried that Duryodhana would force him to use the Brahmastra on Abhimanyu, which he did not want to do.

He signalled to Karna to go behind Abhimanyu and cut his bowstring, instructing Kritavarma to wait for the moment when the bow was destroyed. He told him to then kill Abhimanyu's horses and asked Shakuni to kill the charioteer.

He directed Kripa to destroy the chariot's wheels so that the chariot would collapse. Even as Abhimanyu continued his relentless attack, slaughtering the Kaurava soldiers by the hundreds, the Kaurava heroes sneakily put their plan into operation. Karna directed his charioteer to circle behind Abhimanyu's chariot.

Karna's heart was heavy. He agreed fully with what Vikarna had said and knew that what he was doing was wrong. Abhimanyu had humiliated him by defeating him repeatedly and then, he had killed his brother. He itched for revenge, but he wanted to avenge this by taking on Abhimanyu face to face. The way Abhimanyu was fighting, it seemed impossible to vanquish him today.

This did not mean that he should be killed in such a shameful way. Many warriors attacking a single warrior was a rule of war that they had broken long back. Now he had been given the shameful task of attacking a warrior from behind. This was rank cowardice of the worst type. A warrior like Karna could never participate in such a sinful act.

However, Karna knew that he had no option but to do what Drona had told him. For him, his friend Duryodhana's interest was paramount. When the entire Kuru assembly had humiliated him, it was Duryodhana who stood by him and made him the king of Anga so he could sit in the assembly as an equal to all the kings and princes. He, the son of a charioteer, was given respect and status that had changed his life.

For this one act, Karna was indebted to Duryodhana for life. Duryodhana had lost his son to Abhimanyu and was desperate to end the battle. Karna could not refuse to help him at this stage. He had to choose between letting a friend down and breaking the code of war. The choice was very easy! He would happily suffer the consequences of committing a sinful attack rather than let his friend down.

Karna's chariot was now behind Abhimanyu. He watched in astonishment as Abhimanyu's hands moved like lightning. Karna was proud of his own archery skills, but he had to admit that Abhimanyu's exhibition of archery was unparalleled. He wished that Abhimanyu had been on their side, they would have probably won the war by now!

Pushing these thoughts aside, Karna set out to do the terrible thing he was tasked with. He looked at Drona, who nodded at him. Karna picked his sharpest arrow, and taking aim at Abhimanyu's bowstring, released it.

The unsuspecting Abhimanyu continued his blazing attack and fixed an arrow, taking aim at Ashwatthama. Just then, Karna's arrow whizzed in from behind and cut his bowstring. As Abhimanyu pulled his bow, the arrow fell and the bow snapped. Abhimanyu was shocked by what happened and did not realise how the bowstring was cut. Turning around, he spotted Karna behind him, lowering his bow.

He looked in disgust at Karna and exclaimed, "Shame on you, Karna! What a coward you turned out to be. You do not have the courage or the ability to face me head-on, so you slink behind me like a rat from the sewers and attack! No wonder my father has such contempt for you. Shame on you for calling yourself a warrior!"

Karna's face turned red with embarrassment. Abhimanyu's harsh words hurt him, but he knew he deserved this insult.

Abhimanyu turned back contemptuously and bent down to pick up another bow. Just then, Shakuni shot three arrows at his charioteer, into his neck, heart and stomach, killing him. Kritavarma shot two arrows each at the neck of his horses. Kripa carefully aimed and shot two arrows that hit the chariot's wheels.

The combined effect of the attack achieved its desired result. The chariot's wheels dislodged while the horses collapsed, dead. This made the chariot arch to its left and fall, throwing Abhimanyu off-balance, down on the ground.

Duryodhana laughed maniacally, seeing his arch rival Arjuna's son lying on the ground. Shakuni took aim and shot three arrows at Abhimanyu, hitting his armour. Abhimanyu got up as though nothing had happened and shot an angry glare at Shakuni. He reached into his fallen chariot and saw his sword and shield. He picked them up and charged towards Shakuni.

Drona expertly shot a razor-toothed arrow that split Abhimanyu's sword into two. Simultaneously, Kripa shot two arrows at his shield, breaking it apart. Abhimanyu roared in rage at the two teachers and their wilful conduct. He looked around for a weapon and found none. He spotted the fallen wheel of his chariot and picked it up.

Standing ramrod-straight with the wheel held high in his hand, he invoked the destroyer, Lord Rudra. With the words "Hara Hara Mahadeva", he leapt into the air, swinging the wheel. Abhimanyu's fury was directed at Drona. After all, he was Arjuna's teacher who had taught him not just archery but values. Today, the same Drona was displaying the worst form of valueless behaviour on the battlefield.

Abhimanyu charged at Drona, swinging his wheel. The commander of the Kaurava army was shaken seeing him charge at him. Karna stepped in and shot a powerful missile at the wheel Abhimanyu was holding. It shattered at the impact of the missile, pushing Abhimanyu back, and he fell into his broken chariot. Abhimanyu reached into the chariot and pulled out a mace. It was the mace gifted to him by Balarama.

He lifted the mace high and leapt at Ashwatthama, who stood nearby, and struck his chariot with it. The powerful swing of the mace hit the chariot, causing it to topple. Ashwatthama was thrown to one end of the chariot and he quickly jumped out of it and ran away to the back.

As the Kaurava war heroes watched in astonishment, Abhimanyu wielded the mace as though he were an expert in the art of gadayuddha, swinging it all around and striking soldiers, horses and elephants. He had fought nonstop throughout the day and should have been exhausted but he never showed it in his demeanour as he charged into the Kaurava army, full of energy.

The power in his arms and wide shoulders was transferred to the mace as it dealt a severe blow to whomever it encountered. He swung the mace so hard that it shattered the heads and limbs of all those who came in front of it. Within moments bodies piled up in front of him and he continued his unceasing assault on foot.

A shocked Duryodhana recovered from this stunning spectacle and shouted at his warriors, "What are you doing? Kill him now. Shoot all your arrows at him."

The moment Duryodhana gave his order, the Kaurava heroes strung their bows and shot arrow after arrow at Abhimanyu. While he deflected some with the mace, the others hit him all over his body. Drona, Karna, Shakuni, Kripa, Kritavarma and Bhurishravas relentlessly shot arrow after arrow at Abhimanyu as he charged ahead like an intoxicated elephant.

Abhimanyu kept on attacking the Kauravas even as the arrows pierced his armour. The relentless attack at close range caused his impenetrable armour to crack, and the arrows pierced deep into his body. If he was hurt, he did not show it. He charged ahead, slaughtering infantry soldiers, charioteers and archers on elephants. The way he wielded the mace would have made his uncle Bheema proud.

He now resembled a quilled porcupine. Hundreds of arrows had pierced his body and protruded out from it. He seemed not to care and continued his assault, charging towards the Kaurava heroes. Duryodhana joined in the assault, drawing his huge bow and shooting arrow after arrow.

Abhimanyu was now seriously wounded. Pain permeated into every part of his body; weary, he felt like lying down to rest. He also knew that this was no time to rest. Arrows cruelly hit him one after the other. He could feel his heart and lungs being penetrated by the arrows. A normal warrior would be dead long back. But this was Abhimanyu, grandson of Indra, son of Arjuna and the favourite nephew of Lord Krishna. He would not die so easily.

He ignored the intolerable sensations and continued to attack. By now, he had realised that he was grievously hurt. It gradually dawned on him that, along with his energy, his life force was also ebbing out. He now knew that he was not going to return to the camp. This was his last battle. He remembered his father's words of how the battlefield was the warriors' destiny.

He resolved to die killing as many enemies as possible. Sucking in air into his punctured lungs, he let out a roar and charged at Duryodhana. The Gandhara prince Kalikeya, son of Shakuni, stood in front of Duryodhana with his mace. Abhimanyu swung his mace, sending Kalikeya's crown flying away. With the next swing of his mace, he whomped Kalikeya's mace and struck him on his chest, breaking it. Kalikeya's heart stopped, and he fell dead to Shakuni's anguished cry.

Angry Gandhara solders on elephants charged at Abhimanyu. He swung his mace, striking the elephants one after the other. In no time, there were ten elephants lying dead. The shocked Gandhara soldiers fled the battlefield. There was panic again in the Kaurava camp, seeing the valour of the boy warrior. Many battle-hardened warriors ran away, fearing for their lives.

Abhimanyu had decided to show no mercy to his opponents who had brought the Kuru race to shame with the deceitful attack on him. He massacred his opponents ruthlessly, smashing their chests and heads with his mace. Durmasana blocked his way and shouted at him, "Abhimanyu, be prepared to go to hell. I will now avenge the death of all our warriors."

Abhimanyu laughed arrogantly at Dushasana's son and said, "I will send you to the same place where I sent your cousin Lakshmana."

He swung the powerful mace and demolished the chariot of Dushasana's son. Karna and Shakuni, who were now close to Abhimanyu, kept shooting arrows at him and he staggered from the impact. Dushasana's son leapt from his chariot with his mace in his hand and lunged at Abhimanyu.

Abhimanyu was on his last legs. He had battled throughout the day and had hundreds of injuries on his body. His armour was shattered and his lungs punctured. He gasped for breath as he moved laboriously towards his opponent, who clearly had more energy than he did.

He swung his mace at his opponent and both maces clashed, thundering. Abhimanyu was now bleeding from the mouth and found it difficult to even hold the huge mace. Yet he lifted it high and swung it hard, hitting Dushasana's son on the chest and sending him flying to the ground. Just before he fell, Dushasana's son threw his mace at Abhimanyu, hitting him square on the face.

The sharp end of the mace pierced his forehead and a stream of blood flowed from the wound. Abhimanyu staggered and lost control of his limbs. He suddenly realised that his mace was not in his hands but lying on the ground. He felt like screaming in agony but controlled himself. His head reeled and the entire Kurukshetra battlefield revolved around him. He felt blood rush to his head, and everything slowly became dark. As if in a nightmare, he felt his head hit the ground, and he swooned on the bloodstained battlefield.

The arrows that were stuck on his back pierced his body and came through the front. Blood spouted out from everywhere and he awoke gasping for breath as unimaginable waves of pain travelled throughout his body. His mouth was dry, his vision clouded and his breath laboured. He tried to rise but failed and fell back, his vitality drained.

35

Darkness

The whole world seemed to revolve as Abhimanyu desperately tried to get up but could not. Bleeding from hundreds of wounds, his energy seemed to have evaporated. The lesions from his injuries and the realisation that his life had come to an end caused his tears to flow.

His father's face appeared before his eyes. He remembered Arjuna saying that the warrior's destiny is the battlefield. The bravest warrior is the one who attains veeragati by giving up life fighting on the battlefield and dies being proud of his accomplishments.

The memory of Arjuna's words filled Abhimanyu with a last burst of energy and he struggled to get up. It was torture to even try to get up; he put in a valiant effort to rise but it was too late. Durmasana got up before him, helped by Shakuni and the others. He picked up the mace that Abhimanyu had hit him with, and lunged at Abhimanyu with a wild cry.

He struck the unarmed and helpless Abhimanyu on his head with all his might. The blow on the head from Balarama's mace cracked Abhimanyu's skull and blood gushed out of the wound. Abhimanyu, who was struggling to get up, crashed to the ground, sensing his life ebb out of him.

Durmasana let out a shriek of joy seeing the mortal enemy of the Kauravas collapse. Shakuni and Duryodhana hugged each other happily. The Kaurava princes and their allies let out yells of celebration, beating their chests and jumping around. The Kauravas circled Abhimanyu's body, dancing unrestrainedly, like hyenas celebrating the death of a lion. They blew conches and the soldiers beat drums in celebration.

Yudhishtira's heart sank at hearing the sounds of rejoicing. Jayadratha, who had successfully held off the Pandavas all day long, guffawed, "Hear, Pandavas, how my brave brothers-in-law celebrate. They have felled the son of Arjuna. Victory is ours. Mark my words, this day will change this war. We will win now, be prepared for defeat and destruction."

His words created gloom and despondency amongst the Pandava brothers who dropped their weapons and listened, traumatised, to the revelry. Yudhishtira cried aloud, "I have failed you, my dear Abhimanyu. I sent you to fight my enemies alone and failed to support you. I sent you to your death and I can never forgive myself."

Bheema attempted to console Yudhishtira but failed.

"How can I face Arjuna now? What shall I tell him when he comes back victorious from battle and asks to see his son? How can I tell him that I am the weak and useless king who sent his own nephew to his death?" wailed Yudhishtira.

As the Pandavas mourned and the Kauravas celebrated, Abhimanyu saw his entire life flash before his eyes. He saw his mother singing a lullaby to put him to sleep. He saw his father playing with him. Then, he saw himself playing with his friends and even images of his training with Pradyumna and Krishna. Incident after incident seemed to swim before his eyes.

Then the image of the lovely Uttara appeared before him. Tears rolled down Abhimanyu's eyes, recalling the wonderful moments spent with his beautiful wife. He again heard his wife's protestations begging him not to go to war. With a sinking sensation, he realised that he had to leave his family forever and pass through to the other world.

His father appeared before him again and he heard him saying, "Son, the greatest achievement for a warrior is to become a martyr on the battlefield. He who dies fighting is a true hero. The warrior who fights until his last breath is as great as the one who achieves success on the battlefield. There is no greater satisfaction for a warrior than to close his eyes on the battlefield for the sake of dharma and his country."

Abhimanyu's heart filled with pride, as he knew that he had proved to be the warrior that his father would be proud of. He saw his father and mother before his eyes and suddenly the images seemed to move backwards. His past rushed before him to which he was a silent spectator. He now felt no suffering. In fact, he felt no sensation in his body and existed solely in his mind. His physical body was dead.

As his life proceeded in the reverse direction, he found himself in his mother's womb. He heard the voice of Krishna saying, "It is not impossible to exit the Chakravyuha. Do you want to know how it can be done?"

And then he saw a light before his eyes! It was the moon in the sky far above. His eyes were closed and his body seemed to not exist, yet he saw the moon in the sky. It seemed to be beaming at him. Its light gradually faded away and everything went dark. Blackness enveloped Abhimanyu and took him away gently from the scene of the most heroic battle ever fought.

36

End of the Journey

As Abhimanyu departed the world, so did the sun. It appeared as if it was in a hurry to escape from the sordid scenes that had played out in the past few minutes. As it became dusk, the vanquishing Kauravas departed to their camp, cheering gleefully. The place reeked of death. Tens of thousands of bodies lay on the battlefield—horses, elephants, soldiers, princes, warriors, all mutilated in the battle.

Amid the dead warriors lay the lifeless body of Abhimanyu, and the Pandavas slowly walked up to it, weeping all the way. As soon as the mighty Bheema saw Abhimanyu's body, he slumped to the ground, cradling his face.

"Get up, Abhimanyu, get up! Your father will be here soon, you need to welcome him, please get up," keened Bheema piteously. "What use is my strength and bravery if I could not save you from such a horrifying and tragic death?"

Yudhishtira's knees were shaking. He feared his legs would give way and he would fall. He prayed for the ground to open up and swallow him. That would be preferable to facing Arjuna and explaining why he sent his son to meet his death. Yudhishtira prayed to his divine father Yama to spare his nephew's life and send him back, even though he knew it was impossible.

Nakula and Sahadeva, sobbing, removed the hundreds of arrows sticking out of Abhimanyu's lifeless body, even as Bheema squalled inconsolably. The Matsya king Virat came running and crumpled to the ground on seeing his dead son-in-law. He cried and cursed fate for making his daughter a widow.

Yudhishtira took a deep breath and composed himself. He had to prepare for what lay ahead. He told Sahadeva, "Go fast, Sahadeva, and bring the womenfolk here. Bring Arjuna's wife and daughter-in-law. I know their hearts will break seeing this horrible sight, but we all have to face the inevitable. Let them see our brave prince's face one last time before we consign his body to the flames."

The Pandavas and their allies surrounded the body of Abhimanyu and stood in silence, mourning the greatest tragedy that this war had brought them. Then, they heard the sound of horses galloping. It was Arjuna!

The Samshapatakas had fought valorously with Arjuna all day; they had taken a vow to defeat him or die and death was what they had got. Arjuna had killed more than a thousand of the Samshapatakas and all the Trigarta princes, except their king Susharma. Having vanquished the enemy, Arjuna was returning triumphantly. He was sure that his brothers, son and allies would have won their battles against the Kauravas.

As he moved towards the Pandava camp, a strange sensation came over him—he felt as though he had lost everything, even though he had won. He heard jackals howling in the dark. There seemed to be more bodies on the battlefield.

Arjuna addressed Krishna, “What is this, Krishna? Why is everything so silent? I expected to hear celebrations at our camp. I was looking forward to seeing Abhimanyu at the entrance, eagerly awaiting me. I can only hear the inauspicious howling of jackals. Instead of smelling sweet incense, I can smell only blood and rotting bodies. Why am I feeling so despondent?”

Krishna said, “Arjuna, I fear you must prepare for the worst.”

“What do you mean, Krishna? What has happened? Has anything happened to my brothers or is it my son?”

Krishna remained quiet, driving the chariot as fast as possible.

Arjuna saw the Pandavas in a circle, their heads bent. His heart filled with dread and his stomach seemed to be churning. His legs shook uncontrollably. The moment Krishna stopped the chariot, he jumped out and ran towards his brother. One look at Yudhishtira’s face and he knew what had transpired.

He gazed at his son’s face as he had done every day before he left for battle. Only now, his son did not look back at him, his eyes were closed forever. Arjuna’s legs gave way and he sagged to the ground. He hugged his son’s body and wept bitterly.

“My son, how can you leave me and go? You were just sixteen. You had your entire life before you. An empire awaited you to rule over. Why did you go so early? Your mother didn’t want to send you to war, now how will I face her? What will I say?”

The rest of the Pandavas hung their heads, ashamed that they had been unable to save the warrior prince. Tears ran down the cheeks of everyone assembled.

Krishna walked up to Arjuna and sat beside him with his hand on his shoulder. They sat like that for a long time. It seemed that time itself had come to a stop. No one knew how many hours had passed. It was late in the night. They were all tired, hungry and wounded but no one was ready to leave the battlefield. Finally, Krishna attempted to console Arjuna, "I understand your grief, brave Arjuna. My suffering is as much as yours. Did you forget the lessons I taught you so fast? Death is the only thing that is certain in this world. Everyone has to die one day or the other—you, me and everyone else. My heroic nephew left a bit early. Don't grieve over this body, Partha, this is just an empty shell. Your son has shed his old clothes and moved on to wear new clothes. He is now in a much better place."

"You are the Almighty Lord, why did you allow this to happen? Why did he have to die young? Couldn't you stop it? Don't you have extraordinary powers? Please bring him back to life. I will give my life, please bring my son back to life, Vaasudeva," pleaded Arjuna.

Krishna smiled sadly, "I wish I could do it, Partha, but it is not possible. Let me tell you something about your son that you didn't know—your son was none other than Varchas, the son of Chandra, the moon."

Arjuna looked at Krishna in surprise.

"Yes, Partha, Abhimanyu was the incarnation of Varchas, who was sent to Earth to fight the forces of evil here. It was on Vishnu's bidding that Chandra sent Varchas to be born as your son."

"So, my Abhimanyu has gone to his home in Chandraloka?"

"Yes, Arjuna, your son has returned home after successfully completing his mission. Look around you and you will realise that you gave birth to the greatest warrior that the world has ever seen. In just one day, brave Abhimanyu killed 2,000 princes from the Kaurava camp. He destroyed 8,000 chariots and the warriors who rode them. He killed 900 elephants and their masters. The number of infantry soldiers he killed cannot even be counted. He has achieved his mission of reducing the burden of evil on Earth."

"Why did he have to leave at such a young age, Krishna? He would have been a great king in the future," asked Yudhishtira.

"When Vishnu asked Chandra to send his son to Earth, Chandra hesitated, stating that his son was the apple of his eye and he couldn't spare him. He sent him on Vishnu's insistence but had a condition that his son should come back to him after sixteen years. Vishnu had to agree to his condition, as the Earth needed a hero like him to destroy the enemy and change the course of this war. He was required in the battle for dharma," replied Krishna sadly.

Even as Krishna gave solace to Arjuna, there were sounds of horse hoofs. A chariot was coming towards them, driven by Sahadeva. The Pandava womenfolk alighted, their eyes moist with tears. Subhadra and Draupadi ran to Abhimanyu and hugged his lifeless body. They wept copiously, with Kunti joining them in their mourning.

The women's wailing was like a dagger that tore into the hearts of the Pandavas. Subhadra wept inconsolably at seeing her son's body, "Oh Arjuna, you sent your son to death. I told you to spare this young boy from the horrors of war, but you did not listen to me. All of you sent him to his death. My life has become empty. How can I live without my son?"

Kunti tried her best to console Subhadra and Draupadi. Uttara sat stoically on the ground, clutching her dead husband's hand. Kunti looked at her and murmured, "Uttara, I understand your anguish but do not suppress your grief. Suppressed tears will make you suffer for a lifetime. Do not bottle your emotions, cry and let go of them. That will help you reduce your torment."

Uttara looked at Kunti with her head held high. "I will not cry. My husband has died the way he wanted to—as a hero on the battlefield. I am proud of him. My Abhimanyu has not left me, he is coming back." She took Abhimanyu's hand and touched her womb. "My husband is coming back through my womb."

The thought of Abhimanyu's son having to grow up without his father's love finally had Uttara losing her control and breaking down. The Pandavas' tears made the ground damp. There was not a single dry eye. As Arjuna wept over his son's body one last time, he felt a warm teardrop fall on his back; he looked up.

It was a single teardrop from Krishna's eyes. No one had ever seen Krishna cry, and to see a teardrop fall from the eyes of the Lord wrecked the Pandavas. Arjuna cursed his fate, "What a black day it is that my mother, wife and daughter-in-law cry pitifully and I, the greatest warrior, can do nothing for them! Cursed am I that I have to see this day."

Arjuna let out a roar and got up, "Enough of tears, it is time to avenge my son's death. Yudhishtira! Tell me how a hero like Abhimanyu died like this."

"It was treachery, Arjuna. All the Kauravas attacked Abhimanyu together after he breached the Chakravyuha and defeated them. They attacked a young boy without weapons and killed him in the most shameless way. Guru Drona and Kripa were willing participants to this disgraceful act of adharma."

"Why did you send my son inside the Chakravyuha alone?" demanded Arjuna.

"I have died a thousand deaths in the past few hours, Arjuna. Abhimanyu was confident of breaching the vyuha. All of us came behind him and we were ready to follow him inside but Jayadratha stopped us and used all his powers to block us from entering the vyuha."

"Vaasudeva, they killed my son through cheating. They threw the last shreds of dharma to the winds and slaughtered my brave son. Does the code of conduct still hold good? When the enemy stabs us in the back, should we still insist on waging a fair war? Answer me, Krishna!"

Krishna gave a sad smile.

"From today onwards, there are no rules of war," thundered Arjuna. "I have only one goal—the destruction of the Kauravas. I will end this war very soon. Subhadra, wipe your tears. Your son is now in heaven and I will send his killers to hell."

With these words, Arjuna picked up the great bow Gandiva, pulled back its bowstring and snapped it with all the force at his disposal. The sound reverberated throughout the battlefield so that the very ground vibrated. The joyous Kauravas celebrating in their camp felt the vibrations.

No sooner did he hear the sound than Drona exclaimed, "It is Arjuna! Prince Duryodhana, Arjuna has come to know what has happened. It is time to prepare for his terrible revenge."

The faces of the celebrating Kaurava warriors went pale upon hearing Drona's words.

Arjuna, meanwhile, was not done. "Yudhishtira, I hold Jayadratha responsible for my son's death. He will not survive. I hereby take a vow—by sunset tomorrow, I will kill Jayadratha. If I fail, then I will immolate myself in the same fire that will burn my son's body."

Hearing these words, Krishna took out his divine conch, the Panchajanya, and blew on it, creating a terrific sound. Arjuna lifted his conch Devadatta to his lips and blew on it. Altogether the noise was earsplitting. The vibrations reached the Kaurava camp and the waves seemed like a gale that would blow the camp away. The Kauravas, unable to bear the reverberations, closed their ears as they shook with fear thinking about Arjuna's vengeance.

The Pandava soldiers started beating their drums and the sounds of the conches and drums energised them, preparing them for the battle for the next day to avenge the murder of Abhimanyu.

As the Pandavas prepared for war and the women mourned, Abhimanyu lay still on the holy land of Kurukshetra. Above him, the moon appeared from behind a cloud in its most luminescent form. The moon's rays caressed the body of the great warrior prince, bidding him a final goodbye.

Abhimanyu's journey on Earth had ended.

EPILOGUE

Uttara was a swirl of emotions. Her heart was overcome with pride, and at the same time, tears ran down her face. The tears that she had controlled for thirty-six years rolled down her cheeks as memories of Abhimanyu flooded her mind. Every moment she had spent with her handsome and brave husband were firmly lodged in her mind. She could never forget the few days that she had spent with him and would cherish those memories for the rest of her living days.

She wiped her tears and joy once again swelled in her heart. Before her was the son of Abhimanyu, Parikshith. He was the living image of his father. Uttara had brought him up to be a warrior like her husband. She had always hoped that her Abhimanyu would one day be the emperor, but her dreams had been shattered. She had even thought of jumping into the pyre and joining Abhimanyu.

Fortunately, Krishna had stopped her. He had reminded her that she had no right to kill Abhimanyu's son. He had consoled her and inspired her to live for her son and wait for the day when he ascended the throne of Hastinapura. She had heeded Krishna's counsel.

Her mind returned to the events after the death of her beloved husband. None had slept that terrible night. It was the most tragic moment in the Pandava camp. The next day, Arjuna unleashed his fury on the Kauravas. It was an unprecedented display of warfare. Arjuna had shown a kind of ruthlessness on the battlefield that he had never displayed before.

By the end of the day, he had fulfilled his terrible oath and Jayadratha's headless body lay on the ground of the Kurukshetra battlefield—the same ground where Abhimanyu was brutally murdered. Arjuna's terrifying attack on the Kauravas had led to seven enemy akshauhinis being destroyed. Arjuna, ably aided by Bheema and the rest of the Pandavas, had slaughtered more than 7,00,000 soldiers in one day.

The violation of the code of war had come back to haunt the Kauravas. Drona was beheaded on the battlefield by deception, the same deception he had approved to kill Abhimanyu. Karna stood helpless on the battlefield when Arjuna slew him, the same way in which a helpless Abhimanyu was killed. Bheema killed Dushasana and fulfilled Draupadi's vow. Bheema then killed Duryodhana, again by violating the rules of the war and hitting him below the belt. Truly, Abhimanyu's death had changed the course of the war and brought it to a swift end.

Disaster had struck after the war was over. Ashwatthama had killed the Pandavas' children at night and then, fearing for his life, had hidden himself in the ashrama of the sage Vyasa. Arjuna and the rest of the Pandavas went in search of him, seething in rage. Seeing them, a panic-stricken Ashwatthama pulled out a blade of grass and chanted the hymn to invoke the powerful Brahmashirastra.

He directed the Brahmashirastra to destroy the Pandavas. Arjuna quickly deployed another Brahmashirastra to counter Ashwatthama. As the two missiles rushed through the air, the sage Vyasa, using his divine powers, had paused the weapons. He admonished them for using the weapon of Brahma, which would destroy humanity, and asked them to withdraw their weapons.

Arjuna concurred and withdrew his missile; Ashwatthama was not skilled enough to withdraw his and could only weaken its power. Vyasa asked him to redirect the weapon to another target. A petulant Ashwatthama decided to wipe out the Pandava clan and directed the missile towards Uttara's womb. A furious Krishna cursed Ashwatthama to suffer in misery for 3,000 years as penance for his vile act.

Meanwhile, the missile had hit the unsuspecting Uttara who was agonised. She felt as though her womb had been set on fire. She knew Abhimanyu's child was dead and fainted.

Krishna had then touched her womb with his hand and blessed her and she felt a wave of energy course through her body. Her dead son had come back to life. Krishna pronounced that his birth had prevented the Kuru race from becoming extinct. He would therefore be called Parikshith (the one born in an extinct line). He asked Uttara to bring him up to be a great monarch.

Uttara had abided by Krishna's words and had brought up Parikshith with utter care and love, intending him to be a great king worthy of his lineage. Now Krishna, who had given her and her son rebirth, was not there. A hunter had killed him as his Yadava clan fought with each other. The news of Krishna's death had broken both Arjuna and Subhadra physically and mentally. Uttara had disintegrated with this tragedy.

Now her father-in-law and his brothers had decided to leave the world. Dharmaraja Yudhishtira, after ruling for thirty-six years, was relinquishing the kingdom and placing her son Parikshith on the throne. Once he was named ruler, the Pandavas and Draupadi would leave on their journey to the other world.

Parikshith had given Uttara a grandson named Janmejaya, and she was sure he would grow up and uphold the legacy of his illustrious ancestors. She was tired of life and looked forward to leaving for the forest with her mother-in-law Subhadra to prepare for her final journey. She prayed to Krishna to reunite her with her beloved husband in the other world.

The present moment, however, was one to celebrate. As conches blew, drums rolled and priests chanted the auspicious hymns, Parikshith ascended the throne of Hastinapura and took his place on the great throne after circumambulating it thrice. Yudhishtira placed the crown on his head. Her son now ruled over the kingdom of the Kurus. Uttara looked on, content, as the son of brave Abhimanyu assumed charge as the ruler of the country.

Abhimanyu, that mighty car-warrior, endued with mighty energy, having slain (numerous) foes before the gaze of all bowmen, hath attained to heaven. The great bowman, that mighty car-warrior, struggling on the field, hath fallen in the battle struck with sword and mace and dart, and bow. Sprung from Soma [moon], he hath disappeared in the lunar essence, cleansed of all his impurities.

—Vyasa to Yudhishtira
'Drona Parva (Abhimanyu Vadha Parva), Section LII',
The Mahabharata of Vyasa, English Prose
Translation by K.M. Ganguli

AUTHOR'S NOTE

The story of the tragic hero Abhimanyu is based on the Mahabharata. The primary source of this story is the translation by Kisari Mohan Ganguli. Abhimanyu's heroics in the war have been narrated exactly as per the original story. Some minor creative liberties have been taken by the author to make the tale more enjoyable.

There is a major addition in this novel that is not part of the Mahabharata—the story of Abhimanyu going out in search of his father and meeting Uttara. A folktale that is part of our rich folk tradition is the inspiration for this story. The folk legend is the basis for the love story between Abhimanyu and Uttara.

One of the most well-known legends about Abhimanyu is how he learned the art of breaking into the Chakravyuha while in his mother's womb. The Mahabharata does not have any reference to this. It is again folktales that narrate this incident. Most of them say that it was Arjuna who narrated the story. Some folktales depict Krishna as the narrator. This book makes Krishna the narrator to highlight his important role in Abhimanyu's story.

The role played by Krishna in Abhimanyu's story is very important. Krishna knew what would happen to Abhimanyu, yet he did not save him. It is believed that it was Krishna who ensured that Abhimanyu did not know how to exit the Chakravyuha. He could have brought Arjuna back into the battlefield thus saving Abhimanyu. Just as he brought Parikshith back to life, he could have brought Abhimanyu back to life.

The question is why Krishna didn't do anything to save Abhimanyu. The answer is that Abhimanyu was destined to die young. His life had three purposes—one to exhibit his heroics and destroy many Kauravas, thus aiding in the war on evil; two, to give an heir to the Hastinapura throne; and three, to have his untimely and tragic death change the course of the war.

His death would provoke Arjuna and make him a ruthless warrior, a trait he lacked. This would hasten the process of getting rid of evil on Earth. His death also made the Pandavas break the code of conduct of the war. This helped them kill Drona and Karna easily, thus ending the war.

How Abhimanyu entered the Chakravyuha is a matter of speculation. Nowhere does the Mahabharata talk about the technique used to enter the Chakravyuha. There is also no description of how Drona arranged the formation. The account of the Chakravyuha in this novel is a fictional one. However, the subsequent incidents of Abhimanyu's heroics are as per the original text.

Abhimanyu's story needs to be told. The younger generation needs to know the story of this great hero. The story of Abhimanyu is a tale of unprecedented heroism. It is a narration of love, bravery and sacrifice. It is also a reminder of how unsung heroes like Abhimanyu played a role in the war against adharma.

I hope that you enjoyed reading this novel. Please do let me know your feedback on the tale of the tragic hero by visiting https://deepakmr.com/Abhimanyu/

ABOUT THE AUTHOR

Deepak M.R. is a professional trainer and writer. With master's degrees in commerce and management, he has over twenty-five years of experience in education, training and consultancy. He has been involved in corporate training, teaching, process consultancy and auditing, and has worked at a private university as a dean and controller of examinations.

Deepak has written academic books and technical articles during his career. He writes blogs and is an avid fan of various genres of fiction. He has contributed to the anthology *Unsung Valour: Forgotten Warriors of the Kurukshetra War* (Bloomsbury, 2020) that features tales of forgotten warriors from the great epic. He considers the story of the Mahabharata as the greatest ever told.

At present, he works as a professional writer, tackling subjects such as healthcare, business, finance, lifestyle and technology. He is working on a collection of short stories featuring a great hero from the Mahabharata. He is also working on a fantasy adventure fiction set in the post-Mahabharata period.

He lives in Bengaluru with his wife, daughter and parents.